PRAISE FOR
Sarah Darer Littman

BACKLASH

"Littman pens a raw, frighteningly realistic, and absorbing look at cyberbullying and the damaging effects of airing private trauma in a public forum." — *Publishers Weekly*

"A powerful and credible story." — *Booklist*

"This novel thoughtfully balances the four alternating perspectives, giving an element of humanity even to the perpetrators of severe bullying while maintaining a strong moral judgment." — *School Library Journal*

WANT TO GO PRIVATE?

"A bold investigation of a potentially lethal, if common, mixture for teen girls: emotional immaturity, technology and emerging sexuality." — *Los Angeles Times*

"Littman pens a harrowing cautionary tale about the dangers that lurk online." — *Publishers Weekly*

"This book is a compelling, if not disturbing, read." — *School Library Journal*

LIFE, AFTER

"Convincing and absorbing." — *Publishers Weekly*

"Littman catches the voice of teen readers with her spot-on dialogue and realistic situations." — *The Jewish Journal*

PURGE

"An intimate and powerful novel." — *The Stamford Times*

"With an underlying but not heavy-handed message, this may start a few conversations." — *Kirkus Reviews*

BACKLASH

ALSO BY

Sarah Darer Littman

Want to Go Private?

Life, After

Purge

BACKLASH

Sarah Darer Littman

Scholastic Inc.

This book was originally published in hardcover by Scholastic Press in 2015.

This book is a work of fiction. Names, characters, places, and incidents are either the product of the author's imagination or are used fictitiously, and any resemblance to actual persons, living or dead, business establishments, events, or locales is entirely coincidental

ISBN 978-0-545-92414-6

10 9 8 7 6 5 4 3 2 1   16 17 18 19 20

Printed in the U.S.A.   40
First printing 2016
Book design by Sharismar Rodriguez

In memory of my father, Stanley Paul Darer,
who taught me to observe and, more importantly,
to *care* about the world around me

PART ONE

NOW

LARA

THE WORDS on the screen don't make sense. They can't.

He says: You're an awful person.

He says: You're a terrible friend.

He says: I know you've been checking out dresses for the homecoming dance.

He says: What makes you think I'd ever ask you out?

He says: I'd never be caught dead at the school dance with a loser like you.

He doesn't say it in a private message. He posts it publicly, on my Facebook wall, where everyone can see. Twenty-five people have already liked what he wrote. Even people I thought were my friends. Why would anyone *like* something that mean?

A few people have posted defending me, saying that I'm not a loser, that he's a jerk for posting that.

But my eyes keep going back to Christian's words. I don't understand. I thought we were friends. I thought we were *more* than friends.

Wasn't he flirting with me? Did I get that wrong, too?

My fingers tremble on the keyboard as I IM him.

What did I do wrong? I don't understand.

I wait for him to answer, so numb with hurt and panic that I can't even cry.

When the answer comes, I wish it hadn't.

He says: You're a loser. The world would be a better place without you in it. GOOD-BYE, LOSER!!!

My lungs feel paralyzed. I can't breathe. Why is he saying this? What changed from yesterday to today?

Tears roll down my cheeks as I type back.

Why? WHY?!!!!?????????

But when I press Return, it won't let me send it. He's blocked me.

I hit the keyboard in frustration, shaking my head. *No, no, no.*

I can't ask him why. I can't ask anyone why.

The only person left to ask is me.

SYDNEY

LARA'S HOGGING the bathroom — *again*. I swear it's like this *every single night*. She gets in there first, takes forever, and uses up all the hot water. She better leave me some tonight because I *have* to wash my hair. I've got auditions tomorrow for *Beauty and the Beast*, the eighth-grade musical. Maddie, Cara, and I have spent, like, *forever* practicing our audition pieces, and the last thing I want is for Ms. Brandt to be distracted from my acting and singing talent by gross hair.

I knock on the door for the second time. Okay, this time I'm banging more than knocking. "Lara, come on! Hurry up! You've been in there for forty minutes!"

Tonight she's even more annoying than usual. She doesn't even respond with *Go away. I'll be out in a minute!* or something typically charming and Lara-like. There's just dead silence, which makes me even more angry and frustrated. I give one last loud bang with my fist and stomp down the stairs to complain to Mom.

My mother is in that post-dinner "I'm finally sitting down and reading my boring political papers so don't bother me with your arguments" kind of mood.

"Mom. I swear, if I have to take another cold shower —"

"Sydney, I have been sitting down for all of" — she checks her watch — "three minutes. I am not getting involved until I've had at least ten minutes to unwind."

"But, Mom . . ."

"Ten minutes, Syd," she says, giving me her palm and going back to whatever deathly dull papers she's reading for her position on the city council. She's muttering something about budget cuts as I walk away.

Maybe if I started acting all moody and depressed like Lara, Mom would give me a pass on being a jerk, too. Even now that Lara's doing better, my parents let her get away with stuff because she was so depressed before.

If I were into all that stupid cheerleading like Lara, I'd make them do this cheer:

2-4-6-8

Who's the girl that's REALLY great?

Sydney! Sydney!

HELLO?!!

I stomp back upstairs and bang on the door again. "LARA! GET OUT OF THERE! I need to take a shower!"

Silence. No running water. No splashing. No snarky reply. Nothing.

That's when I get the first tingle of unease, the feeling that something is different tonight. I try turning the door handle, but it's locked. It's not the locked door that freaks me out. Lara always locks the door when she's in the bathroom. It's the silence. It's the fact that she's not yelling back at me through the door.

"Lara?" I call, concern starting to nudge out anger. "Are you okay?"

Nothing. Not even the tiniest movement of water. Panic rises to the back of my throat as I run downstairs, almost tripping on the last three steps.

"Mom — I think something's wrong with Lara!"

That's what it takes to get Mom's attention away from her paperwork.

"What do you mean?"

"She's locked in the bathroom, and she's not answering when I bang on the door."

Mom's face pales. She throws the papers on the table and runs for the stairs, taking them two at a time. I follow her, feeling more scared as I climb each step.

"Lara! Open the door! NOW!" Mom shouts, knocking on the door with both fists.

Nothing. Still nothing.

Mom rattles the handle and shakes the door, like *that's* going to magically make it open.

"Do you hear me, Lara? *Open the door!*" she yells.

More nothing. Scary *omigodwhatishappeninginthere* nothing.

Mom turns to me.

"Call nine-one-one," she says. "And Dad."

I stand there, shocked, staring at her. 911? That means . . .

"NOW, Sydney!"

I race into my parents' bedroom, grab the phone, and dial 911.

"What's the nature of your emergency?" the dispatcher asks.

"My sister's locked in the bathroom and she won't answer. And she's been in there for a really long time."

"What's your location?"

I give her the address, expecting her to send an ambulance, but she's got more questions.

"How old is your sister?"

"She's fifteen," I tell her.

"Are you sure she's in there?"

"Yes!"

"What gives you reason to think this is an emergency?"

"Because she's not answering!" I shout, feeling my throat start to close up.

"Do you have any reason to believe she's come to harm?"

"*Yes!* That's why I'm calling you!"

"Why do you think she might have come to harm?"

No one in my family wants to admit this publicly but . . . "She had depression and saw a shrink and stuff."

"Has she made any suicidal comments?"

"Not recently, at least that I know of, but she did a few years ago."

"Okay," the dispatcher says. "Ambulance and police are on their way to you."

I slam the phone in the cradle and run back into the hallway. Mom's jamming at the lock with some weird metal pin thing.

"What's that?"

"It's supposed to be the key to unlock the door from this side," Mom says from between gritted teeth. "Except it's not working."

That's when I realize I forgot to call Dad. As our resident handyman, he would have had the lock open by now for sure.

I slip into my bedroom and call him on my cell. "What's up, sugarplum?" he asks.

"Come home," I tell him. "It's Lara."

"What happened?"

He's suddenly brusque. Lara's crises do that to our parents.

"She's in the bathroom with the door locked and won't answer. Mom's trying to get the door open. I called nine-one-one," I say in a rush.

Just then the sirens, which had been faint in the distance, start getting loud down the street. I hear him curse under his breath.

"Tell Mom I'm on my way," he says before hanging up on me.

Mom's still struggling unsuccessfully with the lock and is mumbling her own angry curses.

The sirens are now earsplittingly loud — the ambulance must be right outside.

"I'll go let them in," I say just as the doorbell rings.

It's not the ambulance. It's the police. A policewoman, uniformed, with a gun at her hip.

She flashes me her badge.

"Officer Hall, Lake Hills PD. I have a report of a fifteen-year-old female with a psychiatric history who is nonresponsive and locked in a bathroom?"

I nod. "My sister."

"Where?" she asks.

I point up the stairs, and she goes up without asking me any more questions. I hear Mom talking to her, starting to cry, frustrated; she still hasn't been able to get the door open and "Why isn't the stupid key working?" Explaining how Dad got it in case Lara locked herself in and tried to do something stupid.

The police lady says she'll take over with the key thing, speaking in a low, steady voice to calm Mom down.

So my parents expected something like this to happen? Am I the only one who didn't?

I start wondering why I'm always the last to know about stuff that ends up affecting my life, but my brain is too busy being blown into a million shards by a new round of sirens — this time the ambulance. I let the EMTs in and point them up the stairs. This time I follow. By the time we get up there the bathroom door is open, and I glimpse the pill bottles lined up on the edge of the bathtub like birds on a telephone wire.

Oh, Lara. Why?

The EMTs ask Mom to leave the bathroom so they have room to work on Lara. The policewoman leads my mother out into the hallway. Mom is crying. She tries to look back into the bathroom, but the EMT guy shuts the door.

Work on her. I guess that means Lara's still alive. For now at least.

I can't say how many times I've wished that I were an only child. But now I'm whispering frantic prayers, over and over, that I won't be.

BREE

AS SOON as I hear the sirens coming down our street, I know. They're coming for Lara. Don't ask me how I know. I just do. I mean, she's been messed up for a while. Since we were in middle school. Not everyone knows that, because her parents tried to keep it hush-hush, with her mom being a politician and all. But I know, because we used to be best friends. Her being so messed up is part of the reason we're not anymore.

I pick up my cell and call Mom, who's still at work.

"Hi," she says when she picks up. "I've got an important showing in two minutes, so make it snappy."

I look out the window. "There's a police car out front of the Kelleys' house. They came down the streets with lights and sirens."

"That's not good," Mom says, stating the obvious.

Just then I hear more sirens. "I think an ambulance is coming, too," I tell her.

"I hear them," she says. "Listen, my clients just pulled up. I've got to go. Just hang tight and stay inside so you don't get in the way. I'll be home as soon as I can."

"Do you think she's —"

"I don't know, Bree. I've got to go. This could be a huge commission. Just stay in the house."

And the line is dead silent.

"What's going on?" my brother, Liam, asks. His freckled face shows only typical eighth-grade-boy curiosity as he comes to the window. He is alternately red and blue from the flashing lights on the police car.

"Something's going on at the Kelleys'," I say.

"Wow, I never would have guessed that by the *police car* that's parked out front. Thanks, Captain Obvious."

Liam can be such a snot. And him being smarter than me is something my mother never fails to point out.

"So figure it out yourself, Einstein!" I retort.

We can hear the sirens getting closer. I see curtains twitch across the way. Everyone is wondering what is going on.

And then they get louder and louder, and we see the ambulance turn onto our street. Liam sticks his fingers in his ears as sirens scream deafeningly outside the window. Then they stop, with a weird hiccup, as the ambulance screeches to a halt behind the police car.

We watch, our noses pressed to the glass, siren lights still flashing as the medics run to the Kelleys' front door. Curious neighbors have started gathering outside.

"I'm going to go out and see what's happening," Liam says.

"No!"

He stares at me, shocked by my sudden, vehement command.

"Mom said to stay inside till she gets home."

"Why?" Liam asks.

My brother was born asking that question. It's like he's wired to refuse to take no for an answer.

"Because Mom said so, okay? Why can't you just listen to her for once?"

"'Cause she didn't tell *me*," the little brat says over his shoulder as he heads toward the front door. "And because the Kelleys are our friends."

"*Liam.* Mom said to stay inside."

He opens the door, ignoring me. Why does he always have to be such a pain? Especially now.

"I'm going to tell Mom —"

The door slams on my threat.

The Kelleys are our friends.

Were our friends, is more like it.

I watch him drift toward the gathering crowd by the ambulance, sidling up to Spencer Helman from down the street and talking to him. I want to go out, too. I pick up my cell and decide to ignore Mom's instructions. If she gives me a hard time, I'll tell her the truth, which is that Liam left the house first.

As I walk up to the crowd, one of the EMTs comes out of the Kelleys' house with the policewoman. He opens the back of the ambulance and takes out a stretcher.

My stomach turns over. A stretcher could mean anything from a corpse to a sick person going to the hospital, right?

"What happened?" It's one of our neighbors, Mrs. Gorski. She's an old busybody, always looking out her window to see what's happening on our street. A few years ago, Josie Stern skipped school and came home with a bunch of friends while her parents were at work. Guess who called her parents and told on her so she got grounded for a month? You guessed it — Mrs. G.

"We can't release any information at this time," the policewoman says.

The two of them wheel the stretcher back into the house.

"I hope Syd's okay," Liam mutters. He's strangely pale beneath his freckles.

"I'm sure she's fine," I tell him. Because I know this has to be about Lara.

"Maybe Mr. Kelley had a heart attack," he says.

I check the driveway.

"He's not even home," I observe. "See, his car's not here. Besides, Mr. Kelley is in pretty good shape. He's not the heart attack kind of guy."

Unlike my father, who needs to lose weight, as Mom never stops reminding him. Dad has the physique of a middle-aged teddy bear.

"I bet it's the older girl," Mrs. Gorski says, wagging one of her liver-spotted bony fingers for emphasis. "Laura. That one's been giving them trouble for years."

How does *she* know? Does she, like, hide in the bushes and listen to conversations through open windows? Seriously, she can't even get Lara's name right.

It's not like she was Lara's best friend for years. It's not like she had to listen when Lara was depressed and kept talking about how she hated life and hated herself and hated her body and why did she have to be so fat — for *hours*. Not exaggerating. One time we were video chatting and it was 176 minutes of her complaining about life. I timed it. I finally lied and said I had to go, because I couldn't take it anymore.

High school was such a relief. Bigger place, new people. Made it easy to escape, to hang out with other girls.

We were best friends. Then we weren't. It happens all the time. Just read any teen-magazine advice column. There's nothing unusual about our story.

Except now there's a police car and an ambulance parked outside Lara's house.

The front door opens and I hold my breath, waiting to see if Lara is alive or in a body bag.

Two EMTs are wheeling out the stretcher . . . and . . . Lara's strapped to it, with an oxygen mask over her face and an IV in her arm. She's alive.

I can breathe again. Just barely.

But Mrs. Kelley is walking next to her unconscious daughter, holding her hand and sobbing. What does that mean? Does it mean there's a chance she won't make it?

Sydney shuts the door behind everyone and walks to her mother's car, her arms wrapped around herself like she's eaten something bad and got a terrible pain in her stomach.

This is so unreal. What did Lara *do*? Marci won't believe this. *I* can barely believe it.

But Marci doesn't know yet. So I take out my cell and surreptitiously snap a picture of Lara's pale face as they wheel her by on the stretcher.

"What are you doing?" Liam asks, grabbing my arm and staring at me, horrified. "That's sick!"

"Shut up!"

He doesn't. "Bree, what's the matter with you? You better not post that!"

I shake him off and snap more pictures as they slide the stretcher into the ambulance and slam the doors shut. I have to send this to Marci right away, otherwise she's not going to believe me when I tell her. This is just so . . . crazy.

Mrs. Kelley sobs her way over to her car and gets in, obviously planning to follow after the ambulance with Sydney.

Then the siren starts up with a near-deafening whoop. Liam puts his fingers in his ears, and I take some video of the ambulance driving away, lights flashing and sirens blaring.

"Bree, stop it!" Liam shouts over the siren noise. "What is your problem?"

"What's *your* problem?" I shout back. "Just go inside and mind your own business."

"You kids with your smartphones and your Facebooks and what's it called . . . YouTubes," Mrs. Gorski complains, shaking her head as she turns back to her house once the siren noise fades down the street. "No trees fall in your forest unless you've put it online. Everyone has to know everyone's business."

I think the woman is starting to lose it. What is she talking about? And seriously, Mrs. Gorski wouldn't know minding her own business if it stood in front of her and did a kick line like the Rockettes at Radio City.

When I finish taking the video of the ambulance, I head back home. Everything is posted on Facebook before I even walk back in the front door of our house. Now everybody knows.

SYDNEY

LARA'S STILL unconscious. What happens if she doesn't wake up? What happens if she does and she's, like, a vegetable or something? The doctors say they can't give us a prognosis. They say we have to wait and see, something that none of us are that good at doing.

Dad ended up meeting us at the ER. They kept us out of the room while they intubated Lara, which means sticking a tube into her windpipe, and while they inserted a urinary catheter, which sounds totally gross. They took blood and some of her urine (out of that catheter thing) so they could do tests. The ER doctors gave her something called activated charcoal through another tube they'd stuck down her throat into her stomach. It's supposed to help eliminate the drugs she took from her system.

Since they allowed us back into the room, we've been doing what they told us to: talking to her in case she hears us, watching the machines that are tracking her vitals, listening to the slowed beeps of her heart, and most of all, sitting here waiting, hoping and praying that she'll pull through. But the one question we keep asking one another and ourselves in between prayers and hopes is *why?* Why *now?*

Mom sits on one side of Lara, Dad on the other, each of them holding one of her limp hands. Mom alternates between crying, praying, and begging Lara to wake up and come back to us. Dad is a silent, angry rock. He doesn't understand.

"Why would she do this when things were going so much better for her?" he asked Mom right after he got there.

Mom just shook her head and cried harder. Dad comforted her, but he's been asking the doctors and the nurses and the janitor and anyone who walks by the same hurt, angry question.

I can't blame him, because I don't get it, either. Back when she was in middle school and everyone was making fun of her for being fat, Mom arranged for Lara to see a nutritionist so she could lose weight. We all ended up having to change the way we ate — which meant no more cookies for me, even though *I* wasn't overweight. How was *that* fair? Lara and Dad went to the gym together on the weekends, and then he'd take her for low-fat frozen yogurt at Yoglicious. It was their "special time."

And now Lara had just made varsity cheerleading. All she could talk about was her new friend Ashley from cheerleading and how great it was to hang out with her and the rest of the girls from the team.

So why, Lara? I didn't get frozen yogurt treats or "special time" with Dad. But am *I* the one lying unconscious in an ER bed, freaking out my entire family?

Our Lara vigil is interrupted when a policeman comes into the little room.

"Sorry to intrude, but we need to ask you some questions," he says. "Maybe we should step outside?"

Mom glances at Dad. I can tell she doesn't want to leave Lara's side for a second, like her presence alone is what's going to keep my sister alive, more than all the beeping machines. He nods toward the door, and reluctantly she lets go of Lara's hand, kissing it before she lays it back on the bed.

There are two chairs outside the room. Mom sits in one but Dad wants to stand, so I take the other.

"I'm sorry to have to bother you at a time like this," the police officer says. "I'm Officer Timm. This is Officer Hall," he says, pointing to the policewoman, who I recognize from the house.

"Why are you here?" Dad asks. "Can't you see our daughter is . . ."

Dad trails off, because he can't say the words.

"Just the usual follow-up questions in this kind of situation," Officer Hall says in a calm but firm voice.

Mom looks to where Lara is lying on the bed, pale and still.

"Had your daughter appeared depressed recently?" Officer Timm asks.

"No, she was doing really well," Dad says. "That's why I can't understand . . . why she would . . ."

"She made the cheerleading squad," Mom adds. "She was making new friends."

"Did you notice any changes recently in her behavior, or her grades?" Officer Timm asks.

"No," Mom says. "If anything, she seemed happier than usual. Not depressed."

"Has Lara had any history of mental illness?" the policeman asks.

There's that slight hesitation. My parents don't look at each other. They don't need to. They've already got this.

"She got a little down in middle school. Some of the other girls were teasing her about her weight," Dad says.

"But she's fine now," Mom assures them.

We're in the emergency room and Lara is unconscious on a bed, attached to beeping machines while the police are interviewing us. Mom might not be aware of the irony, but Officer Timm exchanges a sideways look with Officer Hall.

They're doing it again. My parents are pretending that we're this perfect family with two perfect parents and two perfect daughters. Problems? Not us Kelleys! We're *totally* electable.

I can't help the loud, exasperated sigh that escapes my lips.

"Sydney, why don't you and I take a walk to stretch our legs while Officer Timm speaks with your parents?" Officer Hall says. "I bet it's tough for you to sit for so long."

"Okay. Sure."

I'm grateful for the chance to get away from the constant beeping of the monitors, from Lara's still, pale face, from my parents, who keep pretending everything is just awesome, despite all the evidence that it isn't. Do they really think they're fooling anyone beside themselves?

As we walk down the hallway, Officer Hall's thick rubber-soled shoes make annoying squeaky noises on the vinyl floor tiles with every step she takes.

"Guess I wouldn't be able to sneak up on a suspect in this place, would I?" she says, giving me a rueful smile.

I wonder if she could read the annoyance on my face or if the sound bugs her, too.

"No. You'd *squeak* up on a suspect."

She laughs. "Can I treat you to a bottle of something?" she says, gesturing to the vending machine a little ways down the hall.

"Sure."

I can't decide between vitaminwater (Mom would approve) or Gatorade (might keep me going for what is obviously going to be a long night). Since I'm mad at Mom, I pick the Gatorade. Officer Hall gets herself a Diet Coke, and we find a couple of chairs in one of the small family waiting rooms located off this hallway in strategic locations.

The Gatorade is cold, sweet, and refreshing. After taking a long swig, I already feel a little better. Or maybe it's just the relief of having a few minutes away from my parents and the desperate, beeping Lara Watch.

"So I'm getting the impression things weren't as rosy with your sister as your parents were making them out to be," Officer Hall says, putting her soda can down on the table between out-of-date copies of *People* magazine and *Car and Driver.* "Am I right?"

"Yeah. My parents are pretending that everything was fine, because that's what they always do, but she was a total mess."

"Do you mind if I take some notes?" Officer Hall asks.

"No. I mean, I guess it's fine."

"When you say 'a total mess,' in what way?"

I pick at the label of the Gatorade.

"Well . . . Lara used to be kind of . . . She wasn't always as . . . thin . . . as she is now. And in middle school, the other girls gave her a really hard time. Like, instead of Lara, they called her Lardo and Lardosaurus. You know, stuff like that."

Officer Hall frowns, her lips a thin, grim line.

"Yes, I do know, unfortunately. And how did Lara take that?"

"Badly. She was crying in her room a lot. And then Mom would nag her about stuff she was eating, because she thought if Lara lost weight, kids wouldn't tease her, but then Lara would sneak food into her room, and then Mom would scream at her when she found the food. It was pretty . . . ugly."

"I can imagine," Officer Hall says, scribbling in her little notebook.

I wonder if she really can imagine what it's like to be in your room, curled up on the bed, clutching the teddy bear you tell your friends you don't sleep with anymore for comfort because the sound of your mom screaming and your sister sobbing scares you. Wishing that they would all just be okay, that Lara would be happy and Mom would be calm and things would be normal like they were in other people's houses.

"Why did you become a cop?" I ask her, curious suddenly.

She puts the notebook down in her lap and fidgets with the pen. "Runs in the family," she says. "My dad's a cop. His dad was a cop. My older brother, too."

"My dad's an engineer," I tell her. "But I don't want to be one. No way."

"What do you want to do?" she asks me.

"How am I supposed to know? I'm in *eighth grade*."

She laughs. "Good point. Just because my future was mapped out, it doesn't mean that everyone else's is." Picking up the notebook, she gets back to Lara — because it's always really about Lara, never about me. "Tell me about the depression . . . When did that start?"

"I can't remember exactly. I think it was when she was in seventh grade? She got mad at me because I asked in front of Mom and Dad why she was crying every night in her room. That's what made my parents send her to a shrink, finally."

"What about friends? Does Lara have many friends?"

"Some. There's Julisa and Luis Cotto — they're twins. And she just made the cheerleading team, and she's been hanging out with this girl Ashley a lot."

"Do you know Ashley's last name?"

"Something beginning with *T* . . . Tra-something."

"Anyone else?"

"Not that I can think of. I mean, she used to be best friends with Bree Connors, who lives next door, but they don't hang out so much anymore."

"Your parents said Lara was doing better. Has she ever shown any suicidal tendencies?"

Immediately, I think of all those nights listening through the wall to Lara sobbing. Hearing her long, tearful video chats with Bree, where she'd say how she couldn't stand another day at school, how she wished she were dead. I'd be lying in bed scared that it might happen, but sometimes wondering what it would be like to be an only child. Hoping God would forgive me, because I hated myself for wondering that.

"Yeah. When she was in middle school — when things were really bad — she used to talk about stuff like that. But not recently. She's been in a good mood lately. That's why this is all so messed up. It doesn't make sense."

"A young person trying to take her own life never makes sense to me." Officer Hall sighs, closing her notebook.

"I guess I should get back," I say, even though the thought of going back to Lara's bedside with my parents' desperation and the slow beeping of the machines makes my stomach clench.

"Sure. I'll walk with you," Officer Hall says.

She squeaks back down the hall next to me to where Officer Timm is waiting outside Lara's room. My parents are back in position on either side of Lara, holding her hands. There's no obvious place for me.

"Thanks for speaking with me, Sydney," Officer Hall says.

"Thanks for the Gatorade."

I have to force myself to go back into the room to join the vigil. I'm too amped from the Gatorade to sit down, so I slouch in the corner, moving my weight from one foot to the other, wishing I could go home and take that shower for my audition.

Mom is reciting the Lord's Prayer. I don't know what to do, so I just keep thinking, *Pleasepleasepleasepleasepleaseplease wakeupwakeupwakeupwakeupwakeupwakeup.*

And then, almost as if she's heard me, Lara's eyelids start to flutter.

"Pete! I think she's coming to!" Mom half whispers, half sobs.

"Lara . . . Lara, sweetheart, can you hear me? It's Dad," my father says, squeezing my sister's hand so hard I'm surprised she doesn't wake up just to tell him to stop breaking her fingers.

She groans. The machines start beeping faster.

"Syd, go get the nurse!" Dad orders.

By the time I get to the door, the nurse in panda-print scrubs is already on her way in. She races to Lara's side, eyeing the monitors.

"Lara, open your eyes for me," the nurse says. "Your parents are here, and your sister. They want to see you."

She tells Mom and Dad to keep talking to Lara.

"Wake up, darling," Mom says. "We love you."

"Come on, honey, you can do it," Dad urges.

"Lara! Wake up!" I shout suddenly, fed up with the waiting, with Lara, with everything and everyone. Mad that it looks like I'm going to miss auditions tomorrow because of my sister and her never-ending drama.

She groans and tosses her head back and forth on the pillow. Dad turns to me angrily and is about to open his mouth to tell me to be quiet or something, but Mom gasps because Lara's eyes have fluttered open.

"Welcome back," the nurse says.

"Thank goodness!" Dad says, grabbing Lara's hand and kissing it.

Mom sobs with relief.

Lara is trying to pull at the tube in her throat.

"Leave that, honey," the nurse says. "We have to wait for the doctor to come to make sure it's okay to take it out."

Lara looks scared and confused, her eyes blinking from the brightness of the lights.

"You're at Central Hospital," the nurse says. "You overdosed on medication."

The nurse shines a penlight in Lara's pupils to see if they contract. As she checks Lara's reflexes, a doctor comes in wearing a white lab coat over his scrubs.

He talks with the nurse, looks at Lara's chart, and then moves to near Lara's head.

"Lara, I'm Dr. Delman. We're going to remove the breathing tube now. I want you to exhale on the count of three. Nod if you understand what I'm saying."

My sister's head moves up and down slowly, her eyes blinking as if she is in pain.

"Okay, here we go, Lara. One . . . two . . . three . . ."

I have to turn the other way and close my eyes, because the thought of it makes me squeamish. But I can't close my ears, and I hear Lara groan and gag, followed by Mom's sharp intake of breath. I guess that means the tube is out, so it's safe to look again.

"Your throat might feel a little sore for a while," the doctor tells her. "You can try gargling with salt water or drinking some warm water with honey and lemon."

Lara looks at him, her eyes wide and shadowed. I get the impression warm water with honey and lemon is the last thing on her mind. I wish I knew what *was* on her mind. I wish I knew what made her do this when everything seemed to be going so well for her.

Why did she have to mess up things for me when I'd been working so hard for auditions? I deserve an explanation.

But I know better than to ask. I'll just get a lecture about how self-centered I am and how can I be thinking of myself at a time like this. Because it's all about Lara. Just like it always is.

Turns out I don't have to ask. My father is the one who can't hold back from uttering the question we're all wondering.

"Why did you do it, Lara? *Why?*"

The heart-rate monitor starts beeping faster. Lara closes her eyes.

My mother hisses, *"Pete!"* and gives Dad an angry look. Better him than me.

A tear trickles slowly from the corner of Lara's eye, down her skim-milk-colored cheek.

When she says the word, it's so faint we barely hear it.

"Christian."

LIAM

I CAN'T believe Bree took pictures.

Even worse, I can't believe she posted them.

Why does she think that's okay?

I check Sydney's Facebook to see if she's posted an update about Lara, but there's nothing. Her last update is from earlier today — a selfie with her friends Cara and Maddie with the caption Break a Leg! Ready for BEAUTY AND THE BEAST auditions tomorrow!

Her bright smile is in total contrast to how pale and totally freaked out she looked as she followed her mom to the car after Lara was put in the ambulance.

I wanted to call out to her. I wanted to say . . . I don't know, that I'm here. That even if we haven't hung out for a while, even if Bree and Lara aren't friends anymore, that I'm still here.

But my friend Spencer was standing next to me, and he's one of the major reasons I stopped hanging out with Syd so much in the first place. He started with the "Syd and Liam sitting in a tree" stuff in fifth grade, hassling me non-stop about whether she was my girlfriend or not. By the time we got to middle school, he'd started telling the other guys I was probably gay because I spent all this time with Syd and hadn't even tried to kiss her.

No way I could let people believe that, because I want to have a girlfriend *someday*. I guess I could have lied and said I did kiss her, but that didn't seem right, either.

So I drifted away from Syd, pretending I was too busy to hang out. And I never told her why, which was a jerk move, now that I think about it.

Some friend.

Maybe I can make up for it. Maybe I'll text Syd to see if she's okay.

I pick up my cell, thumbs hovering above the touch screen.

And then I put it down, sighing, because I'm afraid she'll think I'm trying to get info on Lara's condition to post on Facebook, just like my awful sister.

BREE

A **BUNCH** of people piled onto Christian's post on Lara's Facebook page, saying, **Yeah, Lara's fat and ugly,** and some of the kids who went to our middle school even brought up the nickname she hated so much, Lardo. It's crazy, there are, like, twenty comments, just one thing after another. A few people say Christian's a jerk and ask where does he get off saying stuff like that, but someone else even comes out and says why doesn't Lara kill herself? I wonder if she saw that before she decided to . . . you know, do whatever she did that made the ambulance come. And I wonder — what will happen if she dies?

Oh God. What if she's already dead?

I check my Facebook page. There are fifty likes on the picture of Lara on the stretcher being wheeled to the ambulance, and it's been shared a bunch of times. People are already speculating in the comments.

She looks dead.

Is Lardosaurus dead?

RIP Lardo.

Corpse Girl.

Mom's still not home. I wish she would get here.

And then I remember . . . *Liam.*

My brother is in his room, doing his homework. He's got his headphones on and his foot is tapping to a beat I can't hear. Liam and I have always marched to different drummers, or however that saying goes.

When I tap him on the shoulder, he jumps.

"Sheesh, Bree, why'd you sneak up on me like that?"

"I didn't sneak. You just play your music obnoxiously loud."

"What do you want? I'm busy."

I hesitate, trying to figure out the best way to handle him. I need his help. He can find out what I need to know so badly.

"I'm really worried about Lara," I tell him. "You're still friends with Sydney, right? Can you text her to see how Lara's doing?"

He takes off his headphones and stares at me without saying a word. I get this feeling I'm being judged, and hard.

"Why do you care?" he asks, his eyes narrowed on me like thin green lasers.

I expected him to give me some attitude, but not to ask me that. "What do you mean, why do I care?"

"You haven't been friends with Lara for over a year, and now you're so worried?" Liam says. "Why do you *really* want me to text Syd? So you can post something else?"

I'd be lying if I said that I didn't want to be the first one to post whatever news there was about Lara. Who wouldn't? But that's not the only reason I want him to text her sister to find out how she is. It's because . . . I never thought about death being so . . . real, so . . . permanent. Death's always been for old people, like grandparents, or people far away who are killed in wars that you hear about when your social studies teacher talks about current events or your parents flick past the news on cable.

It's not something that happens to someone I know, that I used to be best friends with.

"It has nothing to do with Facebook," I half lie, pretending to be really offended. "Why would you even think that?"

"Maybe 'cause you posted that picture of her passed out on a stretcher, being taken to the hospital?" Liam says. "I mean, c'mon, Bree, how could you do that? It's so wrong."

"What do you care?"

"'Cause Sydney's my friend," he says. "And because you're my sister, so when you do sick stuff like that, people think I'm a loser, too."

How does it make me a loser when that post already has fifty likes? If anyone's a loser in this family, it's Liam. He just doesn't understand. But I can't say anything because I need him to send that text. So I try a new tack.

"If you're such good friends, why wouldn't you text Syd? Don't *you* want to know if Lara's okay or if she's . . . you know . . ." I can't bring myself to say the word, and without even having to pretend, my voice chokes up and I have tears in my eyes.

My tears are what convince Liam that this isn't just about a Facebook update.

"Okay. I'll do it," he says.

He reaches for his cell and starts to text.

What he doesn't realize is that I'm crying because I'm scared.

LARA

"**OurFather**whoartinheavenhallowedbethynamethy
kingdomcome . . ."

"Pete! I think she's coming to . . ."

BeepBeep. Beep. BeepBeep.

"Lara . . . Lara, sweetheart, can you hear me? It's Dad . . ."

Ow. Hand hurts. Dad. Hurt me. Tell him. Mouth not
working.

Beep. Beep. Beep. BeepBeepBeepBeep.

"Syd, go get the nurse!"

"Lara, open your eyes for me. Your parents are here, and
your sister. They want to see you."

Who's that?

"Wake up, darling. We love you."

Mommy. Love can't fix me. Too tired.

Beep. Beep. BeepBeep. BeepBeepBeepBeepBeep.

"Come on, honey, you can do it."

No, Daddy, can't. Want to sleep.

Parents sound like they're at the end of a bad connec-
tion. Want to hang up. Too sleepy to talk.

"Lara! Wake up!"

Syd.

Everyone else is soft and pleading. Syd is mad. *Why so mad? Doesn't she understand?* Too tired. Shake head no, don't hate me.

Try talking. *Why mouth not working?* There's something in it. Throat hurts.

Have to leave cocoon. Don't want to. But Syd mad. Open eyes. Eyelids stuck. Won't open. Crack open. Lights so bright close again, too bright.

Eyes open. Room so bright.

Beep. Beep. BeepBeepBeep. BeepBeepBeep. BeepBeep.

"Welcome back," a lady says, wearing a scrub shirt with pandas on it. Black-and-white pandas, purple shirt. Happy pandas. Pandas *sososo happy.* I am sad. Sad panda.

"Thank goodness!" Dad kisses my hand.

Mom next to the bed, sobbing.

What happened? Where am I? Why is everyone acting like I died?

Mask over my face. Smells like plastic. Thing in my throat. Hurts.

Try to get it out, but hand shaky and weak, like a newborn baby. Tubes in my hand. Hurts. Everything . . . hurts.

Panda Nurse tells me to leave the tube in my throat; the doctor is coming to take it out.

"You're at Central Hospital," she explains. "You overdosed on medication."

Christian. You'realoseraloseraloseraloseraloser.

Theworldwouldbeabetterplacewithoutyouinit.

I failed. Can't even get that right.

Wanted it to be over and it's not.

Itsnotoveritsnotoveritsnotover. Hurthurthurthurthurtnono nonononononono.

Brightness, a painful spotlight in one eye, then the other. Seeing spots. Want to go back to sleep, get away from the pain, get away from the memory, get away from everything. Panda Nurse taps my elbow with a rubber hammer.

BeepBeepBeepBeepBeepBeepBeepBeepBeep.

Man with glasses standing over me. See shoulder of his white coat.

"Lara, I'm Dr. Delman. We're going to remove the breathing tube now. I want you to exhale on the count of three. Nod if you understand what I'm saying."

Move my head, slowly. So tired. Brain hurts. Hand hurts. Throat hurts.

"Okay, here we go, Lara. One . . . two . . . three . . ."

Exhale . . . less pressure in my throat and then tube slides out.

Moan. Gag.

"Your throat might feel a little sore for a while," the doctor says. "You can try gargling with salt water, or drinking some warm water with honey and lemon."

It does hurt. More than a little. Everything does. Hurts. Especially . . . especially if I . . . no.

"Why did you do it, Lara? *Why?*"

My father's voice.

Daddy. No.

Shut my eyes. Want to go back to sleep. Don't want to

think. Don't want to feel. Don't want to remember why. It hurts. *Daddy, Mommy, it hurts too much, to remember.* I want to go back to sleep.

Moving head side to side, trying to shake away thoughts, trying not to remember again.

But then I see his face.

See the words he wrote.

See them on my computer screen.

See them etched into my brain.

Feel them etched into my heart.

Know them deep in my soul.

Remembering.

Don't want to remember.

Don't want to live.

Tear rolls down my cheek.

"Christian."

"Was that *Christian* she said?"

Doctor is asking. Are they going to do something to him?

I shouldn't have said it. Open my eyes.

This is real. This is happening.

It was supposed to be over.

Instead of making it better I've . . . just . . . made . . . it . . . worse.

Panda Nurse tapping my knees with the rubber hammer.

Involuntary movement.

I'm awake involuntarily.

I want to go back to sleep.

"Is Christian her boyfriend?" That sounds like Panda Nurse.

BeepBeepBeepBeepBeepBeepBeepBeepBeepBeep.

He hates me. He told me the world would be a better place without me in it. I still don't know why. But it hurts. It still hurts so badly I don't want to be awake. I don't want to be here. I wasn't supposed to be here.

"Not that we know of," Mom says. "She doesn't have a boyfriend."

"She's friends with someone named Christian on Facebook and — What?! How can people —"

Sydney's talking, but now she's crying.

"Give me your phone!" Daddy. He's angry.

Daddy's swearing. "Who are these sick punks? What kind of kids would write this stuff?"

I don't want to know.

Please don't make me know.

I don't want to feel.

PleaseletmegobacktosleepbacktosleepbacktosleepLetme forgetIthurtsithurtsithurts.

I hurt.

SYDNEY

MOM'S ON the phone with the police, who've left the hospital, telling them about this Christian DeWitt, which is his full name according to his Facebook profile. She tried to get Lara to tell her as much as she could, but Lara's pretty out of it, so Mom hasn't been able to get much info. Dad wants to go find this Christian guy and rip him limb from limb, and then when he's done, go find all the other jerks who wrote nasty stuff about Lara on her wall and do the same to them. He made me take a zillion screenshots on my cell of Lara's profile and Christian's profile and his friend list and all the people who commented on Lara's wall and then email them to him so he can start his personal investigation and vendetta. Mom keeps telling him he has to calm down and let the police deal with it.

"Calm down? Our daughter almost *died*, Kathy!" Dad hisses. "And these animals are telling her she's fat and ugly and saying she's better off dead? Who *does* that? What kind of sick world do we live in?"

"I don't know." Mom sighs. "But getting yourself arrested

for assault isn't going to help Lara. Or me. Don't forget I've got an election coming up in November."

As if any of us could forget that for a second.

"Our daughter is lying in a hospital bed and you're bringing up *the election*?"

Dad's voice is starting to rise. Mom tells him to lower it so he doesn't make a scene.

Hate to break it to you, Mom, but I think the scene has already been well and truly made.

I take out my cell to check the time. There are, like, a gazillion texts from Maddie and Cara, but I'm not up to reading them now. I just want to go home. It's already so late I can forget about washing my hair. I'll be lucky if I even get any sleep before auditions. Like, I know this is a crisis, and my sister is in really bad shape — *again* — but I'm so sick of being treated like a second-class kid just because Lara is messed up. It's not fair!! I'm probably going to win the Worst Daughter in the World Award for asking to leave, but I decide to do it anyway.

"Mom . . . Dad? I know it's a bad time, but when are we going to go home? I have auditions tomorrow."

Mom looks like she's about to explode and is trying very hard to hold it together.

"Sydney, do you understand what is going on here?" she says to me like I'm a three-year-old, which just sets my teeth on edge.

"Yeah. I understand perfectly, Mom. Lara tried to kill herself, which is really, really awful. I was scared she was going to die just like you were. Now she's going to be okay. I'm happy and relieved about that, honestly, I am. But that doesn't take away from the fact that Lara's messing my life up again, just like she always does."

Mom opens her mouth, probably to tell me how awful and selfish I am, but Dad gestures to her to be quiet.

He puts his arm around me and guides me down the hall away from Lara Watch and my angry mother, who, as usual, doesn't understand me.

"I need a snack. How about you?"

"I want to go home," I tell him, my voice cracking despite all my best efforts to stay cool. "I want to be able to audition for the musical tomorrow. I don't want Lara to ruin this like she does everything."

Dad stops and turns me so I'm facing him, with his hands on my shoulders. He looks down at me, and when I notice the shadows and lines around his eyes, I feel bad for causing him more problems. But then my fists clench, because why should I always have to be the one who feels bad? I've worked hard and now Lara's screwing things up for me. Story of my life.

"Honey, I know this seems unfair to you," Dad says. "It *is* unfair. There's nothing fair about it."

"So? How come we can't go home, then?"

I've got two parents here, and they each have a car. One of them could drive me home.

Dad sighs heavily.

"Because we're a family, and we love and support each

other. We're part of a team. Sometimes," he says, patting my shoulder, "you just have to take one for the team."

I shrug his hand off my shoulder. I can't believe this is happening, again. Actually I can. That's what's so messed up about it.

"How come it's always *me* who has to take one for the team?" I ask, fighting a lump of angry tears in my throat. "When's it going to be someone else's turn?"

Someone else like *Lara*, for example. But of course, I can't say that, especially not now.

"Oh, honey, I know . . ."

Dad hugs me, but I stand stiffly. I don't want his hug right now. I just want him to take me home. But *that's* not going to happen.

My phone buzzes with an incoming text.

"Go back to Lara," I say. "I'll be *taking one for the team* in the family waiting room."

I can tell he's torn. He wants to be by Lara's side, but he's trying to make it up to me for missing auditions. Like taking me for some crummy hospital cafeteria food could actually do that. Nice try, Dad.

"Are you sure you're not hungry?" Dad asks.

"I'll come get you if I am."

He kisses the top of my head and heads back to Lara, the important child.

I walk to the visitors lounge to read my text. I need time away from the family drama to be angry on my own.

The text is from Liam.

>Hey, Syd. Saw Lara taken in ambulance. Is she
>okay? Are YOU okay?

I hesitate before texting Liam back. Ever since Lara and Bree stopped being friends, it's been kind of awkward for us. Like, before, our families used to hang out and do stuff together all the time. Our dads even built a tree fort in the huge oak tree in the Connors backyard when we were younger. It was supposed to be for all of us, but Lara and Bree made it theirs, telling Liam and me that we weren't welcome because we didn't know whatever stupid secret passwords they'd made up. Back then, it was Lara and Bree against the two of us despised younger siblings.

Until Lara started having problems in middle school, and eventually they started hating on each other instead.

Even after Lara and Bree stopped being friends, Liam and I still hung out. But then once we got to middle school, he started acting all weird, like I'd suddenly developed a highly contagious disease. It's only recently we've started talking again. Still, it's kind of out of the blue for him to text me.

It's only because he asks about me, not just about Lara, that I decide to text him back. Because he cares about how *I'm* doing, too.

At least someone does.

>Lara awake. Mom's talking to the police.
>Me = wanna go home.

Wow. Glad she's okay. Hope u can go home
soon. Do you know what made her do it?

Did u see her FB page? What that guy
Christian wrote?

No. Hold on.

I flip through the pages of a two-month-old *People* magazine while waiting for him to look up Lara's page. I skip
anything that has to do with real-life stories. The Kelley
family has its own *People* drama going on, thanks. I'll stick
to deciding who wears it better in the Fashion Faceoff.

My phone buzzes.

I can't BELIEVE it . . . Man, people are sick.
I'm so sorry.

It's not your fault.

Well . . . I'm REALLY sorry for that pic Bree
posted on her FB page. I swear. I'm
embarrassed we're related right now.

Picture Bree posted? What picture?

I go to Facebook on my phone and look up Bree's page.
When I do, I want to throw up. Or throw the phone away,
or, better yet, at someone, namely Bree Connors.

Bree posted a picture of my unconscious sister being wheeled toward the ambulance. As if that weren't bad enough, it has seventy-seven likes and, although there are some expressions of concern and sympathy, some of the comments underneath are so awful, so cruel, that they make me hate Bree, hate Liam, hate everyone in the entire world.

Syd?

I switch off my phone. I don't care if he's sorry. I can't text with him right now. I want to shut off the entire disgusting, mean, insane world.

And as I think that, I suddenly understand what might have made Lara do it.

It's not easy being Lara's sister. If she weren't my sister, I probably wouldn't be her friend. But she *is* my sister. And nobody, *nobody*, sister or no sister, deserves what I just saw on that page.

BREE

My picture of Lara has 104 likes and 15 shares by the time Mom gets home. That's the most I've ever gotten on any picture or status update, ever. Wonder if I should Instagram it? #Call911

"Tell me everything," Mom says, putting a bag of groceries on the kitchen counter.

"How could you stop and wheel a cart around the supermarket like nothing happened?" I ask her. "Aren't you at all . . . you know, *freaked out* by this?"

Mom has her hand in the bag, starting to unload it, and she stops and gives me an exasperated look.

"I assume you want dinner, Breanna. And if that's the case, then someone, namely me, had to get food to make it with." She takes out a package of chicken. "Unless you have a better idea."

Which of course, I don't, and Mom knows that when I blush and say nothing.

"Just tell me what happened," she says.

"We heard sirens. Like, when I called you. The police car came first. Then the ambulance. All the neighbors were outside the Kelleys' house watching. Then the medics wheeled Lara out on a stretcher, put her in the ambulance, and drove away with lights and sirens. She tried to . . . kill herself."

"Yeah, and Bree took a picture of her and posted it on Facebook."

My brother is standing in the doorway of the kitchen, narrow-eyed, cell phone in hand.

"You *what*?"

When I see my mom's expression it's like when you're at the beach and you see that really huge wave coming toward you, and you don't know if you should try to ride it or dive under, and if you hesitate too long, you get nailed by it. I wait a second too long to answer and Mom goes nuclear.

"Breanna Marie Connors, what part of 'hang tight and stay inside' didn't you understand? I told you to stay in the house and make sure Liam did, too. Simple instructions. Not rocket science."

It's so unfair. Liam was the one who disobeyed Mom first, but *I* get the grief. And she makes out like I'm stupid, as usual.

"Liam wouldn't *listen*! I *told* him you said to stay in, and he completely ignored me and walked straight out the door! *He's* the one who went out first."

"Is that true?" Mom turns to Liam, who's still leaning against the doorjamb.

He glares back at her defiantly. "Yeah. They're our friends, right? I thought they might need help. Isn't that what friends are *supposed* to do?"

Mom's lips purse, and I know he's got her there. Sure, Lara and I have drifted apart, but at least on the surface my parents and the Kelleys are still friendly.

"*Helping* doesn't mean taking pictures and posting them on Facebook," Mom snaps.

"I wouldn't do that," Liam says, not hiding his disgust with me. He nods in my direction. "That's Miss 'I'll Do Anything No Matter How Sick to Get Likes on Facebook.'"

Mom takes off her suit jacket, slowly and deliberately, and I feel acid in the back of my throat, because I know I'm about to be hit by another wave of her anger any moment.

"Liam, I need to speak to your sister privately," she says.

Here it comes.

"Wait . . . before I go, I wanted to tell you . . . I texted Syd, and Lara's awake," Liam says.

I feel tears well up, but this time they're ones of relief. "That's . . . so great to hear," I say. "Thanks for letting me know, Li."

"Yes, it is," Mom agrees, looking at me from the corner of her eye.

"Mrs. Kelley is talking to the police," Liam adds, like it's just some random factoid that's he's just happening to mention.

That is so NOT great news.

"What do you mean, the police?" I ask, trying to keep my voice steady.

Liam looks at me like I'm some kind of an idiot.

"The police always ask questions in the event of a suicide attempt, Bree," Mom says, giving me a hush-up look.

"Syd says it's because of some guy named Christian. Did you see what he wrote on her wall?"

The sound that comes from the back of my throat escapes despite my attempt to stifle it.

"Don't tell me you're friends with that guy, Bree," Liam says. "What a jerk!"

"Christian who?" Mom asks. Her voice is calm, almost nonchalant. Like she's never heard of anyone named Christian, ever.

"Christian DeWitt. He wrote all this sick stuff on Lara's page, Mom," Liam replies.

My eyes are trained on the point where the wooden table leg meets the floor. It's where food and dust bunnies collect if you don't clean the floor enough, which sometimes Mom doesn't because she's too busy at work, so she makes me do it. Once, I did a halfhearted job of sweeping and mopping the kitchen floor, and that's the first place she checked because she knew I'd do a lousy job because "that's the kind of kid you are." As in I'm not a "go-getter who makes her own luck" like she is, so I'm "never going to get anywhere in this world." She knew all that because of two missed Cheerios and a small dust bunny.

If I keep my eyes focused on that spot, they can't give anything away.

"I know this is very unsettling, Liam, but Lara has never

been the most stable girl, has she?" Mom says. "Remember what a mess she was in middle school?"

Mom's finished unloading the groceries, and she takes out the chopping board and a knife to start preparing dinner.

"To be honest, I wasn't that unhappy that she and Bree started drifting apart," Mom continues. "I was worried it might get unhealthy for Bree to continue to hang around with her so much."

Weird. She never told me that. In fact, if anything, I felt the opposite, because Mom has always been so obsessed with Mrs. Kelley. She started copying the way she dressed and the way she spoke. And she always laughed a little too loudly whenever Mr. Kelley told a joke. If Lara and I weren't going to be BFFs anymore, it gave *her* less reason to be BFFs with Mr. and Mrs. Kelley.

"I don't get it. How does that matter now?" Liam asks. I abandon my table-leg staring to look at him, because he's taking this so seriously. "Are you saying just because Lara was kind of a head case in middle school it's okay for all those kids to write that stuff on her wall?"

"No, but —"

"Because that's just wrong." Liam interrupts Mom before she can even finish her sentence. "Like, 'to the end of the universe and back' wrong."

"Liam, I'm not saying it's right for anyone to write things on Lara's wall," Mom says. "But let's face it — a more stable child probably wouldn't have ended up in the hospital."

Liam crosses his arms over his chest. He's not buying what Mom's selling.

"They're our friends. Dad and Mr. Kelley built the tree fort together. How can you be so . . ." He trails off, searching for the words to describe the ways he finds Mom and me lacking. Unable to find it, he punches the doorjamb and shouts, "Forget it," before stomping upstairs and slamming his door.

And then it's just me and Mom.

She glares at me, eyes narrowed almost to slits, and hisses, *"What were you thinking?"*

LARA

CHRISTIAN SAID I was a loser.

He said the world would be a better place without me in it.

And now I'm a loser at trying to make that happen.

Everyone expects me to be happy that I failed.

But I'm not.

Which is why I can't have shoelaces. Or a belt.

And they make me open my mouth after they've given me my pills to make sure I've swallowed them.

And they do bed checks every few hours to make sure I haven't hanged myself with the sheets, so I can't even get a good night's sleep.

And I want to sleep all the time, because when I'm asleep, I'm not here. Not here in this place, where every movement is watched. Where everything I say is being turned over and analyzed, making me want to curl up into myself and say nothing.

But it's bad if I say nothing. It means they'll just keep me here longer.

So I have to say something.

I'm searching for the magic words to get out of here . . .
Abracadabra? Alohomora?

There are get-well-soon cards on the dresser from my
family and friends.

Mom said my friends Julisa and Luis want to visit.

I told her that I'm not up to visitors yet. Not even them.

The truth is, I don't want Julisa and Luis to see me in
this place. This prison, filled with crazy people.

Crazy people like me.

Luis thought I was crazy enough when I tried out for
cheerleading. He must think I'm completely *loco* now.

The cheerleading team sent flowers. They're beautiful —
roses and carnations and daisies in cheerful yellows, pinks,
and whites. But they're arranged in an ugly plastic male
urinal.

"I'm sorry, Lara, glass vases aren't allowed," the nurse
told me.

I pretend to be excited about the flowers and the cards.

I pretend that I can't wait to get out of here to see my
friends.

I have to find the words to convince them that I'm fine.
That everything is perfect.

Maybe I should ask Mom.

She's the expert on that.

LIAM

"**In conclusion,** science, technology, engineering, and math are more important than the arts," my friend Oliver says. "The future of our country depends on graduating students who are proficient in STEM subjects, so if we have limited resources to spend on education, we shouldn't waste them on unnecessary subjects like music and art."

Today's debate club topic is "All Public Schools Should Provide Students with Music and Arts Education."

I argued the premise.

Last night, Mom heard me practicing and said, "No one better raise *my* taxes to pay for kids to waste time finger painting."

I closed my bedroom door and practiced in a quieter voice, almost a whisper. I knew there was no point telling Mom about the research I'd found to back up my argument, about how arts education helps kids develop creative-thinking, problem-solving, and communications skills. Mom's more convinced by dollars and cents than common sense.

"Liam, your rebuttal," Mr. Phillips says.

I go up to the podium. Oliver smirks from the front row. He's convinced he has this debate in the bag.

"Those who say that music and arts education is unnecessary don't recognize that the arts are a language spoken by everyone, reaching across cultural, social, economic, and racial barriers," I say, thinking of my mother. "They help us learn empathy, to understand how someone else feels and to experience his or her emotions as our own. And in an increasingly global and interconnected world, this is essential to achieve both economic and political success."

People clap when I'm done. *Yes!*

Not only that, as I sit down, I notice I've wiped the smirk off Oliver's face. We may be friends, but we both like to win.

I guess I got that from Mom. You know how some parents let their kids win when they're little so they feel good about themselves? Not my mom. Dad would, but Mom was like, "If you want to win, you have to earn it. All this 'give everyone a trophy' garbage is ruining this country."

When I finally beat her at Monopoly, I took a picture of the board, and then I never played with her again.

Mr. Phillips calls for the votes. We're judged on how we argue the point, how we rebut the opponent's points, how well our arguments are structured, and our presentation skills.

As he's tallying up the scores, I remember when Dad came to my first debate. I was arguing for the death penalty. My team won.

In the car on the way home, he said, "I never knew you were in favor of the death penalty, son." He glanced over at me. "Have to say, I'm surprised."

I stared at him. "What makes you think I'm in favor of the death penalty?"

"Liam, you just won a debate arguing in support of it," Dad said. "Not only that, you did such a good job you almost made me think *I'm* in favor of it."

"Dad, that's just the side I took for the debate," I explained. "Mr. Phillips told us we had to start off arguing a position we don't agree with because it's harder to do."

My father shook his head slowly. "Wow . . . Smart man, Mr. Phillips," Dad said. "Teaching you to play devil's advocate."

"I'm not sure Mom agrees," I muttered.

Dad laughed. "Maybe not. But remember, you inherited your way with words from your mom, not me."

I'm hoping my way with words pays off as Mr. Phillips finishes tallying the points on the voting sheets.

"We have a winner," he says. "Congratulations, Mr. Connors."

I turn and hold out my hand to Oliver. Mr. Phillips is big on us being gracious when we win — and not being sore losers when we don't.

"Good debate, Mr. Steiner," I say.

Oliver shakes my hand and says, "Nice work, Mr. Connors."

Then we both laugh because it still seems so weird to call each other mister, but we're supposed to at debate club because Mr. Phillips says it's a way of showing each other respect. But as soon as the announcement crackles over the loudspeaker that the late buses are here, Oliver fake punches my shoulder and says, "Crush you next time, sucker."

"Yeah . . . in your dreams," I tell him.

Guess we can only keep up the respect thing for so long. But that's okay. We're just messing with each other. It's way different from the stuff people have been saying to Lara Kelley.

We talk about our fantasy football picks on the way down to the front circle.

"See you tomorrow," he says as we part ways for our late buses.

"Not if I see you first," I retort over my shoulder.

The late bus is half-empty, as usual. The lucky ones have parents or older siblings who pick them up.

Even if Bree had her license and use of one of the family cars, I can't see her going out of her way to do me a favor.

But today I don't mind so much, because Syd is sitting on the late bus, staring out the window. I slide into the seat in front of her.

"What's going on?"

"You don't want to know," she says. "Nothing too special."

But you're pretty special . . .

Stop, I tell myself. Syd needs a friend, not a creeper.

"I just wonder if I'll ever stop feeling like I want to punch everyone in the face." She sighs.

It's so unlike Syd to say something like that that I can't help putting my hands up to block my face, laughing as I do so.

Syd swats my arms down playfully.

"Not *you*, silly," she says. "Just . . . the rest of the world."

"Whew!" I breathe an exaggerated sigh of relief. "You had me so scared for a moment there."

"Yeah, right," Syd says. "Because I'm so tough that huge football players have been known to wet themselves when they see me walking down the hall."

Being able to make her laugh is even better than beating Oliver. Mom would slap me upside the head for even *thinking* that, but luckily for me, she can't read my thoughts.

"Seriously . . . is everything okay?" I ask. "I mean . . . I know that's a stupid question but . . ."

"Heh . . . yeah." She looks out the window, avoiding my gaze, and her lower lip trembles. "No . . . everything isn't okay. Pretty much nothing is okay, if you want to know the truth." Her voice wobbles, like she's about to cry.

Crying girls freak me out, because I don't know what to do to make them stop. Thankfully, Syd turns mad instead.

"But of course I have to pretend like everything's fine, because Mom's running for reelection to city council. I'm just so *mad* all the time. Like, every time I stay after school for rehearsal and work on crew instead of being in the cast . . . I was *good*."

"I know," I agree. "I ran lines with you."

"It's not fair," she says. Syd's speaking quietly, so only I can hear over the noise of the bus engine, the driver's radio, and the chatter of the other kids, but there's so much anger in her voice I feel like it could drill a hole in the seat back between us. "I didn't even get a chance to try out. Because Lara's drama always messes up my life."

And then, as if she's just realized what she's said, she covers her mouth with her hand and looks at me, wide-eyed with horror.

"You probably think I'm awful, right?"

The fingers over her mouth muffle her words. Her other hand grips the seat back.

I pat that hand hesitantly, gently, with my own.

"I don't think you're awful, Syd. I think you're . . . you know . . . human."

Her eyes get all watery, and I'm scared she's going to start crying, but then she takes a deep breath and smiles.

"Whew," she says. "Human, huh? Well, that's a relief. And all this time I've been worrying I was some kind of alien."

Who could blame me for crushing on her?

SYDNEY

BEING BUZZED into the psych ward is like being let into prison — not that I've been to prison, but I've seen movies. I can't believe Lara's been in this place for two weeks.

She's in her room, sitting on her bed, wearing sweats — the kind with an elastic waist, because she's not allowed the ones that tie with a string. Her skin is pale, almost gray in color, and her hair hangs limply around her face, like she hasn't brushed it today. Like she doesn't care about her appearance — or anything for that matter.

My sister looks kind of like the flowers wilting in the plastic pee bottle on the dresser — she's seen better days. I wonder why no one has thrown those flowers out. Dropped petals litter the top of the dresser, and the water in the pee bottle is green.

"The doctor tells us you can come home tomorrow," Mom says.

Wait, what? How come nobody told me *that?*

This place is so awful that I feel like the world's worst sister for even thinking this, but I've been kind of enjoying being the only child at home these last two weeks. No having to wait to use the computer or the bathroom. No Lara using up all the hot water before I get to take a shower. And best of all, even though my parents still talk about Lara constantly, they seem to notice me more.

"I can't wait to get out of this place," Lara says with the most emotion I've seen her show since the night in the hospital. "It's horrible. I hate it."

I *am* the worst sister ever.

"But they're helping you," Mom says. "And that's the most important thing."

Lara opens her mouth, but then shuts it like she's thought better of what she was going to say. She looks down at her hands and starts picking at her cuticles instead.

"You seem a lot better," Mom says. "They tell us you're making progress. Of course, you have to continue with intensive therapy when you come home."

How exactly does Lara seem better? I wonder. Okay, she's not passed out in a bathroom, but she still seems pretty miserable to me.

"Should I throw out these flowers?" I ask, walking over to the dresser, because the green water in the pee bottle is really starting to gross me out.

"No!" Lara says with vehemence that startles me.

"Fine! Jeez, chill, will you?" I say, backing away from the dead flowers that for some reason my crazy sister wants to keep.

"Honey, I want you to have a look at these," Dad says, taking some papers out of his pocket and moving to sit next to Lara on the bed.

"Pete, are you sure this is a good idea?" Mom asks, her brow creased with worry.

"It's fine, Kathy," Dad snaps.

Lara flinches slightly at his tone, and she looks from one parent to the other, eyes wide.

I don't have a good feeling about this.

My father is obsessed with vengeance and has little or no confidence in the competence of our local police force. Having watched a gazillion reruns of *Law & Order*, he considers himself just as qualified to run this investigation as they are, no matter how many times Mom tells him to back off and let them do their job. He's been spending every night glued to his laptop, creating a spreadsheet of everyone who commented on Lara's wall, which he's cross-referenced with Christian's friend list. Organizing and systemizing things are his specialty. I think it's something to do with being an engineer. The problem is, he gets confused and frustrated when we don't fit into the systems he creates.

"I want you to look at this list," he said. "I've made a list of the comments and who made them and if they were a friend of yours and that . . . person," Dad says.

"I don't want to look at them," Lara says. "I can't."

"Pete —"

"Lara, we need to find this jerk. He has to pay for what he did to you," Dad says. "Just look at it."

"I can't, Daddy," Lara says, her voice starting to break.

"Of course you can, honey. Just for a minute or two," Dad urges her. He's so focused on his spreadsheet and revenge that he's completely oblivious to the signs that Lara's losing it.

"I can't!" Lara screams. She takes the paper and rips it into shreds and starts crying hysterically.

Dad stands there looking completely dumbfounded, the way someone who's poked a stick in a nest can't understand why he's getting stung by a swarm of angry bees.

"It's okay, Lara, you don't have to look," Mom says, going to Lara and trying to put her arms around her, but Lara shakes off my mother's embrace and seems to shrink into herself, curling up and burying her head in her arms, her shoulders heaving from the force of her sobs.

"Lara? What's happening?" A nurse stands in the doorway. She gestures for us to get out of the room. My parents don't want to, but she doesn't take no for an answer. She closes the door in Mom's face as soon as we get out, and we can only hear the murmur of voices from behind the closed door.

"Pete, I told you it wasn't a good idea," Mom bites out from between clenched teeth. "Just because it's your way of coping with what happened doesn't mean it's the best thing for Lara."

"Are you sure she's ready to get out of the hospital?" Dad deflects.

And they're off. My parents are arguing about my sister again. I walk down the hall and thumb a text to Maddie and Cara.

It's official. My entire family has lost it.

But I pause before hitting Send. And then, with a sigh, I backspace and erase it.

It's hard enough at school being the sister of "that girl who tried to kill herself." Add to that being stuck backstage doing crew at play rehearsals while my friends are onstage together. Why add to my problems by being honest about how crazy things really are with my messed-up family?

The nurse comes out of Lara's room, and my parents stop arguing and pretend everything's fine.

"We need to talk," the nurse says. "But first, I'm going to give Lara something to calm her down."

"Can we go in?" Mom asks.

"She doesn't want to see you right now," the nurse says. "Only her sister. And we need to set up a family meeting for the two of you with Lara's psychiatrist before she is released tomorrow. If her doctor still feels that's appropriate."

Then she walks away to get Lara's medication.

Me? Why me?

I can tell my parents are wondering the same thing as I open the door to Lara's room and slip inside. She's lying on the bed, curled up in the fetal position. I'm not sure what I'm supposed to say or do, and I'm afraid to do anything that might set her off again. I sit on the edge of the bed.

"Hey . . . are you okay?" I ask in a quiet, and what I hope is calming, voice.

Duh. Stupid question. If she were okay, she wouldn't be in this place.

"Do you have your phone?"

Her voice is muffled, because her face is still half buried in the pillow.

"My phone? Yeah, why?"

"I want to . . . They won't let me use the computer in here and . . ." My sister sits up and faces me, reaching out and taking my hand. "I have to see if he wrote to me."

I'm about to say, *"Seriously?"* but I bite the word back.

"Lara, I can't let you use my phone. Mom and Dad would kill me."

I try to pull my hand out of her grasp, but she holds on.

"Come on, Syd, *please*," she begs. Her fingers are white-knuckled around my wrist, gripping so hard it hurts. "I need to know."

"Lara, no! I can't do it. You shouldn't be asking me to."

"Shouldn't be asking you to do what?" It's the nurse, carrying a tray with a small paper cup containing pills and a plastic cup filled with water. She looks at Lara sternly.

My sister's fingers become limp on my arm and fall off, and her eyes plead with me not to rat her out.

I don't know if I'm doing the right thing by covering for her, but I say, "Nothing," and I get up to leave.

As I walk out the door, I hear the nurse quizzing my sister — was she asking me to do something that was against the rules?

"See you tomorrow, Lara," I call out.

As bad as I feel for my sister being stuck in this awful place, part of me hopes the nurse tells the doctor that she was trying to break the rules and that she has to stay in longer.

I'm the worst sister in all eternity.

———

Mom and I have to stop at the pharmacy on the way home from the hospital to pick up prescriptions they've called in for Lara so we'll have them when she's released. We bump into Mrs. Helman, Spencer's mom. She asks how Lara is doing.

"Much better," Mom tells her, beaming at Mrs. Helman with what I've started calling her Paranormal Smile. "She's improving every day."

Considering we've just left Lara having to be given something "to calm her down" because she was crying her eyes out, I have to wonder if my mother is living in some kind of alternative reality.

"I'm so happy to hear that," Mrs. Helman says. "Let me know if there's anything I can do to help."

And then Mom asks her if she's planning to go to the city council election debate, and I have to walk away, because it's just too weird to hear Mom talking about her opponent, school funding, and property taxes like nothing is wrong. Going on like life is normal when we'd just left Lara behind locked doors that they have to buzz you in and out of like a prison. Pretending that everyone at school, everyone on our street isn't talking, isn't wondering what's so wrong with us that would make Lara do it.

———

Dad went back to work after the hospital, and Mom and I have already eaten by the time he gets home, so he grabs a plate and comes to sit with me and watch TV. I'm watching a rerun of some old rom-com movie because I don't want to think about anything other than laughing.

"Can I switch to the news?" Dad asks.

"Dad, I'm watching this!"

"You've seen that movie at least five times already, Syd," he says. "And it's not exactly intellectually stimulating."

"I don't *want* intellectually stimulating," I say, throwing the remote control in his lap and getting up off the sofa. "I want something that's going to take my mind off this crazy house and all the crazy people in it!"

I stomp up to my room and hurl myself on the bed. I wish I were old enough to drive so I could get in the car and just *go* somewhere. Not that I have a destination in mind. Anywhere but here.

Unfortunately, I don't have that option. The closest thing I have is a book. I pull one of my favorites off the shelf and start reading it again, hoping that reading about other people's problems will help me forget my own.

———

My sister is home from the hospital by the time I get back from school the next day.

"Shh!" Mom says when I let myself into the kitchen. "Lara's resting. She tires very easily."

"Is she in the family room?" I ask. "Because I have homework to do and I need to use the computer."

"No, she's in her room," Mom says.

"So . . . why do I have to shush, then? She's upstairs. I'm downstairs. I can't even talk in my own house?"

We're inside the house, so the Paranormal Smile is nowhere to be seen. Mom gives an exasperated sigh. "Sit down, Sydney. I need to explain a few rules going forward," she says.

This doesn't sound good. I slide into a chair at the table and perch on the edge, waiting for the axe to fall. What are my parents going to take away from me this time because of Lara?

"Your sister is still in a . . . fragile state," Mom says. "We have to keep a close eye on her to make sure she doesn't come to any harm."

"Wait, you mean she might try to kill herself again?"

"There's no immediate risk but —"

"If they thought she might try to do it again, why'd they let her out of the freaking hospital?" I ask, my voice rising in anger at the doctors who made the decision.

I don't want to knock on my sister's door or the bathroom door and get no answer and wonder if she's okay or if she's dead. I don't want to feel that sick, gut-wrenching panic ever again.

"Sydney, keep your voice down!" Mom hisses. "Lara's sleeping."

"How am *I* supposed to sleep knowing my sister might try to kill herself in the next room at any random moment?"

"Can you just listen to me before you start with the drama?" Mom says.

Oh, I'm *the one with the drama? Wow, Mom.*

"Lara will be seeing a therapist regularly, and I have to keep her under constant observation," Mom continues. "That means she has to keep her bedroom door open and even the bathroom door has to be kept cracked open when she's inside."

"What, even when she's, you know, *going*?"

"Yes, even then," Mom says, her face grim.

"That's kind of creepy," I say.

"It's a whole lot less creepy than finding her unconscious in the bathtub surrounded by pill bottles," Mom says.

I have to admit she has a point there.

"Wait — those rules don't apply to *me*, though, do they?"

Mom looks confused.

"No. Why would they apply to you?"

"Because last time, when Lara was trying to lose weight, you made *me* stop eating cookies, too."

The look on Mom's face would be comical if it wasn't my life we were talking about. It was like this was some huge revelation to her, when *she* was the one who made the freaking policy.

"I didn't do that!" she protests.

"What do you mean, you didn't do that? Of course you did! You don't buy cookies anymore. You don't make any. This house has been a Cookie-Free Zone since Lara was in middle school."

"But . . . that was because I was trying to create a supportive environment for Lara to lose weight," Mom protests. She looks down at her fingers and fidgets with her engagement ring. "I never intended it to feel like a punishment for you, sweetheart."

"Sure doesn't feel that way."

"I'm sorry."

She says it so softly I think I've misheard. I've never heard Mom say those words to me before. Apologies are a one-way street in our house, a street that goes in the parental direction. Until now.

But when I look at Mom her eyes are glistening. There's no Paranormal Smile. I think this is the real deal.

"I'm doing the best I can, Syd. I try, but I don't always get it right," she says, an unfamiliar wobble in her voice.

I'm not used to seeing her like this. Hearing her admit that she's not right all the time, that she's sorry, that she's not the Paranormal Queen of Perfection, is what makes me get up and hug her, even though I'm still mad.

"It's okay, Mom. Nobody's perfect."

She hugs me back, and I breathe in the scent of the perfume she always wears and the smell of her shampoo. So what if Lara is falling to pieces — Mom still puts on makeup and dresses like she's on a photo shoot. Maybe that's the glue she uses to hold herself together.

Mom releases me and sighs heavily.

"I don't have to tell you how having to be here to watch Lara constantly is going to impact my campaign," she says.

And that's when our little "moment" ends with a thud.

"Maybe you can get Lara to apologize for the poor timing of her suicide attempt," I say before taking my backpack and stomping upstairs, ignoring the stricken look on my mother's face.

LIAM

"**DID YOU** hear? Sydney Kelley's sister got let out of the hospital."

"You mean the girl who tried to kill herself?"

"Yeah. My sister said some dude dumped her on Facebook and that's what made her do it."

That's the kind of buzz going around the cafeteria at lunch.

I see Sydney walk in with her friend Cara. She stands in line to get her food. At first she's chatting with Cara. But then I watch as her back tenses up and her hands clutch the tray tighter. As she starts hearing what people around her are saying. Then she says something to Cara and rushes out of the cafeteria, leaving her tray.

"Yo, Liam — you zoning out or what?"

Oliver waves his hand in front of my face to get my attention.

"What?" I ask.

"Did you hear anything I just said?"

"You asked me if I was zoning out."

He gives me an "Are you kidding me?" look.

"Duh. *Before* that."

"Uh, no."

"Are you going to debate club after school?"

"Yeah," I tell him, but my mind isn't on debate. Or on the fantasy football league, which is what the other guys at the table are talking about. I'm wondering where Syd is and if she's okay. I want to find her and ask, but I'm afraid she'll think I'm weird if I do. So instead I pretend I just got a text, and under the pretext of replying, I send one to Sydney.

Hey, saw you rush out of the caf. You okay?

She doesn't answer right away. I start to think she isn't going to, so I force myself to join in the fantasy football league discussion and act like I care.

And then my phone vibrates.

Not really.

Anything I can do?

Tell everyone to shut up about Lara? Make
the world go away?

I wish I could do that. But I can just see me standing up in the middle of the cafeteria and shouting, "Could you all just shut up about Lara Kelley? And now, back to your regularly scheduled programming . . ." That would only make people talk about it more — and then they'd be talking about me, too, and how crazy *I* am.

Wish there was something that I could ACTUALLY do, I text back, before saying, "Are you serious? I can't believe you played the Bills running back over the Bears last week. You left twenty-five points on your bench."

As Roger Cohen launches into his reply, Syd texts back.

> There's nothing anyone can do. That's the
> worst part of it.

My fingers tighten around my phone. I feel like throwing it at the wall. *Someone* should be able to do *something. I* want to do something. But I don't know what to do or how to do it.

So I just type, Hang in there, Syd, and go back to talking about fantasy football.

LARA

THE ONLY time I've been out of the house since they released me from the hospital is to go to see Linda, my therapist, which I have to do every few days until she decides I'm sane enough to reenter society and, more importantly, go back to school. Part of me hopes that's never. Every time my parents bring up the subject of if I want to go back to Lake Hills or transfer somewhere else it makes me want to take more pills. Like that's even a possibility. Anything that might resemble a pill is under lock and key in our house. The next time I get my period, I'm going to have to ask Mom's permission to even take Midol. She's probably going to ration my use of tampons in case I try to make a noose out of the strings.

The problem is the alternative is staying home, bored out of my head, under Mom's watchful eye. On the therapist's advice, I'm not allowed to use the computer or my cell phone "until my emotional state is more stabilized," so even if someone *did* care — like, say, if Christian changed his mind after he heard I tried to kill myself — no one can contact me. Mom turns off the router when I have assignments so I can't get online. The only thing I can use is Microsoft

Word. If I need to look anything up online to get my schoolwork done, Mom stands over me, breathing down my neck till I'm done. I'm not sure which of us hates the new arrangement more.

I've tried reading, but the words bounce around the page like Dad when he's had too many cups of coffee. The doctor warned me there might be some neurological effects from the overdose. He said that hopefully they'll just be temporary, but only time will tell. Great. Imagine if they're not. That'll make going back to school even worse. Now everyone will call me *Stupid* Lardo.

So I've been watching a lot of daytime TV, mostly kid programs, because in those, everything has a happy ending. Even though I know that's a lie, that in reality everything goes downhill once you get to middle school, and things never really get tied up in a neat bow after half an hour in real life, it's better than watching *Maury* or *Jerry Springer*, where the whole point of the show is to see people whose lives are so messed up that they're willing to find out who is *really* the father of their baby on national TV. Why would anyone want to find out something that personal in front of an audience? Don't they ever think about how someday that poor little baby will be a teenager and see his or her screwed-up parents fighting on YouTube?

I'll take *Sesame Street* over that in a heartbeat.

While I'm counting with the Count, I list the reasons why I wish the pills had worked.

1. *I wouldn't have to face going back to school.*

2. *I wouldn't spend the rest of my life being known as the girl who tried to kill herself and failed at that, too.*

3. *I wouldn't have to remember, and so, because of that, and here's the biggie:*

4. *I wouldn't have to feel. Anything. Ever again.*

But what I'm doing is putting me on Dr. Hospital Shrink's Naughty List, because I'm not supposed to be engaging in "destructive negative thought patterns" like this. Instead, I'm supposed to be making a Gratitude List of three things I'm grateful for every day.

I was like, "How am I supposed to do that? My life sucks. That's why I'm here in the first place."

Dr. Hospital Shrink just smiled and nodded, like yeah, yeah, he'd heard it all before.

"It doesn't have to be a big thing, Lara. It can be something as small as being grateful that you got the right flavor Jell-O on your dinner tray."

"If I liked Jell-O, which I don't."

"But you get the idea," he persisted. Dr. Hospital Shrink was annoyingly persistent.

As much as I pretended not to, I did. This was my list for the first day:

1. I'm grateful for water. I'm thirsty.

2. I'm grateful that Mom and Dad went home
   to shower and change so I had a break from
   them sitting by my bedside, sighing and
   making me feel like I'm their Problem Child.

3. I'm seriously grateful for toilet paper. That
   activated charcoal they gave me to help get
   the drugs out of my system is making me poop
   a lot, and it's making my poop beyond gross.
   Like, I mean, even more beyond gross than
   poop usually is. It's totally black, like coal.

This episode of *Sesame Street* is brought to you by the letter *W* for *Waste of time.*

Making the list hasn't been getting easier, even after being out of the hospital for a week. I'm still stuck on number one for today's list.

Oh wait:

1. I'm grateful for Sesame Street *so I don't have
   to watch "Mothers who sleep with their son's
   girlfriend's brothers" on* The Jerry Springer Show.

One down. Only two more to think about in the endless hours that stretch between now and when I go to sleep and this all starts over again.

2. *I'm grateful for naps, because they help pass
    the time and let me forget.*

Except when they don't. Except when I dream about Christian.

Last night I dreamed that he *did* ask me to his dance and I bought that ivory dress I loved on Wanelo. He looked hot in his tux, and he told me I was beautiful when he slipped a pretty corsage of tiny pink roses with a small spray of baby's breath onto my wrist — the touch of his hands on my wrist sending shivers up my spine.

In my dream limo, he put his arm around me and rested his hand on my bare shoulder, gently touching my skin with his fingertips. He whispered in my ear that he loved me and this was going to be the best night ever. In my dream, I believed him, my heart beating faster in excitement and anticipation, because just by being there with him and having his arm around me, it already was.

But when the limo pulled up at the dance, it wasn't at his high school; it was at my middle school. And all these people outside dressed in tuxes and beautiful dresses were holding big signs that said *Lardo* and *Lardosaurus*. I was scared Christian would see them and change his mind, so I tried to kiss him to distract him from the signs. But instead of leaning in to kiss me with his perfect, warm lips, he pulled away from me in horror.

"Why would I want to kiss *you*?" he asked, his handsome face distorted almost beyond recognition by disgust and loathing. "*Lardo*. You repulse me. I would never want to be seen with you in public *anywhere*, let alone a *dance*."

"But . . . *why*?" I pleaded, reaching for him, still feeling the warmth of his fingers on my skin. "A few minutes ago, you said . . ."

"The world would be a better place without you in it, *Lardo*," he said, and he was no longer handsome. His eyes made me shiver, but with fear, not anticipation; his mouth was a thin line of cruelty. But worse still were the words that came out of it. "You should just do us all a favor and kill yourself."

I woke up, my heart racing, with tears streaming down my cheeks. In the stillness, in that lonely quiet of three in the morning when no one else was awake, I cried into my pillow so my sister wouldn't hear through the wall, and I wished once again that the pills had done their job.

And the question that I asked myself, over and over, as I tried to get back to sleep, staring at the shadows on the ceiling was: *What did I do wrong?*

Until I understand that, making these stupid gratitude lists is just a homework assignment in fakery, because I'm mad that I still have to wake up every day to a world where nothing makes any sense.

No way am I going to be able to come up with number three today. Linda, the therapist I see now that I'm out of the hospital, is just going to have to deal. Just like she expects me to. Just like everyone else thinks I should.

Mom knocks on the door: her attempt at pretending I

have privacy. I'm not allowed to shut it anymore in case I harm myself. They're protecting me from me.

Even when I shower I have to leave the bathroom door ajar, which is totally awkward when Dad's home. My parents promised that when I take a shower he's not allowed to come upstairs.

But still . . . the faint draft coming in from the open door reminds me that I'm not to be trusted.

Now I know how zoo animals feel, always watched, always observed, never able to escape except in their heads. Except now everyone's trying to watch me in there, too.

"Lara, honey?"

"Yeah?"

She inches into my room and takes a seat on the edge of my bed. I shove the stupid gratitude journal under the covers. No way I want Mom prying into that.

Elmo is telling kids about how great it is to share. Oh, Elmo, you poor, deluded little red fur ball. You don't have a clue, do ya, li'l buddy? Kids are *way* meaner than Muppets.

"Can you turn down the TV a little?" Mom asks.

I push Mute. Elmo's relentless optimism is starting to grate on my nerves anyway. He doesn't get it. Wait till you hit puberty, Elmo. Just you wait.

"The police called," Mom says. "They're coming over in half an hour to talk to us — well, specifically to talk to *you*. I thought you might want to take a shower and get dressed."

Not particularly. I'm happy to stay in my pj's, with unwashed hair and no makeup and unbrushed teeth. Because

I really don't care. I know I'm supposed to, but I don't. But here's the thing with Mom: When she says, "I thought you might want to . . . ," what she *really* means is *I want you to . . .* If I say what *I* really feel, namely that I want to remain slobby and unwashed, she'll ask me twenty questions about why (answer: because I don't care about how I look) and don't I worry about the impression I'm giving the world (answer: no) and doesn't it make me feel better to be clean (answer: nothing makes me feel better).

I wish she would come straight out and say, *Go take a shower and get dressed*, instead of pretending I have any say in the matter.

"What do they want to talk about?" I ask, instead of telling her that.

"They want to ask you some questions about Facebook."

Ugh. Just what I'm trying to forget about. Just what I'd rather not think about ever again.

My father is *obsessed* with the subject. The other night he printed out his stupid spreadsheet for what feels like the millionth time and wanted me to look at it so I could tell him something about every single person on the list. I tore it up again without even glancing at it. He yelled at me, saying that I owed him my cooperation "after everything you've put this family through." Then Mom yelled at him for yelling at me when I'm "still so fragile and unstable." Syd yelled at both of them because she's "sick of living in such a messed-up family where everyone yells at each other all the time while I'm trying to do my freaking homework."

I curled up, wishing that I were a turtle with a hard shell that I could retreat into and hide when things got difficult or scary. And I stuck my fingers in my ears, asking myself again why I had to be such a failure, why I couldn't even get a simple thing like taking too many pills right.

What Dad doesn't understand is that I just want to forget. Every time he tries to ask me questions, I pretend to have a relapse, except the reality is I'm half pretending. My parents think that trying to commit suicide was the hardest part. They still don't get that *failing* is what's hard. How from the moment my brain starts to work again in the morning, I have to start trying to make sense of why I'm still here and to figure out how to survive another day.

Mom is alert, as always, trying to read every tiny change of expression on my face.

"Are you up for this? I spoke to Linda and she said she thought it would be okay. You have an appointment with her this afternoon anyway to process whatever might come up."

Process. Murray Monster, can we *ixnay* the word *process* for the rest of my life? There are word processors and food processors and processed meat, but apparently all my thoughts and feelings also have to be processed, like spray cheese or SPAM.

"Whatever. I'll go take a shower."

I might have to keep the door cracked, but at least Mom won't follow me in there.

In the shower, I twist the hot tap up until the water turns my skin pink. If only hot water could sterilize me; if only it could boil the thoughts out of my brain. At least it fills the bathroom with swirling mists of condensation. I close my eyes and try to visualize my brain as the fog: grayish white, fluffy, with no form, no thoughts, no pain.

It works for about four seconds before Christian's face emerges from the mist. *The world would be a better place without you in it.*

I might as well do what Mom says and wash my hair, since I'm an epic failure at my own life.

———

"You look refreshed, dear," Mom says when I walk into the kitchen.

Refreshed. Rebooted. Reprogrammed. Re*processed.*

Ignoring her, I open the fridge and scan the contents for something that might make the Gratitude List. But there's no cookie dough, no gooey chocolate cake, no unhealthy snacks. Mom thinks I still care about not being Lardo, that I still think all those trips to the nutritionist and all that extra exercise and the weighing food and mindful eating and stuff were worth it. Nope. If there were a big chocolate cake in the fridge, I would eat the whole thing and wash it down with a quart of milk. Because what does it matter? What does anything matter when the world would be a better place without me in it?

"Don't leave the fridge door open. Can I make you something?"

If she could make me understand about Christian, that

would be something useful. But she can't. I mumble, "No thanks," and grab a yogurt that I don't really want, just to stop her from nagging me.

"They should be here in a few minutes," Mom says. She's watching my every movement, even as I go to get a spoon for the yogurt, hypersensitive to the weapons for self-harm lurking all around me. Kitchen knives. Matches. Glass. You name it. It's all here in our kitchen.

I don't respond. I just sit and eat the stupid yogurt. It's banana, which makes it even less appealing. This is definitely not going to be one for the Gratitude List, unless I can write that I'm glad that eating it is over. Luckily for me, the doorbell rings.

Mom looks from me to the direction of the front door, her brow furrowed. She's obviously worried about leaving me alone in the presence of So. Much. Danger.

"I'll just get the door," she says. "Back in a sec."

As soon as she leaves the room, I ditch the rest of the yogurt in the garbage can, making sure to hide it under something so Mom doesn't see. If there's one thing being in the Shrink Hospital of Horrors taught me, it's that I have to play the game.

When Mom comes back, she's followed by a police lady and a guy wearing a worn jacket and khakis instead of a police uniform, but you can still see the gun holstered under his arm and the badge at his waist.

"Lara, honey, this is Detective Souther and Officer Hall. Officer Hall was here the night you were . . . taken to the hospital. Officer, Detective, can I get you anything? Coffee? Water?"

"No thanks," Detective Souther says. "Are you most comfortable chatting here, Lara?"

I'd be most comfortable not chatting at all, but nobody is giving me that option.

I shrug. "Whatever."

We all sit down at the kitchen table. Detective Souther takes out a little black notebook. Something tells me he doesn't have to make useless Gratitude Lists in it.

"We've been looking into the activity on your Facebook profile the night of your . . ." He hesitates for the briefest second. "Hospitalization. We're here to ask you about a young man named Christian DeWitt."

If there is one thing in the world I don't want to talk about to the police, especially in front of my mom, it's a young man named Christian DeWitt.

Math equation: Christian + talking = pain.

But if I show that I'm freaked out by the idea, Mom will get even more freaked out, creating a vicious vortex of freaked-outness.

"Oh? Like what?" I ask with pretend nonchalance.

"How long have you been friends with Mr. DeWitt?" Detective Souther asks.

Before he turned on me? Two months, four days, eleven hours . . .

"About two months."

"Have you ever met him in person?"

I avoid looking at Mom.

"No. But he was friends with a bunch of kids from my school, so I figured he had to be okay."

Mom exhales her disapproval.

Yes, Mom, I know. I broke the rules. Don't you think I've learned my lesson?

"Did he friend you or did you friend him?"

This guy clearly must have forgotten what it's like to be in high school. Like I *ever* would have had the courage to friend someone as good-looking as Christian.

I couldn't believe when I got the friend request from him. He's so gorgeous, like, seriously, he could be an Abercrombie model. I looked at his profile picture for ten minutes, unable to believe that he actually wanted to friend me.

"He friended me."

"And how did you develop a relationship?"

What relationship? There is no relationship, Detective. Somehow — I don't know how or why — I screwed it up.

"We started chatting. You know, by IM."

"Did you ever video chat?"

"No. I wanted to, but the camera on his laptop was broken."

"Did you ever speak to Mr. DeWitt on the telephone?"

"No."

"And on the night of your hospitalization, he sent you this message?"

Detective Souther nods to Officer Hall and she takes a piece of paper out of a folder. It's a printout of the Facebook direct message Christian sent me. The one that said the world would be a better place without me in it. The one that said, "GOOD-BYE, LOSER!!!"

I realize, horrified, that they'd been reading my chats and my emails. They know everything. How stupid I'd been. How I believed someone like Christian could actually like someone like me.

But they're still asking me questions instead of giving me answers. Like everything else that's supposed to be helping me, this is just another royal waste of time.

I'm beyond sick of it. I'm furious.

"Why are you even bothering to ask me questions when you've already pried into my personal life and read everything?! When you already *know*!" I snap. "Huh? Why don't you answer *my questions* for a change?" I stand up and grab the paper, crumple it up into a ball, and throw it on the table in front of the spying detective.

"Lara!" Mom exclaims. "Calm down!"

She grabs my wrist and tries to pull me back into my chair.

"Why should I?!" I shout at her, trying to pull my arm out of her grasp.

Don't I have a right to be mad? Why does she always shut me down?

"Maybe this was too much, too soon," she explains to the police, pasting on a warped version of her Politician Smile. Even Mom can't manage full-watt fakery right now.

"This must be incredibly painful for you, Lara, and I

understand that our questions feel intrusive," Officer Hall says in a calm, gentle voice. "But we want to help you find answers."

I still.

It's the hope, however unlikely it might be, of finding an answer that makes me slump back into my seat and answer the question. Trying to understand why Christian turned on me is an obsession.

"Yeah. He sent me that message. I don't know what happened. I don't know what I did wrong, why he suddenly changed like that. He went from being so sweet to . . ."

This is why I don't want to let any kind of feeling start — because I have no control over the size of it, or how to control it or stop it if it gets too much. Emotion pours over me like a tidal wave, drowning me with primitive force. I lay my head down on my arms on the table and sob until the sleeves of my T-shirt are wet.

Mom flutters around me, panicked by the force of my grief, stroking my back, trying to give me tissues, telling me everything is going to be okay, which I know isn't true. I know full well it's a lie, because how can things ever be okay after what's happened?

When my sobs have slowed to sniffles, Mom sits holding my hand, and I face Detective Souther and Officer Hall with red, swollen eyes.

"Lara, you didn't do anything wrong to make Christian turn," Officer Hall says. "The thing is . . ."

She glances at Detective Souther. He takes over.

"What we've learned from our investigation, Lara, is that there is no Christian DeWitt. The profile was deleted a week after you were hospitalized. According to the administration at East River High, there is no student of that name registered. No family by the name of DeWitt lives in the town of East River. And we cross-checked the few profile pictures — they are all of a young man named Adam Bernard who models for Abercrombie and Fitch, the clothing store. We contacted Mr. Bernard and he has no knowledge of anyone named Christian DeWitt."

I stare at his mouth as the words come out, my mind unable to believe what he is telling me can be true. It can't be.

This is a dream. A really bad dream. The worst dream ever. I'll wake up and it won't be true, just like the one I had where I went to the dance with Christian in the limo and we ended up at my middle school with everyone calling me Lardo.

I start pinching my leg, hard, with my left hand, over and over to try to wake myself up. Mom sees me and takes my hand.

"Lara, stop. You're going to bruise yourself," she says, thinking that I care.

And that's when I know beyond all shadow of a doubt, this isn't a dream. The horror of this is that I'm awake, and it's all too real. Even worse, it's not going to go away.

I thought my world had already shattered when Christian sent me that message, but I realize now that was only the appetizer, the prelude to *this* moment, which is the main course.

Because Christian isn't even real. He's fake. I tried to kill myself over a boy who doesn't even exist. It's official. I am the stupidest person alive.

And I wish, even more now, that I were dead.

PART TWO

TWO MONTHS EARLIER

LIAM

EVER SINCE I can remember we've had a Sunday afternoon family football-watching ritual. If Mom makes appointments to show a house during game time, Dad gets mad because he says it's supposed to be our "sacred time" or whatever. Mom's a bigger believer in the sacred principle of making money and paying the bills — at least that's what she says whenever they fight about it, which is often.

But today, the sacred gathering around the big screen is on — well, kind of. At least we're all in the same room, sitting around in front of the television, with the game on, pretending that we're watching it together. Bree checks her cell phone every few minutes. Mom has her iPad on her lap to check work emails and browse real estate websites, but she's smart enough to look up and comment about game plays often enough to keep Dad happy.

I don't know why Dad insists on this whole family football deal. If you ask me, everyone would be a whole lot happier if he just let us do our own thing. But gathering around the TV to watch guys throw the pigskin is Dad's thing with a capital *T*. So we do it.

The camera focuses in on the cheerleaders, who are totally hot in their short shorts, crop tops, and knee-high leather boots.

"Don't they get cold when the game's in, like, November?" I ask. "I mean, they're not exactly, you know, *wearing a lot.*"

"Is that so?" Dad chuckles, glancing over at Mom. "I can't say I noticed."

My mother makes a *pfft* sound and rolls her eyes.

"That reminds me, cheerleading tryouts are this week," she says to Bree. "Do you want to go through your routine with me before dinner?"

"No," Bree says right away.

She couldn't be more obvious about wanting to kill that idea in a hurry.

Still, I don't blame Bree. Mom's a frustrated cheerleader. She shows up at all the games with the school colors painted on her cheeks, like she's trying to live out her regret that she didn't make the cheerleading squad in high school through my sister. It makes me want to crawl under the bleachers — but if I say anything, she's like, "Come on, don't you have any school spirit?"

"Why not, Bree?" Mom persists.

"I just don't, okay?"

"Bree, I —"

"Can't this wait till halftime?" Dad says.

I can't tell if he's really upset that we can't hear the commentator, or if he's trying to shut them down before this turns into World War III, like so many conversations between Bree and Mom do these days.

"Yeah, it totally can," Bree says, giving Mom a pointed look. "I'm gonna make some popcorn."

"Don't forget the butter," I remind her.

"Not too much," Mom says. "It's already butter flavored."

"But that's fake butter," I complain. "Real butter tastes better."

Bree makes a disgusted noise and escapes to the kitchen to avoid the butter war.

Dad says, "Can we go for five minutes without arguing about something so I can actually watch the game? Timer starting . . . now."

He looks at his watch. I turn my attention back to the game. Dad must be feeling lucky today. I'm pretty sure the longest we've ever gone without an argument is three minutes, ten seconds.

LARA

IF THE mayor's speech goes on much longer I'm going to fall asleep on the stage. And seeing as how there are photographers from local papers and online news sites here, that will *not* go down well with Mom. Or His Honor, Mayor Robinson. But seriously, how many political speeches can one teenager be expected to stay awake for at a single event? So far we're at eight and counting . . . Any more have got to count as cruel and unusual punishment.

It would be one thing if they actually said something interesting. But every single speech consists of the politician thanking all the other politicians and the people gathered to listen, before wrapping up with five minutes or more of bland generalizations about how proud they are to serve and democracy is great and blah blah blah God bless our town and the United States of America.

Because we're in the front row, I can't even check Facebook or Instagram or even send #Imbored selfies to my friends. I have to try to stay awake and look attentive, like the perfect politician's daughter.

Syd, who is on the other side of Dad, looks like she's struggling, too. We exchange a glance of mutual misery. I hope none of the photographers catch it. If they do, *we're* going to be the ones who catch it from Mom.

When the thing is finally over, Mom makes us go over and say hi to the mayor.

"I can't believe how much you've grown," he says. "Two beautiful young ladies you've got there, Kathy."

Mom gives him her high-wattage smile.

"I know. Smart, too."

"Just like their mother," the mayor says.

Gross. Political flirting, and in front of Dad, too.

One of the photographers asks if he can take a picture of us with the mayor.

So we pose with him — the perfect Kelley family. #LOL

"Can I take a picture with you?" I ask Mayor Robinson. I figure if I have to sit through hours of political speeches then I should at least have something to show for it.

Mom shoots me a disapproving look, but the mayor laughs.

"Sure," he says. "If world leaders can do these cell-phone selfies, then I reckon it's okay for Mayor Robinson of Lake Hills."

I stand next to him and take a picture of us with my phone. When I check it, I realize Syd has photobombed it — there's half of her face with a cheesy grin and one of her hands giving a thumbs-up.

But I can't yell at her because we're being a Perfect Family, and Perfect Siblings don't argue with each other — especially not in front of the mayor and the assembled press, who have just snapped pictures of him and me taking a selfie.

"Thanks, Mayor Robinson," I say.

"My pleasure," he tells me, smiling.

We're all smiling around here. My face hurts from having to smile so much.

While Mom drags Dad around for more political chitchat, Syd and I retreat to a corner and check our phones. I post my pic on Instagram and Facebook with the hashtag #chillinwithMayorRobinson.

And I count the minutes until we can go home.

BREE

"WOW, SHE'S turned into such a show-off," I say when I see Lara's #chillinwithMayorRobinson picture on Instagram.

"Who?" Mom asks.

"Lara," I tell her, handing her my phone.

She reaches for her glasses, but she can't find them. I don't tell her they're on the top of her head, because it's kind of funny watching her look for them when they're right there.

"What does it say?" she asks.

"Chilling with Mayor Robinson," I say, disgusted.

"Is that Sydney in the background?" Mom asks.

I look closer. "Yeah, looks like she photobombed it."

"Let me see," Liam says.

He studies it intently. "I wonder if Syd posted anything," Liam says, pulling out his phone to check.

"Hand it over here," Dad says, dragging his attention away from the game. "I want to see what all the fuss is about."

"Why does she always have to brag about hanging out with the mayor?" I say. "She's always posting pictures of them at the grand opening of some new restaurant or whatever."

"It's part of being a political family," Dad says. "I bet you anything Pete Kelley would rather be hanging out watching the game than listening to speeches."

"Maybe . . . ," Mom says. "But Kathy's gotten pretty full of herself since she got elected to the city council."

"She seems the same to me," Liam says.

"That's because you don't have to deal with her in business," Mom says. "I've been lobbying her about the tax breaks that would benefit my clients since I worked my butt off to help get that woman elected. Now that she's in office does she help me, her friend and constituent? All I get are excuses about 'balancing developer interests with environmental concerns.'"

Dad and Liam aren't close enough to hear her when she mutters "The two-faced . . ." Her voice fades away before I can hear the end of that sentence. But it shocks me to hear her say something so horrid about Lara's mom.

Still, at least she's stopped nagging me about showing her my cheerleading routine.

I forward the picture to Marci and Jenny. #whoyouchillin with #notthemayor

Jenny sends us back a selfie of her and her dog. #chillinwithBailey

Marci sends a picture of herself with a mannequin at Victoria's Secret. #chillinwiththePinkdummy

Making a joke out of it makes me feel better. Like I don't have to be jealous of Lara anymore.

LIAM

WHEN BREE tells Mom she's thinking of skipping cheer-leading tryouts at dinner Tuesday night, you'd think Bree announced she'd killed someone by the way Mom reacts.

"What do you mean you don't want to try out for cheerleading?"

Mom sounds like her head is about to explode. She's been sending Bree to cheerleading camp since she was practically old enough to walk. When Bree was on JV last year, Mom was at every game taking pictures and video.

"I was just thinking . . . maybe I want to try something else," Bree says, but now she sounds a little less sure. "Like dance team."

"When you have the chance to make varsity cheerlead-ing?" Mom nearly shouts. "Why would you do that?"

Bree looks to me for support, but I'm not about to stick my neck into this fight. Mom's like one of those crazy stage moms, except it's about cheerleading. And it's not like she even made the squad herself.

"I'm bored of cheerleading," Bree whines. "I've been doing it forever."

"You want to give up because you're *bored*?" Mom says. "You're never going to get anywhere in life if you drop things the minute you get bored, Breanna."

Uh-oh . . . Here we go . . . We're in for another lecture about how we have it so easy and we need to get some grit, otherwise we're not going to succeed at college, jobs, life, you name it. We might as well just give up and die because we're so freaking soft and lazy. Okay, maybe she doesn't go *that* far, but the whole time Mom's on one of these rants you start feeling worse and worse about yourself. You just wait for it to be over so you can escape to your room, put on headphones, and listen to music that lifts you up again.

Except now I'm stuck at the dinner table and Dad's working late tonight, so he's not here to cut Mom off, which he does when she starts getting out of hand. So thanks to Bree, I have to listen to the full-length tirade.

Bree stares at her plate, picking at her food with her fork.

"Colleges and employers don't take kindly to quitters, Bree," Mom continues. "I want you to think about that before you make an irrational decision."

If Dad were here, I could ask him if people really look at what you did after school in high school when you apply for a job. He's okay with those kinds of questions. But Mom takes it badly when you dispute her Truth. Very badly. So I don't.

But I kind of wish that Bree *would*. I mean, this is her life. Her fight. If she really wants to try out for dance team, then why doesn't she speak up instead of letting Mom lecture her out of it?

Whatever. I eat as fast as I can and ask to be excused, leaving Bree to fight her own battles. Or not.

LARA

I'M SO nervous the morning of cheerleading tryouts I can barely eat.

"Are you sure this is a good idea if it's making you so stressed you're losing your appetite?" Mom asks.

"I'm *fine!*" I snap at her, and shove a few more spoonfuls of cereal I'm not really hungry for into my mouth just to prove it to her.

Syd slams her cereal bowl down on the table.

"What's the matter?" Mom asks.

"Nothing," Syd says. She pours her cereal and milk and starts eating with quiet determination, ignoring Mom and me.

My sister is such a drama queen. But at least Mom's annoyed at her now, so I manage to finish breakfast and get out the door to catch the bus without her giving me any more grief about trying out for cheerleading.

———

Bree is waiting at the bus stop when I get there. She nods hello as I walk up. There was a time when we would have started talking nonstop the minute we saw each other, even though we'd been texting and chatting for hours the night before. But that was before we got to high school, and she decided I wasn't worth being friends with anymore. She started hanging out with Marci Liptak and Jenny Cole, two "cool girls" who had gone to the other middle school. Bree made it very clear I wasn't invited when they went to the mall or the movies.

That wasn't the best time of my life. But I've moved on, too.

"Hey," I say. "You going to cheerleading tryouts after school?"

Bree looks surprised that I'd ask. I guess it is kind of a dumb question, because she was on JV cheerleading last year, and she's been doing cheerleading practically since she could walk.

"Yeah," she sighs.

"Me too," I tell her.

Her look of surprise turns to shock.

"*You're* trying out for cheerleading? *Why?*"

"Why not?" I say. "I've always wanted to do it. I just wasn't in good enough . . . you know, *shape* to do it before."

What I mean is that Lardosaurus would never have been allowed on the cheerleading team. But I'm not her anymore. I've changed.

"But it's not like you know any moves or anything."

"That's not true. You taught me, remember?"

Bree shrugs, because it's true. Back when we were friends, the minute she'd get home from cheerleading camp, we'd get together and she'd show me what she learned that day. I begged my parents to send me to the same camp, but they wouldn't. They thought I should be more "well rounded." But I think the real reason was because Mom was afraid I was *too* rounded.

"Well, good luck," she says as the bus pulls up. She doesn't sound like she means it.

"You too," I tell her, but it's to her back because she's already getting on the bus. She goes to sit in the back with someone else, making clear that our mutual cheerleading tryout isn't something to re-bond over.

Whatever. I tried. I guess you can't repair some friendships, no matter what.

———

"Hey, if you're not going to eat your potato chips, can I have some?" Julisa asks me at lunch.

"Me too," Luis, her twin brother, says. "What's with you anyway? You buggin' about something?"

I hand him the bag of potato chips. "Share them with Julisa. And yeah, I'm bugging about cheerleading tryouts."

"Oh yeah, they're today, right?" Julisa says.

"Yup. I'm *sooooooooo* scared I'm going to mess up," I tell them.

Luis observes me intently as he crunches on a mouthful of potato chips.

"What?" I ask.

"I just don't see it. Why are you trying out for cheerlead-ing?" he asks. "You don't seem the type."

Is he saying I'm too fat to be a cheerleader?

That's the first thought that goes through my head. I cross my arms defensively over my belly to hide it from his view.

"I mean, going from yearbook and debate club to try-ing out for varsity cheerleading?" he continues. "That's . . . different."

"Shut up, Luis," Julisa says. "Lara can do whatever she wants."

"I'm not saying she can't," he says, keeping his brown eyes trained on me. "I'm just curious. Why?"

Luis and Julisa also went to the other middle school in town. They don't know the sad, painful history of Lardosaurus, and the last thing I feel like doing is going on an archaeological dig so they do. I don't want to explain that, for me, getting on the cheerleading team would mean that Lardo was well and truly gone and that all the hard work I did to get in shape was worth it.

"It's something I've wanted to do for a long time," I tell him. "And I guess I figured . . . now or never."

"Good for you, Lara," Julisa says. "Go for it. You'll be awesome."

"Yeah. I'm sure you will be," Luis says, even though I'm pretty sure he still doesn't get why I'm doing it. "Good luck."

When the bell finally rings and it's time for tryouts, I go down to the locker rooms to change into my shorts and T-shirt. Even though I've lost weight, I still get really self-conscious changing in public, worrying that everyone is still looking at me and thinking, *Lardosaurus*.

"Are you new?" the girl next to me asks. "I don't remember you on JV last year."

"I was here at Lake Hills, but I wasn't on JV," I tell her.

"Oh," she says. "What made you decide to try out this year?"

"I've always wanted to," I confess. "And I finally got up the courage. Well, except that I'm so nervous now I'm not so sure about the courage part."

"I'm sure you'll do great," she says. "My name's Ashley, by the way."

"I'm Lara," I tell her as I bend to tie the laces on my sneakers.

"Well, good luck!" She heads off into the gym with a bounce in her step, looking way more confident than I feel.

I walk over to the sinks and take a final look in the mirror, making sure my hair is neatly tied up so it won't get in my face when I do tumbles.

Bree completely ignores me when I walk into the gym. Whatever. I'm here to try out for the Lake Hills High Varsity Team, and I'm not about to let Bree Connors psych me out. I just hope I make it.

BREE

"**DON'T FORGET** to text me," Mom says for what must be the twentieth time since we left the house.

"Omigod, Mom, I *will*," I snap, slamming the car door on whatever else she was about to say, because I'm so sick of her nagging me.

She cares more about me making the varsity cheerleading team than I do.

Because Mom didn't make it as a cheerleader in high school, it's super important to her that I do. Ever since I can remember, she's told the story of the Mean Girls and the Evil Coach who came between her and her dream of wearing a short skirt and waving pom-poms. It was her favorite fairy tale, but without the usual happily-ever-after ending.

"But it toughened me up" was how the story ended instead. "It gave me the grit that made me the successful real estate broker I am today."

Still, when I made JV last year you'd think I'd gotten into Harvard she was so excited. She took me out shopping at the mall and then for frozen yogurt to celebrate. I began to wonder if she'd be half as excited if I actually got into

Harvard, not that there's the slightest chance *that* will ever happen.

The whole reason she drove me today instead of making me take the bus is because Ms. Carlucci might post the list before school, and she wanted to make sure I got in early enough to check. Personally, I could have waited until lunch, but I'll take any excuse not to have to ride the bus.

Marci and Jenny are hanging out on the wall near the front door, playing Fashion Firing Squad before the bell rings.

"Hey," I say, settling my butt on the cool concrete next to Marci.

"What's up? Awesome day, right?" Marci says. "Well, it would be if I didn't have to look at Maribel Agesta's muffin top explosion. *Ugh.*"

"Seriously," Jenny groans. "Doesn't she look in the mirror before she leaves for school?"

I wonder what they said about my outfit before I walked into earshot, or if being their friend gives me a pass from judgment. The thing is, even if Marci and Jenny aren't judging me, I know there's always someone at our school who will. You walk into the wild jungle of judgment every time you open the door to the student center.

"Check out Tim Daniels. He's expecting a flood," Marci says. "I think he's been wearing the same pair of jeans since sixth grade."

"And that shirt — did he get it at *Nerdcrombie?*"

Marci laughs at Jenny's lame joke. They both look at me because I'm not laughing. They expect me to say something — to agree, to make fun of him, too.

The thing is, even though he wears the same pair of high-waters every day and he's kind of strange, Tim's okay. Last year when I was struggling with algebra, he helped me with my homework in study hall a bunch of times.

Still, if it's a choice between Tim Daniels and me, guess who's getting thrown under the bus?

I giggle, but it's a couple seconds too late.

"What's with you this morning, Bree?" Marci asks.

"Oh, I'm just nervous because the lists go up for cheerleading today," I tell her, even though that's not what's really the matter.

I wonder: Is there anyone I can tell that sometimes I want to crawl out of my own skin and be a different person than who I am? Be someone other than the Breanna my mother wants me to be?

"Ohmigosh, when?" Jenny squeals. "I'm sure you'll make it."

"Not sure," I mumble. "Maybe before school. Maybe during the day. Maybe not till after school."

"Why aren't you there checking now?" Marci asks.

I don't have a good answer. So I pick up my book bag and stand up.

"I guess I better go and look before the bell rings."

"Good luck!" Jenny calls after me.

I'm not sure if I want it. Because I secretly half hope I don't make it, even though it would suck if I didn't because it would just give Mom another reason to think I'm not good enough. What I really want is to make it, and then tell Mom I'm not going to do it. That I'm going to try out for the dance team, no matter what she says.

If I could actually get up the courage to do it.

I can see from down the hall that there's nothing posted on the cheerleading trophy cabinet yet, so I turn around to head to my first-period class. Lara Kelley is coming down the hallway, obviously going to check if the lists are up. I could tell her that they aren't yet, but I don't. I just nod in her general direction and keep walking.

I can't believe we were best friends once, running back and forth between each other's houses like there were no doors to stop us and sharing secrets up in the tree fort. I'd been so excited when Mom sold the Kelleys that house and told me a girl my age was going to live there. Dad always used to look over at the big oak tree in our backyard when we had cookouts and say how it would be great for a tree fort. Mom would laugh and say she'd never trust us in a structure that Dad built up in a tree. It was different some-how when Lara's dad said the same thing. Dad said, "That's what I've always said," and Mom suddenly changed her mind. Our dads worked together on the tree fort for months, and all these years later it's still standing.

That's more than you can say for our friendship. Every-thing is different now. Awkward. Ever since seventh grade when Lara got all crazy and depressed, and I had to spend night after night listening to her go on about her awful life. High school gave me a chance to break free.

Now she's lost all this weight and tried out for cheerleading. Why is she trying to force her way back into my life? I've made other friends now. Like, I'm happy for her that she's managed to get her act together and all that, but I've moved on. Can't she get a life of her own?

Mom texts during second period, asking if the list is posted yet.

No. STOP. I'LL TXT YOU! : /

I press Send.

Shouldn't she be busy selling houses or doing her volunteer work with Habitat for Humanity or whatever? She should know better than to text me during school anyway.

I'm trying to pay attention while Ms. Blackstock reads from *Julius Caesar,* "'A friend should bear his friend's infirmities, but Brutus makes mine greater than they are.'"

She tells us that means Caesar thinks friends are supposed to put up with their friends' faults, but that Brutus exaggerates all of Caesar's.

It makes me wonder if that's how Lara feels about me. It's not that I didn't feel bad about pulling away from her when we got to high school. But seriously, I'm not exaggerating what she was like in middle school. The girl was totally cray-cray.

How long do you put up with someone's faults before you get sick of it and give up? I totally get why Brutus stuck it to Caesar. If you ask me, Brutus got a raw deal. The play should have been named for him.

I check to see if the list is up again during lunch. It's not. I send Mom a text telling her that so she doesn't text me during class again.

What's the matter with Coach Carlucci? This is her JOB, Mom texts back. Maybe I'll call her.

NO!!!! DON'T!!!!!!!!!!!!!! I text back.

Ugh. My mother isn't just a Tiger Mom. She's a freaking Great White Shark Mom. She should have her own week on the Discovery Channel.

By the time the end-of-school bell rings, Mom's texted me three more times, even though I told her I'd text her as soon as I knew anything. You'd think it was her who was waiting to hear if she was going to make cheerleading, not me.

When I walk down to the trophy cabinet, there's already a bunch of girls hanging around the list. Lara is one of them, and I hear her let out a shriek as I approach the group. I'm not sure if it's of disappointment or excitement, but then she turns around and starts jumping up and down. It makes my stomach clench tighter as I draw closer to read the names.

They're in alphabetical order and . . . there's no *Connors*. It skips from *Chapman* to *Dresner*. I read it twice, just to make sure. There's *Kelley, Lara*. But no *Connors, Breanna*.

I can't believe it. Am I being punked? *Lara* made the squad and *I* didn't? This is just wrong.

Lara is talking to Ashley Trapasso, a junior on the team, and she is all giggly and happy. As if she senses my gaze, Lara looks in my direction and laughs.

Seriously?! After all the time I spent listening to her whine about how much her life sucked, she has the nerve to laugh at me when I get cut from cheerleading? I turn on my heel and head out of there. I feel my phone buzzing — probably another text from the Great White Shark. I ignore it. I can barely handle myself right now. The one thing I *do* know is that someday, somehow, I am going to make Lara pay for laughing at me when my life sucks after all those times I listened to her whine when hers did.

———

When I get home I fling myself onto my bed and blast music and decide to repaint my nails. I can't believe I didn't make the team, even if deep down, there's a part of me that's relieved, because now I have an excuse for not doing cheerleading. But I just can't believe Lardo made the team over me. Something has to be seriously wrong with the universe for that to happen.

My phone is buzzing constantly. Mom's probably flipping out, wanting to know if I made the team. But I'm not up for the sigh, the rant, the way she'll make this all about her. Because this isn't about her. It's about me. And Lara. And her laughing at me for getting cut. This is about me figuring out how to get my revenge for that, somehow. The question is: How?

"Bree!" my brother shouts from downstairs. "Pick up the freaking phone! Mom wants to talk to you!!"

Guess I can't avoid talking to the Great White Shark Mom any longer. Time to be reminded of what a disappointment I am. Always *such fun*.

"Yeah," I say when I pick up the phone.

"Breanna, your father and I don't pay for you to have a cell phone so you can play stupid apps. We pay for it so we can communicate with you when we need to. That means you pick up the phone when we call and answer our texts when we text. Do you understand?"

"Yes, Mom."

"So? What happened? Why have you been avoiding me?"

I take a deep breath and exhale the answer into the phone. "BecauseIdidn'tmakeit."

"What do you mean you didn't make it?"

"I mean, I'm not a varsity cheerleader. I got cut."

"That can't happen!" Mom shouts into my ear. "I paid for all those camps! You were on junior varsity! You can't get cut!"

"Apparently I can, Mom," I point out. "My name wasn't on the list."

"Did you go to Coach Carlucci and ask her why?" Mom asks.

"No," I say.

"Why not?" Mom asks. She's sounding increasingly irritated, and I can tell that she's winding up for a lecture.

"I didn't feel like it, okay? I just wanted to come home."

"You didn't feel like it?" Mom repeats in a scathing tone. "You have to start advocating for yourself, Breanna. You'll never get anywhere in life if you stay a doormat."

"Wow, thanks for the pep talk, Mom," I say, feeling a lump rise in my throat. "You always know just what to say to make me feel better."

And I hang up on her.

Picking up the nail polish and turning my music back up to loud, I finish painting my nails bright red and start adding glitter stripes.

"Hey, can you turn that down or use headphones?" Liam says, sticking his head into my room. "I'm trying to do homework."

"Can you do it? I don't want to ruin my nails."

My brother rolls his eyes and grunts but stomps into my room to reduce the volume on my Jambox. And just before he does, I hear the chorus of the song that was playing:

You said you loved me, but it was all a liiiie.

Now I'm so lonely, all I do is crrrry.

That's when I get the idea. The genius idea of how I'm going to get my revenge on Lara for laughing at me.

———

The first step is to set up a new Gmail account. That takes all of, like, two minutes. Then I use the new Gmail account to open a new Facebook account. I search Google images for a really hot guy, the kind of guy I know that Lara would think is gorgeous. The kind she'd totally flip out over if he showed the faintest bit of interest in her.

This is where I have an advantage from being her former best friend. I know her taste in guys. We used to sit in the food court at the mall, rating guys on a scale of one to ten. She'd sigh every time we went into Abercrombie, because the models were so hot. Not that it did her any good. The salespeople in that store looked down their noses at her because she was overweight. She usually ended up more depressed after we went in there, and then I'd have to hear about it. It got to the point that if I wanted anything from Abercrombie, I'd make sure to go there with ABL — Anyone But Lara.

I end up picking an Abercrombie model, but just his face, because he's got to look like he's still in high school and there aren't that many guys at our high school who have washboard abs like this dude. His name's Adam Bernard, but I create a new identity for him. I search for some other pictures of him and upload them so it looks like he has a reasonable profile. On his new fake Facebook profile, I call him Christian. Christian DeWitt. He goes to East River High, which is about an hour away from here — far enough that Lara wouldn't know him and close enough that she'd think they might have a chance of meeting someday. I give him some of the same musical and TV likes as she has and then have him friend me. I send a bunch of friend requests from him to other kids I know at our school, and then a whole bunch to freshmen and sophomores at East River

High. East River is a big school and he's supposed to be a senior there, so they might not know him, and since he's good-looking I figure they'll probably just friend him.

Sure enough, by the time I finish my homework, Christian already has 150 friends. That's when I figure it's safe for him to send the friend request to Lara.

LARA

KELLEY, LARA.

It's there. My name. On the list of girls who've made the cheerleading squad.

I'm on the team. I'm part of the group. It's official. I'm not Lardo anymore.

I read it again to make sure I'm not seeing things and then let out a shriek of excitement.

"I can't believe it! I made it!"

"Awesome! I had a feeling you would," says Ashley.

I can't believe she's talking to me. Smiling at me.

"Welcome to the team," she says.

Being friendly to me. This wouldn't have happened two years ago. Maybe not even one year ago. But it's happening now, and I almost have to pinch myself to believe it's real. That it's happening to me, Lara Kelley.

"I'm *so excited*," I tell her. "But also kind of nervous, to tell you the truth," I confess.

"Don't worry," Ashley says. "Everyone's nervous at first. You'll do great."

She gives me a hug, and for the first time in years it

feels like I'm a part of something special. I wish I could take this moment and put it in a bottle to save in my memory box so I can remember it whenever I start feeling like Lardo again.

I smile my thanks back at her.

"Hey, are you busy on Saturday?" Ashley asks. "A few of us are going to the mall."

"Yes!" I exclaim. And then I realize that came out wrong. "I mean, no, I'm not busy, and yes, I'd love to come."

We both laugh, and as we do, I glance over and see Bree giving me a death glare. Like, seriously, if looks could kill, I'd be pushing up daisies. I try to ignore her, but I can't help wondering why she's mad at me. Then I see her turn and stomp off down the hallway, looking at her phone.

"What's up with Bree Connors?" I ask. "She just gave me a totally evil look."

"Oh, she's probably pissed she didn't make the team," Ashley says.

"Wait . . . she didn't?"

I'm genuinely surprised. I'd have thought Bree would have made it before I did. She was on JV and has been doing cheerleading way longer than me.

"Nope," Ashley says. "She's pretty good technically, but Coach said she didn't have a great attitude in JV. Like she was going through the motions instead of really putting her heart into it, and it showed."

"Oh . . . I just . . ."

"Don't let her bother you," Ashley advises me. "Haters gonna hate."

Ha! Don't I know it . . . But for once, I'm on the inside, not on the outside, being hated on. And I'm loving the way it feels.

"Yeah. I guess so," I say. "Well, I better run, or I'll miss the bus."

"I'll Facebook you my cell," Ashley calls down the hall after me. "So we can make plans for Saturday."

———

Bree is sitting in the back of the bus, and she gives me another killer glare when I get on before turning her face away and pretending I don't exist.

I get that she's pissed she didn't make the team, but what I don't understand is why she's so mad at me. It's not like I'm the only one who made the team when she didn't.

Besides, Bree of all people knows how hard things have been for me. I know we aren't such good friends anymore — well, hardly friends at all anymore, if I'm honest — but that's not my fault. *She's* the one who dumped *me*, not the other way around. Still, you'd think even if she can't bring herself to be happy for me, she could at least not be mad that my life is finally taking a turn for the better.

Whatever. Like Ashley said, "Haters gonna hate." It's her problem, not mine.

I get most of my homework done and then go on Facebook. I make my status *OMG!!!! I'm A CHEERLEADER!!!!! :)* Then I wonder if it's too dorky and if I should delete it. But it gets three likes pretty much right away, so I leave it.

Dad brings home takeout from my favorite Chinese restaurant to celebrate me making the squad, although Mom makes a point of measuring my portions, because she wants "to make sure you don't put the weight back on if you're going to be wearing those short cheerleading skirts."

Like I wasn't already worried about how I was going to look in them.

"So does this mean you'll get takeout when I get a lead part in the eighth-grade musical?" Syd asks.

"*If* you get a lead," I say.

Syd ignores me.

"Well, does it?" she asks Dad again.

"I will buy takeout to celebrate my little Drama Queen, too," Dad says, smiling at her.

"Good. Because Maddie and Cara and me are already planning our audition pieces," Syd says. "I'm going to get a lead."

"Maddie, Cara, and *I*," Mom corrects her. At least it's not just me she's nitpicking tonight.

Syd gives an Oscar-worthy sigh of irritation.

"*Maddie, Cara, and I*," she repeats, in what I have to

admit is a spot-on imitation of Mom. Maybe she might get a lead after all. "And when I *do* get a lead, we are *not* having Chinese. We're going to have yummy Italian from La Dolce Nonna."

"Well, let's celebrate Lara's good news while we eat her choice tonight," Dad says.

"Then she'll celebrate your good news while she eats your choice when the time comes," Mom adds.

IF the time comes, I think again but don't say.

———

Right before I go upstairs after dinner, I check Facebook again. I've got a friend request from some guy I've never heard of, Christian DeWitt, who's a senior at East River, a high school in a town an hour away from here. I have no idea why he's friending me, and I normally wouldn't friend someone I don't know — my parents are real freaks about that. But he's gorgeous. I mean, like, model hot. And he's friends with a lot of my friends, so I figure maybe it's okay. Even Bree's friends with him.

Still, if my parents find out I've friended someone I don't know, it's a grounding offense. Like I said, total freaks. That's why I'm not allowed my own laptop, and Syd and I have to share this computer in the living room, which is *so annoying*.

With Mom being on the city council, she's all about "setting examples" of how to be the Perfect Parent. And of course she knows the police chief personally, so Syd and I always have to be a Perfect Example of everything. Nothing less than perfection will do when you're the daughters of Councilwoman Kathy Kelley. Being fat and depressed definitely didn't fit the profile.

I gaze at Christian DeWitt's picture, the cursor hovering over the Confirm button. He's seriously hot. I can't believe he wants to friend me. *It can't hurt*, I tell myself, clicking Confirm.

I'm about to get off the computer when I hear the plink of Facebook chat.

I can't believe it. It's *him*. Hot-as-anything Christian DeWitt! Hey, congrats on making cheerleading! he writes.

Thanks! I'm pretty pumped. :)

So, how was the rest of your day?

Pretty good. How about you?

Better now.

What was the matter before?

Stuff. You know, it happens, right?

Don't I know it!

At least you're having a good day . . .

Good doesn't even begin to describe it. I made varsity cheerleading team, and now this amazing-looking guy is chatting with me. When I think about where I was a year and a half ago, I can't even believe this is happening.

Yeah. Pretty awesome day.

And my day just improved because I'm
talking to a cute girl like you.

He. Thinks. I'm. Cute. !!!!!!!!!!!!!!!!!!!!

I suddenly worry, though, that this is so weird and sudden. What if he's some middle-aged creeper pretending to be a teenager, like when the police come to school to give us those "Be Very Afraid of the Internet" talks?

But if he's friends with all these people I know and all the kids at his own high school, he must be legit. *Do you need glasses? ;P* I type.

Come on, don't be modest. You're
really pretty.

Pretty? He seriously must be blind or something.

"Lara, are you done yet? You're not the only one who has homework, you know!"

Figures, just as I finally have some gorgeous guy telling me I'm cute and pretty, my sister butts in and tells me she needs the computer.

Gotta go, I type, hoping that this isn't the last time I ever hear from him.

Chat soon! he writes.

Smiling, I log off Facebook.

"It's all yours," I tell Syd, and I head upstairs. My life really is turning around, and I couldn't be happier.

LIAM

YOU'D THINK it's Mom who didn't make the cut for varsity cheerleading by the way she's stomping around the kitchen, breathing fire and smashing pots and pans down on the counter.

"I'm going into school tomorrow morning to talk to Coach Carlucci," she fumes. "This is ridiculous! How can she cut *you* and let *Lara Kelley* on the team?"

"Mom! *No!*" Bree shouts. "Don't do that! It'll just make things worse!"

"Worse, how?" Mom asks. "How can things be worse than you not making the team?"

Bree stares at Mom. Her fists are clenched, her face is turning red, and I see a tear escape the corner of her eye. She looks like she's either going to let Mom have it or start crying hysterically. I wish she'd finally let Mom have it. I mean, it's not like she *wanted* to make cheerleading that much anyway. Maybe it's a good thing she got cut.

Her mouth opens and I think, *Come on, Bree . . .*

But then she starts crying and runs out of the room. A minute later we hear her door slam.

Another typical evening in the Connors house.

Mom picks up the phone and calls Dad. "Sean — how long till you get home?"

Yeah, Dad — we need you here to bring on the sanity.

"Oh, Bree's in her room having another tantrum." Mom sighs. "I just don't know what's got into her . . . Yes, I know hormones, Sean. But there's more to it than that . . . Okay, see you soon."

She hangs up and takes out the potato peeler.

"Liam, peel these potatoes for me, will you, please?"

Great. That's what I get for hanging around to watch the drama. Stuck peeling potatoes while Bree has another tantrum and does nothing.

I start peeling the stupid potatoes.

"At least you're not giving me problems right now," Mom says.

But like an idiot, even though it's not my fight, I start doing just that.

"Bree didn't even *want* to do cheerleading, Mom. Maybe it's a good thing she didn't make it. Now she can try out for something else."

The look on my mother's face when she turns to me makes me curse myself for opening my big mouth.

"A good thing? Is that what you think, Liam?"

"Forget it. Never mind," I mumble.

"No, let's hear this," Mom says. "Why, Liam? Why is your sister getting cut from the team after we've made sacrifices to pay for her to go to cheerleading camp every year a good thing?"

"Because . . ."

Why did I say anything? This isn't my problem. It's Bree's. And you never win an argument with Mom, especially when she's in a mood like this. I sigh.

"Really, Mom, forget it. You're right. It's bad. Whatever."

She's not happy with me, but at least she lets it go, so I can finish peeling the potatoes and escape to watch TV until Dad comes home.

I turn on the news, which isn't much of an escape, but Mr. Phillips tells us we should keep up with what's happening in the world if we want to be part of debate team. I flip from one cable news channel to another, wondering how the same story can sound so different depending on which channel I'm watching.

I always thought the news was supposed to tell it like it is.

There's only so much news I can take before I switch to one of the science channels. Watching things get blown up in the name of science makes me feel better.

My father sticks his head in the living room when he gets home.

"Hey, buddy — how's it going?"

I roll my eyes. "Great — if you like living in the middle of a war zone."

"Yeah, I gathered there's been a disturbance in the Force," Dad says. He's a *Star Wars* geek, but he leaves it up to me to figure out who's Darth Vader in this particular episode.

He sits down on the sofa next to me, just as there's a really epic explosion on the TV. "Wow. That was awesome!" he exclaims.

"Yeah. It was kind of like that between Mom and Bree, but I'd rather watch it on TV than in real life at home."

"I hear you, Liam." He gets up from the sofa with a grunt. "I'll try to go impart some Jedi wisdom to the warring parties."

"Good luck with that," I mutter.

But I lower the volume on the TV so I can overhear his conversation with Mom. He's the calming one. Maybe I can learn something.

"I'm going to go into school tomorrow and talk to Coach Carlucci," Mom's telling him. "It's ridiculous that Lara Kelley made the team and Bree didn't, and you know it."

"I don't know anything, Mary Jo," Dad says. "Maybe Bree had an off day and Lara was in top form."

"But if she just had an off day, Coach should take that into account," Mom says. "Everyone has off days."

"Honey, you told me Bree said she wanted to try out for dance team. Maybe she didn't give the tryouts her best shot," Dad suggests.

"That's not the way I've brought up my daughter," Mom says. "I've told her she's always supposed to give everything her best shot, no matter what. Did I get to where I am today by half measures?"

"Of course you didn't. But she's a teenager. She has to learn these things for herself," Dad says.

"So you want me to let our kids fail?" Mom says. "Is that what you're asking me to do?"

I hear her stirring something on the stove; the metal spoon is clanking angrily against the side of the saucepan.

"I don't want the kids to fail any more than you do," Dad says. He's starting to lose his Yoda-like calm. "But they're going to face disappointments in life, and they need to learn how to cope with them without us rushing in to try to make it better."

"So then they'll be disadvantaged," Mom argues. "You think Kathy Kelley isn't pulling strings with the mayor to get whatever she can for *her* kids?"

"Yeah, and do things always go so well with Lara?" Dad says. "Just because other parents are doing it doesn't mean we should."

Score one for Dad by bringing up Lara's imperfections.

Mom grumbles her response, so I can't hear what she says. But from the tone of her grumbling, I can tell that Dad's won this round. Now he'll go up and talk to Bree, and hopefully peace will be restored in the Connors household in time for dinner — which is good because I'm starving.

BREE

I HATE my mother. Nothing I do is ever enough because I'll never be *her*.

What if I don't want to be her? Does she ever think about that? What if I want to be *me*, whoever that is?

Like I'll ever get a chance to even find out, living with the Great White Shark Mom.

If she goes to talk to Coach Carlucci tomorrow, I'm never going to speak to her again. Ever. I will *die*. Seriously, die.

There's a knock on my door.

"Go away, Liam!" I shout.

"It's Dad. Is it safe to come in?"

He says it in a joking way, like he knows how mad I am at Mom. Dad's gotten used to acting as the United Nations peacekeeping force between us.

"Yeah, okay."

Dad comes in and closes the door behind him.

"Doing your homework?"

"Trying to."

"It's hard to concentrate when you're upset, huh?"

I nod.

"Heard about cheerleading."

I don't say anything. I don't even look at him. I don't want to talk about it.

"Look, Breenut," Dad says, calling me by a nickname from when I was a baby. "I know Mom's upset you didn't make the team, but it's not the end of the world."

That's when I turn to him. "Do you mean that?"

"I wouldn't say it if I didn't."

I have to swallow a lump in my throat. At least one of my parents doesn't think I'm a total disappointment.

"In a way, I think this could be good for you. It'll give you a chance to try something new. Didn't you say you wanted to try dance?"

"I did. But it's probably too late to try out now."

"Well, how about exploring some other interests?"

That would be good if I could think of any. But it's pretty much been cheerleading all the way my whole life.

"Like what?"

"Anything. Newspaper. Debate. Volunteering. School dance committee. At last year's open house, they had a list of clubs as long as my arm. Longer, even."

"I'm not going to do debate like Liam, Dad," I tell him. "Forget it."

"I just used that as an *example*, Bree," Dad says. He sounds a little irritated. "Choose whatever strikes your fancy. But try something new. Experiment while you're young, before you get stuck in a track and it's too late."

He sighs, and I wonder if he feels like he's stuck and it's too late. Did he dream of owning his own plumbing supply store when he was my age? Didn't he ever want to get out of Lake Hills and go somewhere else?

"Okay, okay, I'll think about it. Thanks, Dad," I say, turning back to my desk. "I've got to finish my homework."

Dad comes over and kisses the top of my head.

"Go easy on your mother, Breenut," he says. "She means well."

Whatever feelings I had of being understood disappear. As Dad walks out of the room, I can't help wondering if he asked Mom to go easy on me, too.

———

I've been chatting with Lara as this Christian DeWitt guy for a few weeks now, and it's getting kind of weird because Lara is flirting with me. I mean *really* flirting. It's a side of her I've never seen before. I'm like, *Who IS this person?* This isn't the Lara I knew. This definitely isn't the Lara you see in school.

Okay, so I'll admit I started flirting with her first. I mean, *Christian* did. *I* would never flirt with another girl. It's not like I'm gay or anything. I guess that's why this all feels so weird.

But like I said, it's not *me* who's really flirting with her. It's Christian, or, as Lara's started calling him, *sweetie* (barf), *honey* (puke), and *babe* (awkward).

Sometimes it creeps me out so much to be flirting with her that I don't know how much longer I can keep doing it. I wonder if I should shut down his profile and the Gmail account without saying good-bye. Just disappearing

Christian DeWitt from the face of the Internet. A few clicks here, a few clicks there, and His Royal Hotness Mr. DeWitt is virtual toast.

But then Lara walks past me at school with Ashley Trapasso, the two of them in their little cheerleading outfits with matching purple-and-gold hair ribbons, and Lara ignores me like she's better than me all of a sudden.

That's when I realize I have to continue, and I laugh to myself as she passes, because I know that the guy she's seriously started crushing on is just make-believe. That actually, that guy is *me*, her old BFF Breanna Connors. How do you like *that*, Lara, sweetie, honey, *babe*?

I think it was because I was getting bored of flirting with Lara that I decided to let Marci in on the secret. Until then, my alter ego as Christian DeWitt was a secret between Gmail, Facebook, and me. But Marci was over one night around the time Christian would normally be chatting with Lara, and I was getting tired of having to keep thinking of nice things to say to the girl. I decided that Marci might be a source of useful inspiration.

At first I was really nervous about how Marci would react. I was worried she would think I was some kind of freak for doing this to Lara. Turns out she thought it was hilarious.

"Wait — Christian DeWitt is *you*?" she said.

"Yeah. Well, actually, he's this Abercrombie model," I told her, bringing up the model's website. "But the 'guy' Lara is crushing on? That's me."

Just then, I noticed that Lara had come online.

"Check it out. She's online," I said. "Want to flirt with her?"

Marci giggled. "Oooooh yeah! Flirting is my specialty!"

She was speaking the truth. It's one of the reasons I hang out with her. I keep hoping her flirting skills will rub off, and I'll be able to interact with guys without coming off as a total dork. I mean, I'm great at flirting from behind a computer screen when I'm pretending to be Christian, but put me in front of a real boy and I get tongue-tied.

I started off the conversation, asking Lara how her day went. She went on and on with all her boring cheerleading stuff: how she'd mastered some new tumble and she was going to be second from the top of the pyramid. Like some guy would actually care about any of that. If there were an Olympics for Boring, Lara would be the all-time gold medalist.

Marci was cracking up. "You'd think she'd never talked to a guy before," she said. "Let me have a turn!"

Marci doesn't know about Lara and me and how we used to be best friends, and about Lara's problems in middle school. She doesn't know what I know: that Christian probably *is* the first guy who has ever shown interest in Lara. And he's not even real.

"Sure," I said, letting her sit in the chair.

"I know!" Marci said. "Why don't we pretend Christian's got a big dance coming up at his school and have him hint that he's going to invite Lara?"

"Why didn't I think of that?!" I said. "I've been getting so bored of flirting with her. At least this will give us something else to talk about so I don't have to keep lying and telling her she's cute and pretty."

"Lara's kind of cute," Marci said. "I mean, she's not a total dog."

For some reason this annoyed me. She didn't know Lara when she was Lardo. I was the one who was friends with that girl. I was the one who had to listen to Lardosaurus cry and complain.

"Well, she's not my type," I said, trying to cover up my annoyance with a joke. "Anyway, let's look on the East River High website and see if they have an actual dance coming up, just in case Lara thinks to check."

We were in luck. The weekend before Thanksgiving there's the East River High homecoming parade, football game, and dance. That gave us plenty of time to string Lara along with the hopes of a fake date.

So do you have any big plans the weekend before Thanksgiving? Marci (as Christian) asked Lara.

> *Not really. I think we march in the*
> *homecoming parade. The cheerleaders,*
> *I mean.*

> You don't have a dance?

> *Well, there's a dance, but I doubt I'll go.*

Why not?

Oh, you know. Not my scene.

So . . . if we had a dance at East River, that
wouldn't be your scene?

Marci and I laughed as we watched the cursor blink,
picturing Lara completely freaking in front of her computer
as she tried to figure out how to respond. It took her long
enough.

*I guess that would depend . . . on who I was
there with.*

So, hypothetically, if you were there with
someone like . . . me?

"I wish I could see her face right now," I said. "I bet she's
peeing herself."

"I know, right?" Marci said. "Come on, Lara, tell your
boyfriend what he wants to hear!"

"I'm not her boyfriend *yet*," I said. "Don't rush things."

"You're not her *boy*friend at all!" Marci said.

She had a point. But *I'm* the real Christian. He's *my*
creation. I wanted to be the one in control, the one setting
the pace.

If it were . . . hypothetically someone like you,
then it would definitely be more of my
scene. :)

"Look! She went smiley face on him!" Marci said.

"DON'T ASK HER YET!" I said frantically. "Tell her you've got to go."

Marci looked at me like I'd flipped.

"Why? We were just starting to have fun."

"It's more fun to string her along," I said. "That's what Christian would do if he were a real guy, right?"

"Yeah, I guess." Marci sighed as she typed, Talk soon, gotta go.

I could just imagine Lara's disappointment as Christian logged off so abruptly after teasing her with the idea of the dance.

A few years ago, my phone would have been ringing right away, and we'd have dissected every sentence of the chat for meaning. But that's the beauty of this whole thing. I know exactly how Lara thinks.

———

Two days later, I tell Marci she has to come with me to the media center during our open period because I've got something to show her.

"This better be worth it," she says. "Because Taylor Goodhew is in the student center, and no offense, but he's a lot cuter than you are."

Marci's one of my best friends, but when she's pursuing a hot guy, she'll dump Jenny and me in a heartbeat. That's just the way she is. It's annoying, but you learn to live with it because she's fun to hang out with the rest of the time.

"You'll have time to go to the student center afterward," I tell her. "Trust me, you want to see this."

I find a free computer that isn't close to other students and go to Wanelo. I know Lara's screen name from back when we were friends. And I show Marci the "Cute dresses for the Dance" list she's set up.

"Oh. My. God," Marci says so loudly I have to tell her to shush before the librarian does. She lowers her voice. "The girl is, like, *totally delusional*. She's making lists of dresses to go to a dance with a guy that *doesn't even exist*!"

"I know! Isn't it hysterical?" I tell her. "And look at the dresses!"

"This one just screams loser," Marci says.

"What about this one?" I say. "It's like she wants to be Ariel from *The Little Mermaid* but *in tenth grade*."

We go through the entire list, shredding all of Lara's choices. Marci's having so much fun dissing Lara, she spends the whole open period with me and doesn't even care that she missed going to the student center to hang out with "way cuter" Taylor Goodhew.

SYDNEY

NOT A-FREAKING-GAIN. I am *so sick* of this! Every time I need the computer to do homework, Lara's on it. I thought since she made varsity cheerleading she'd be out of the house more and getting a life.

To be fair, she *is* out of the house more at practice and stuff, but the problem is when she comes home, she's glued to the computer. And judging from how she's all smiley and smug, I'm betting you anything she's *not* doing homework all the time she's on it, even though whenever I say I need to get on she swears she is.

Type, type, type.

Plink!

That's Facebook chat. She *so* isn't doing homework, the giggling, lying dork.

That's it. It's *my turn*.

"Lara, I need the computer *now. I've* got homework to do. You're just messing around."

"I'm *not,*" she says. "I'm chatting to someone *about* my homework."

Seriously, I can't understand why God doesn't just strike

her down with a lightning bolt. It's *so obvious* she's telling great big whopping lies.

"I'll give you twenty minutes, and then I'm calling Mom," I say, furious that, as usual, I'm the one who ends up giving in and letting Lara get her way.

Being the younger sister stinks. Especially when your older sister has "issues," and everyone expects you to tiptoe around her in case she loses it again.

Especially when she's completely fine now. But everyone got so used to her *not* being fine that my parents still treat her like a piece of fragile porcelain.

Me? I'm their beef jerky kid. As far as Mom and Dad are concerned, I'm a nonperishable item, tough as old boot leather.

I'm going to ask for my own laptop for my birthday. I don't care what the stupid police chief says. And if my parents say no, I'm just going to save up the money my grandparents give me for birthdays and Christmas and whatever until I can afford to buy one for myself. Then I can do my homework whenever I want to, instead of having to work around my faking-it fragile sister.

I have to get away from Lara and her annoying giggling, but I don't want to go all the way upstairs. I want her to know I'm hovering in wait. So I go out on the patio to text Cara and Maddie.

The sun is sinking behind the trees, and I see the silhouette of the old tree fort, the one my dad made with Mr.

Connors, where Lara and Bree used to spend so much time together before they stopped hanging out.

I spot movement in the shadows beneath the tree, a faint rustle of the dried leaves piled around its base. And then I see a person climbing up the wooden rungs nailed to the trunk. *Liam.*

These days we smile at each other on the bus and when we see each other in the halls, but since our families stopped hanging out, we don't see each other as much as we used to. I suddenly find myself wondering why. It's not like *we* ever had a problem with each other. I guess we were used to our friendship just happening. Or maybe he got embarrassed about hanging around with a girl because his friends were teasing him. I swear, the minute I started wearing a bra, some of the guys at school started acting all weird.

I glance inside. Lara's still on the computer. She's still got eighteen minutes, according to the time on my cell, so I figure, what the heck? I walk over to the bottom of the big old oak, hoping I don't scare Liam with the sound of my feet crunching through the leaves.

As I start climbing up the wooden rungs, I whistle so he knows someone is coming up. His head pops out of the doorway, and he shines the flashlight app on his cell down in my face, almost blinding me.

"Do you mind?" I complain.

"Oh, it's you," he says. "I was afraid it was Bree."

I climb up the rest of the way and crawl in to join him. The tree house seems so much smaller than I remember. A spiderweb catches in my hair as I lean against the wall, breathing in the must and mold of disuse. Liam lights a candle, and it glows, flickering, showing the boy-band posters my sister and Bree had tacked up on the wall back when they were into that kind of thing. Back when they were still friends.

"So what brings you up here?" Liam asks.

"I had to get away from Lara," I say. "And I saw you climbing up so . . ."

"Funny that," Liam says with a wry grin. "I came up here to get away from Bree."

"Remember how they always used to keep us out of here, even though it was supposed to be for all of us?"

"Oh yeah," Liam says. "And we'd be stuck down below complaining about how not fair it was, but not knowing how to do anything about it."

"How did they get away with being so mean to us?"

"'Cause they're the older sisters?" Liam suggests. "Because that's the way it is in families?"

"I guess. So is Bree still mean to you?"

"Not mean. Just . . . annoying. Seriously annoying. Sometimes it feels like the house isn't big enough for the both of us — that's when I escape out here. Bree hasn't been up here for, like, two years or something."

"It looks like no one's been up here. It's gross. You should clean the place up if you're planning to hang out here regularly."

He laughs, the candlelight reflecting on the whiteness of his teeth.

"Wow. You're such a *girl*, Syd."

"Duh, really? I hadn't noticed."

Some guys get all weird when I joke around with them. But not Liam. Even though we hadn't hung out in a while, he definitely gets my humor. We used to play Mad Libs and do silly stuff like try to make all the words have to do with farts and poop. It made us laugh so hard our stomachs hurt. Our parents called us the little hyenas, because we were always cracking up about something.

"Why did we stop getting together as families just because Lara and Bree got all teenage girl and fell out?" Liam bursts out suddenly. "Does the whole freaking world revolve around my sister?"

Yes! It's as if the candle's glow has reached to the very deepest part of me, the part that I don't want to let people see because I'm afraid it makes me an awful person. But suddenly, the person I'm so afraid of, Deepest Darkest Syd, realizes she's not alone.

"Tell me about it," I say. "When you're normal in my house, you might as well be invisible."

"How . . . is . . . Lara?" he asks.

"Oh, *she's* fine and being totally annoying and inconsiderate, not that my parents would ever see that. That's why I was outside. She's hogging the computer every night, pretending she's doing homework, but really she's chatting."

"'Totally annoying and inconsiderate.' Wow. Sounds just like Bree," Liam says.

We sit, watching the flickering candle, enjoying a moment of silent younger-sibling solidarity.

"Why didn't our moms stay friends?" he asks. "Or our dads?"

He doesn't say, "Or us?" but it's there, hanging unspoken like a ripe fruit unpicked, and now that I'm sitting here with him in the candlelight, I wonder, too. Because unlike all my other friends, Liam gets it.

"Mom got all caught up in the city council stuff, I guess."

"Yeah, she's, like, a big politician these days, huh?"

"Ugh, I know."

"And my mom's determined to be the real estate queen of Lake Hills," Liam said. "You can't go past a bus shelter without seeing her face."

"Tell me the truth . . . Have you ever felt like drawing a mustache on her poster with a Sharpie when you've been really mad at her?"

Liam bursts out laughing. "How did you know? That was the one secret I thought I was taking to the grave."

"Probably because I've felt like defacing Mom's campaign posters once or twice," I admit. "But at least I only have to deal with that every two years. You have to see your mom on the bus shelter all the time."

"Yeah, tell me about it. I mean I love Mom and all, but . . . 'Everything I touch turns to sold'? Cringe!"

"Well, what about *my* mom? 'Kathy Kelley — Putting the *public* in public service.' As long as she doesn't have to admit that there's anything the matter with our family in public, that is."

Speaking of things wrong with our family, I check the time on my cell. It's been more than twenty minutes.

"I've got to go. I told Lara she had to get off the computer in twenty minutes so I could do my homework, and her time is past being up."

"Wait," Liam says. "I . . . it's just . . . even if our families aren't friends anymore, do you think you and I could maybe still . . . you know, hang out sometime?"

Even in the candlelight, I can see him blushing through his freckles. *He means like friends, right?*

"Yeah," I say, hoping that's what he means, because I'm not sure how I'd feel about anything more. "See you in school. G'night."

"Careful going down. I'll shine the light for you."

I climb down the slat ladder bathed in the light from his flashlight app. We call good night to each other again when I reach the bottom. I crunch through the dead leaves back to my house. When I let myself in through the sliding door, my cold fingers and cheeks tingle from the warmth.

When I get into the living room, though, it's my temper that flares when I realize Lara is *still* on the computer, giggling and typing and so obviously *not* doing homework.

"Lara, get *off*! It's my turn."

"Just give me two more minutes," she says.

"I'm calling Mom," I say, pressing her number in Favorites.

Lara's still typing.

My mom picks up and she's *not* happy.

"Sydney, I'm in the middle of a council meeting. What is it?"

"Lara won't get off the computer, and I need it to do my homework. She's not even doing work, she's chatting."

"You interrupted me at a meeting —"

"*Mom*, I need to do my homework!"

"Put her on."

I hand Lara my phone. "Mom wants to talk to you."

I can hear Mom yelling at Lara, furious that we interrupted her while she's busy doing oh-so-important city council business at her meeting. Lara's typing as she's listening, but she finally says, "Okay, FINE!," hangs up, logs off, throws my phone onto the table, and storms upstairs.

I'm fuming with anger and frustration as I start my homework.

But then I think about hanging out with Liam earlier and how that was the best part of the day. At least Lara can't ruin that.

BREE

THERE ARE pros and cons to having told Marci about Christian. In the pro column, she's been giving me ideas on how to keep my flirtation with Lara going. I guess it helps that she's got a lot more experience with flirting than I have. Marci's way more advanced than I am on the guy front. She's done stuff that I only think about — and even then I feel guilty.

When we were all talking one night at a sleepover, Marci, Jenny, and me, I lied and said I'd done stuff I hadn't.

Afterward, I wondered why. Why couldn't I have just said, *I haven't done that yet?* What would have been the big deal?

I guess I was worried if I did, they might have made fun of me for *not* having done stuff, or they might think I was judging them for the stuff they'd done. What would have happened if I'd just told the truth?

Marci's totally into the Christian deception. She checks out Lara's dress list every day, and she judges up a storm. Marci makes the team on the show *Fashion Firing Squad* look like Girl Scouts. She texts me as soon as Lara posts something new, along with her biting review.

ZOMG, the latest one looks like a red velvet
cupcake with chicken pox! Hideous!!!

The funny thing is, Lara's getting more and more excited
about a dance that I haven't even asked her to yet. Or more
accurately, Christian hasn't. He's been hinting that he's
going to ask her, but he hasn't pulled the trigger. It's kind of
fun to watch Lara squirming like a worm on a fishing hook,
wondering if and when he's going to do it.

So Lara keeps herself busy picking out new dresses,
and Marci gets to play Fashion Firing Squad. It's a total
win-win-win.

One evening, I'm so busy multitasking, chatting to Lara
as Christian in one window on Facebook, laughing with
Marci about Lara's dress choices in another, and trying to
actually get homework done in a third, that between all that
and the music I'm blasting, I don't notice that my mom is
standing behind me, reading the screen over my shoulder.

"Why are you flirting with Lara Kelley?" she asks.

I jump and quickly minimize all my windows.

"MOM! Did you consider knocking?" I complain, but
my heart is beating furiously because I am *so busted*.

She sits on my bed.

"Is there anything you want to tell me, Breanna?" she
asks. "I know being a teenager can be . . . confusing, and
especially with all . . . well, those shows on TV and . . . well,
all I'm saying is, do you need to tell me something about
your . . . uh . . . preferences?"

It takes me a second to realize what my mom's saying, or not saying. And when I do I groan. Because, seriously? It's like she doesn't know me at all.

"I like *boys*, Mom, if that's what you're asking."

"I don't understand. Then why are you talking about going to a dance with Lara Kelley?" My mom glances between me and the now-blank computer screen, her brow wrinkling in confusion. Well, wrinkling as much as it can after the Botox she had done before she had the photos taken for those awful "Everything I touch turns to sold" bus shelter posters.

If I'd had some warning, I could have come up with an excuse, but I'm blanking, so I go with the truth. Well, truth-ish.

"It's a joke I'm playing on Lara, 'cause I was pissed she made cheerleading and I didn't," I explain, fully expecting the grounding guillotine to be lowered the minute I'm done. "I've been pretending to be this guy Christian for a month or so, and she's developed a major crush on me. Well, I mean on *him* . . ."

I trail off, expecting Mom to start her tirade about how I'm irresponsible and such a disappointment and how I should be more like her — all the usual complaints she has about how I don't measure up. But to my amazement, she smiles. And then she starts *laughing*.

"That's priceless," she says. "Lara actually *believes* you're this guy?"

"Uh . . . yeah. She's been, like, flirting with me. Well, him. She even thinks I'm going to invite her to my school dance, and she's picking out all these really fugly dresses just in case. I've kind of been stringing her along and . . ."

"Now this I have to see. Kathy Kelley's daughter flirting with a fake boyfriend. C'mon, show me!"

I'm totally glad she's not mad and grounding me, but . . . Suddenly, I have this crazy feeling that maybe I wish that she was. Because this feels kind of weird.

Reluctantly, I maximize the Facebook chat window. Lara's asking, *Christian? Are you still there?*

Yeah sorry. Had to step away for a sec.

Oh. Thought I said the wrong thing. :)

Lara is so insecure it's pathetic. Every time Christian shows the slightest bit of coolness to her, she thinks it's because she did something wrong. It makes it so easy to play her.

"Oh dear. Poor Lara. She's so needy and gullible," Mom says. "Tell her, 'You could never say the wrong thing, baby.'"

"What?"

"Go on. Type it."

You could never say the wrong thing, baby, I type slowly on the keyboard. Just a few moments ago I felt powerful, like Lara was my puppet on a string. Now, all of a sudden, the tables are turned. Now it's like I'm the puppet and Mom's the one pulling the strings.

"Type how cute that picture of her is, and how just looking at it gives you the warm fuzzies," Mom says.

"Christian wouldn't say 'warm fuzzies,' Mom. That's totally lame."

"Just type it," she orders.

My fingers pound the keys angrily.

Aw, you're so sweet. :) Lara types back. I seriously want to puke.

"Let me have a turn," Mom says.

I stare at her. "What?"

"Come on, move over. I want to be Christian for a while."

Okay, this has now officially moved into Beyond Weird territory.

"No. Mom . . ."

"Oh, come on, Bree. It's just a little fun."

I slide out of my chair. Mom sits down and immediately starts typing.

I feel like I'm going to throw up. It's one thing for me to do this. It was bad enough when Marci got involved. But now *my mother* is doing it.

"Kathy Kelley always walks around with her nose in the air like she's better than everyone else," Mom mutters as she's typing. "Pretending she's the perfect mom. Ha!"

She turns to me and smiles.

"We know better than that, don't we, Bree?"

"Um . . . yeah. We do. If she's such a perfect mom, then why is Lara such a screwup?"

I've heard Mom say those exact words so many times I just repeat what she expects me to say.

"I'm so sick of seeing her fake smile on those campaign posters," Mom says. "You should have made the cheerleading team, not that crazy daughter of hers. I bet it was all about politics. Kathy probably pulled strings with the coach. I knew I should have called Coach Carlucci."

I started this whole Christian thing because I was mad that Lara laughed at me when she made the team and I got cut. But listening to Mom, I try to remember *why* I was so mad. It wasn't me who was that into cheerleading to begin with. It was my mom. I've kept it going because I was bored, and to be honest, I'm curious how far I can take this. How long it takes before Lara realizes that she's been tricked into baring her heart to a fake guy.

But now that Mom's involved, I almost wish I'd never started.

"Chill, Mom, she didn't," I say. "I just didn't make the team, okay?"

"Oh, look, Lara has to get off the computer, but she sent us *xoxo*. How cute," Mom says. She types, Love you.

"What?!" I shriek. "What did you do that for? I'm not ready for the *L* word!"

"It's not *you* saying it," Mom says. "It's Christian."

Aaaaaaaaaaaaaaaargh!!!

Now I really wish she'd grounded me instead. It's always like this with Mom. I can't have anything for myself without her ruining it. I'm glad I didn't make the stupid cheerleading team. It's worth it just to spite her.

"It's about time someone took those Kelleys down a peg or two. I'm proud of you, Bree."

I've tried so hard and for so long to get my mom to say those words. But now that she does, they leave me feeling hollow.

LIAM

SYDNEY KELLEY and I haven't sat on the bus together for a long time, but after she climbed up and hung out with me in the tree fort last week, something's shifted. Today she gets on the bus before me, then slides over and smiles when I get on, inviting me to sit next to her.

I hesitate for a second or two, wondering about what Spencer and the rest of the guys are going to say. But then I remember how good it felt to chill with Syd again, and I sit down next to her, our shoulders touching as the bus lurches forward onto the next stop.

"How's it going?" I ask.

"Okay," she says. "Lara's still being annoying, but that's not exactly breaking news."

"Well, if it makes you feel any better, Bree is, too," I tell her. "But let's not talk about our stupid sisters, okay?"

"Good thinking," Syd says. She pulls some papers out of her backpack. "Hey, can you run some lines with me? *Beauty and the Beast* auditions are on Friday after school, and I'm trying out for Belle."

"Sure," I say, hoping I don't get carsick. I mean, we're on a bus, so maybe it'll be different.

"Don't worry, I won't embarrass you by singing any-thing," Syd says.

"I don't care if you sing, as long as you don't expect *me* to," I tell her.

She laughs and seems to shift a little closer to me. Our knees touch, and she doesn't move hers away.

"You read the Beast. Start here," Syd says, pointing with her finger.

"Okay. Here goes," I say, clearing the morning froggi-ness out of my throat.

"Belle? Are you happy here with me?"

"Yes," Syd answers tentatively.

"What is it?" I read.

Syd looks at me with wide, sad eyes. I feel queasy. I think it's just because I'm reading on the bus.

"If only I could see my father again, just for a moment. I miss him so much."

"There is a way," I read. I pretend to hand her a magic mirror. *"This mirror will show you anything, anything you wish to see."*

"I'd like to see my father, please," Syd says.

According to the script, this magic mirror shows Belle's dad stumbling around in the woods, lost, sick, and in pretty bad shape.

"Papa. Oh no. He's sick, he may be dying. And he's all alone."

Syd's good at this acting thing. I turn to look at her, because she sounds like she's starting to cry. But she smiles at me, so I carry on reading.

"Then . . . then you must go to him," I say.

I feel sorry for the Beast dude. He obviously likes this Belle chick, but he's going to have to let her go.

"What did you say?"

"I release you. You are no longer my prisoner."

I wonder — if I had a girl I liked as my prisoner and I thought maybe she was starting to like me back, would I let her go? I mean, I know it would be the *right* thing to do, but if I were some Beast guy living all alone in the middle of the woods, would I still care about doing the right thing? Who would be there to know if I did the wrong thing except for me?

"You mean . . . I'm free?"

Syd sounds so amazed that you'd think I *was* really keeping her prisoner.

"Yes."

"Oh, thank you," she says. And then she tells the pretend magic mirror, *"Hold on, Papa. I'm on my way."*

"Take it with you so you'll always have a way to look back and remember me," I read. I'm really feeling this dude's pain now. I don't want her to go.

"Thank you for understanding how much he needs me," Syd says, and the warmth and gratitude in her eyes is so genuine I almost feel like she's going to lean forward and kiss me.

"Did I get all the lines right?" she asks.

"What? Oh yeah," I say, half disappointed that she doesn't, even though I'd *really* catch crap for that. But it would be worth it.

"You make a pretty good Beast," Syd says. "If you could carry a tune, I'd tell you to try out."

"Yeah, well, *that's* not going to happen. No way, no how," I assure her. "The only place *I* sing is in the shower."

"Coward," she says. "I've heard you sing before — when we were younger. You weren't *that* bad."

"In case you haven't noticed, my voice has changed since then."

"Yeah, it's not as high and squeaky," Syd says, but she's grinning, so I know she's teasing me.

"My voice was never squeaky," I tell her.

She starts making squeaky mouse noises, and so I tickle her side, in the place I remember from when we were little that she's really ticklish, and then she's laughing and gasping. "Stop! Truce!"

So I do.

"Seriously, do you think I've got a chance?" she asks. "I want the part of Belle so badly. I've been practicing for over a month."

"I'm no expert, but I think you're great," I tell her, and I mean it.

"It's hard, because Maddie and Cara are trying out, too, and they're my best friends. I want the part, but I'll feel bad if they're upset that they don't get it."

I like that about Syd. She's ambitious, like Mom, but she's not just out for herself.

"Well, you know what they say . . . all's fair in love and theater."

She laughs. "I don't think that's *exactly* what they say, but theater can feel like war sometimes."

The bus pulls up in front of school.

"Well, good luck with the auditions," I tell her.

"Break a leg," she says. "That's what you say in theater."

"Break a leg, then. Break both of them."

"No, don't say that!" Syd giggles as she follows me off the bus. "Breaking *both* legs *wouldn't* be so great!"

"Definitely only break one, then."

The last thing I want is to wish bad luck on Sydney, just when we're starting to hang out again.

LARA

WHEN MR. JONES asked for my math homework and I didn't have it, I wanted to sink through the floor, because I'm not the kind of student who does that. Honestly, I'm not. I *always* do my homework.

Except last night I didn't, because how could I possibly think about logarithms after Christian said he loved me? It wasn't a long, romantic protestation of love — just a simple *Love you* right as he was signing off. But still — he said it. The *L* word.

I tried to concentrate on my homework, I really did. But it was impossible. It's the first time anyone has said *Love you* to me other than my parents or my grandparents. The first time a *guy* has said it to me. That's a pretty memorable moment, right? I printed out the chat convo and put it in the carved wooden box Grandma and Grandpa brought back from their trip to Canada. The memory box, where I keep my treasures — things that remind me of important events or special moments that make me happy. There aren't many things inside it.

I bet Christian isn't letting his grades slip. He's super smart, as well as hot. He's taking *four* AP classes this year. I can't even imagine. I don't want him to think I'm not smart enough for him. It's bad enough wondering if I'm pretty enough every time I look at his profile picture.

I worry whether I'm enough for him, period, all the time. I know he doesn't spend as much time worrying about me. I asked him once why there were so few posts on his Facebook wall and he said he's so busy with APs that he really only ever logs in to talk to me. He just doesn't have the time to keep up with everyone else's posts.

If only I were that focused.

But he still hasn't asked me to his dance, even though he's been hinting at it for weeks. That's another thing that's been driving me crazy, and, if I'm honest, affecting my schoolwork. I've been spending a lot of my time on the computer either chatting to Christian or searching for dresses instead of doing what I should be doing. And Syd is being such a pain, always bugging me to get off because she thinks her homework is more important than mine, even though she's only in middle school and I'm in high school.

I don't understand why Christian doesn't just come out and ask me. If he can say he loves me, then asking me to the dance should be a no-brainer, right? Why does he keep stringing me along? It's *soooooooo* frustrating, not to mention crazy-making. I just want to *know for certain* so I can pick my dress, get some shoes, figure out how to wear my hair, and all that stuff — and also because then I'll finally get to meet Christian in real life. The thought of walking into the dance with him, dancing to some slow song, being in his arms knowing that all the other girls are wishing that they were me . . .

My daydream is interrupted by a text from Ashley.

> Don't forget to wear uniform to school
> tomorrow!

Oh shoot! I forgot. I have to go throw my cheerleading uniform in the wash. I'll wait till later, because Syd's going to want the computer.

Plink!

Facebook chat window. It's him . . .

> Hey, babe — how's it going?

> *Pretty good. But can't chat much. Too much*
> *homework. Got to catch up.*

> : (Homework more exciting than me?

> *Trust me, I'd SO much rather talk to you than*
> *do math. But I have to keep my grades up*
> *or the 'rents will freak.*

> Yeah, I know. My dad is always on my case
> about grades.

> *It's more Mom with me. Dad, too, but Mom's*
> *much worse. Anyway, I better go . . .*

>Wait! Quick question before you go. Tell me,
>who's your best friend?

I don't want to admit that I haven't got a real best friend anymore — not since Bree. I mean, I've made other friends, sure, like Julisa and Ashley, but I don't know if I'll ever be as good of friends with anyone as I was with Bree, telling them everything, all the time. Maybe it's because I'm getting older — or maybe just wiser. I couldn't understand how she could just dump me when we got to high school, after we'd been besties for so long.

Still, Christian's not going to know if I lie — at least not till we actually meet. So whatever, I figure.

>*This girl Ashley. We're on the squad together.*
>*She's awesome.*

I really need to get going on my math homework, but I see he's typing.

>What were you like in middle school?

Is he serious? Didn't I just say I had all this work to do and I don't have time to chat? Besides, if there's anything in the world I'd rather do less than math homework, it's talk about middle school.

I really have to do homework, I type.

Come on, baby, please? Tell me a little
something and then you can go. I really
want to get to know you better.

I want to go, but I can't. Maybe if I tell him something,
he'll finally ask me to the dance. But . . . middle school? Ugh.

I don't really like to think about middle
school, much less talk about it.

Why not?

Oh you know. Bad hair. Bad clothes.
Whatever. I've moved on.

What about friends?

That's the part I want to talk about the least. He's picking a scab on a wound that's only recently healed — if it
even has healed all the way. Why the sudden inquisition?

In middle school, I was best friends with this
girl, Bree.

There, satisfied?

What happened?

I'll tell him this one last thing, and then I'm signing off to do my homework.

> I don't know. She just kind of dumped me
> when we got to high school. Like all of a
> sudden she didn't want to know me
> anymore. And now . . .

I hesitate, wondering if I should tell him about Bree. She's one of his Facebook friends. I wonder how well they know each other.

> Now what? Go on, tell me . . .

> Now she's acting like a total brat. Like, when I
> made cheerleading and she didn't, she
> gave me a death glare. Seriously, if looks
> could kill, I'd be dead.

> Why can't she just be happy for me?

> After all this time, I'm —

I pause in the middle of typing this last thought because I was about to write *getting my life together*, but that would tell him that my life in middle school had fallen apart, and I don't want him to know that. I'm trying to figure out what to say instead, when he types, Well, I guess you better go do your homework. Later.

And he goes offline.

What?!

He could see I was in the middle of typing something to him. And he didn't sign off with anything like *Love you*, not even *Later, baby*. Just *Later* like I'd said something to offend him.

I have to catch up on my homework and get my cheer-leading outfit in the wash, not spend the rest of the night worrying about why he quit our chat so suddenly and went offline.

Like I'm actually going to be able to do *that* easily now.

BREE

WHEN I log out of Christian DeWitt's profile, I'm fuming.

So I'm "being a total brat," am I? Maybe Lara Kelley should look in the mirror! *I'm* not the one who was a total porker in middle school. *I'm* not the one who was so psycho I had to see a shrink. And to top it all off, Lara expects me to be *happy* for her? *WOW*. That girl is *totally delusional*.

I print the chat out and put it in my backpack to show to Marci tomorrow in school. I'm going to talk it through with her, but I'm pretty sure I already know what I'm going to do. It's time to bring this prank to an end and finally give Lara the lesson she deserves.

I'm tired of chatting with that girl every night. That's why I stopped being friends with her in the first place — because I was sick of listening to her whine about her miserable life.

Another reason I'm ready to end this is because now that Mom knows she keeps making all these little suggestions about how I can flirt with Lara better, which is weird and freaks me out on too many levels to count. Last night after I broke off the chat with Lara, she came into my room and wanted me to start it up again so she could be Christian for a while and "have a little fun."

I was like, "Are you *insane*?"

Mom got mad and told me to show her some respect, which just pissed me off even more. Seriously — this was my thing and now Mom's trying to take it over. Story of my life.

Sighing, I look out the bedroom window and notice a light flickering in the window of the old tree fort. *Who would be in there?* I haven't been up there in, like, forever. It reminds me too much of Lara. I wonder if all those posters of bands we liked in middle school are still on the walls, and if the book of secret passwords and rules we used to keep Liam and Sydney out is still hidden under the remnant of carpet that Mom got from one of her clients after they moved into their new house.

I just hope it's not some crazy axe murderer or a stinky hobo or something living up there. That would suck. I better make sure to close my curtains from now on. I don't want to give some random tree-fort freak an eyeful.

———

The next morning before school, I pull Marci aside and show her the chat convo printout. Jenny tries to horn in on our conversation, but Marci says, "Do you mind? This is private," and Jenny huffs away. I can't help feeling good about that. Jenny's always trying to make out like Marci's *her* best friend and I'm this unwanted cling-on.

"Wow," Marci says after she reads the chat. "I can't believe you didn't let her have it then and there."

"Well, they say revenge is a dish best served cold, right?" I tell her.

"So are you going to dump her tonight?" Marci asks.

"After school," I say. "I'm going to do it publicly. On her Facebook wall. So everyone can see."

"I can't *wait*," Marci says, grinning. "It's going to be *epic*."

"Don't tell anyone," I remind her.

"Top secret," she says, pretending to button her lips shut. "My lips are sealed. Text me when it's done, promise?"

"Yeah, I promise."

———

As I walk to the cafeteria at lunchtime, I pass Lara in the hallway. She's wearing her cheerleading uniform and she's with Ashley, her new BFF, and some other cheerleaders. She doesn't even acknowledge I'm alive.

I don't care. Because I know what's going to happen to her later today, and she doesn't. So let her giggle with Ashley and the rest of her stupid cheerleader friends, all their ponytails bobbing as they laugh with their matching purple-and-gold ribbons, like a bunch of horses' butts on a merry-go-round.

My classes after lunch drag even more than usual. Now

that I've made the decision to break up with Lara — or that *Christian* is going to break up with her — I want to get it over with. Not just think about it, do it. Everything has been leading up to this; the fake account, the fake flirting, it's all been a setup for what's going to go down later on today.

Deep down, I wonder if Lara has any clue that Christian isn't who he says he is. Deep down, I wonder if she has any idea that *he* is really *me*.

No way. I've covered my tracks pretty well. The only people who know are Marci and Mom. Marci is totally for it, and strangely, so is Mom. It's all good.

As anxious as I was to get it over with all afternoon in school, when I get home, I find myself hesitating. Once I do it, I can't go back to pretending I'm him anymore. Once I do it, I lose that power. This will really be the end.

So I make myself a snack — Nutella on toast with a glass of milk — and watch a few episodes of a reality show about crazy stage moms.

"Why do you even watch that show?" Liam asks, coming into the family room chomping on an apple. "Those people are seriously messed up."

In my head I hear Mom urging me to log back in to chat with Lara so she can pretend to be Christian again.

"Ya think? They're no more screwed up than our parents. Trust me."

Liam stares at me, goggle-eyed, his mouth hanging

open, filled with unchewed apple. It's gross, like looking at a train wreck in a tunnel.

"No way Mom and Dad are like those crazies," he says.

"Can you at least finish chewing before you talk so I don't have to look at your food debris?"

He swallows.

"Okay, fine, but I'm serious. I wouldn't want to be one of those stage kids. No way."

I would. Even with an ambitious, pressuring stage mom. 'Cause I already have a pressuring mom, but at least then she'd be pressuring me to do what *I* want, instead of what she wants me to do.

Too bad, Mom. I failed, too. Guess we're both losers, huh?

I wonder if my failure is going to give me "grit" so I'll be more like Mom. But is that what I really want? Dad's the one who's always understood me more. Or at least he's the one who tries.

I switch off the TV and get up off the sofa. "Don't worry," I tell Liam. "You're not talented enough to be onstage anyway."

He nabs the sofa and the remote and turns on some geeky science show that's just an excuse to blow things up and call it an "experiment." I've caught a few episodes when I haven't had anything better to do, and the explosions are pretty cool, especially in slow motion.

Showtime, I figure, as I walk up the stairs. Time for Christian to teach Lara a lesson. Time for the final curtain in the Christian and Lara Show.

I log into Facebook as Christian and go to Lara's wall. I type, look it over once, and add one more thing. My finger hesitates over the mouse button for a moment. I take a deep breath, and click Post.

Then I log out, log back in as myself, and wait for the fun to start.

LARA

IF YOU hold the mirrored door of the medicine cabinet toward the bathroom mirror there are hundreds of versions of you, like clones created in a secret lab by white-coated scientists. The first time I did it I thought it was so cool — an infinite tunnel of possible Laras. But now my hand trembles on the mirror as I watch a tear ice its way down all of my cheeks. I guess you could say each one of those faces is either the Lara that I once was, that I am now, or that I would be in the future, if I had one.

I don't.

Christian just messaged me that the world would be a better place without me in it. He's right.

I wish I knew what I did to make him change his mind about me so suddenly, without any warning. One minute I think he's about to ask me to his school dance, the next minute he's posting on my wall that I'm an awful person and a terrible friend. That he would never consider being seen with a loser like me at his school dance.

He didn't even know me in middle school, before Mom took me to the nutritionist and the shrink and I lost thirty pounds.

Why? What did I do? I just want to understand. I *need* to understand. If I only understood, then I could change, I could be a different Lara, a nicer Lara, a *better* Lara. A Lara that people didn't like one minute and then hate the next. A Lara that didn't make friends, then lose them.

But it doesn't matter now, I guess. This way is better for everyone.

Mom will freak out if I make a mess, so I take all the pill bottles and line them up on the edge of the bathtub, neatly, like soldiers. I've got Mom's sleeping pills, the ones she pretends she doesn't take and hides in her bedside table under the latest copy of *Vanity Fair*; the painkillers Dad has for when his back plays up; and the acetaminophen with codeine from when I had my wisdom teeth removed over the summer. I grab the plastic cup that holds my toothbrush and bring it with me as I stand by the bathtub, trying to decide if I should get undressed or be fully clothed. I don't want to be naked when they find me dead. That would add insult to injury, having policemen taking pictures of me and making comments about how I could lose a few pounds and stuff.

In the end, I strip down to my underwear and T-shirt.

Making the Lake Hills High varsity cheerleading squad is probably the most awesome thing I've ever accomplished in my life. It made me feel like I'd finally turned the corner from miserable to happy.

That didn't last long.

I settle myself in the tub and turn on the water. I thought

about doing this in the bedroom, but locking my bedroom door is too out of the norm. This way it's less obvious.

It feels weird when the water starts to soak into my underwear and T-shirt, and I wonder if I should have just laid on the bathroom floor and pretended to be in the bath, but once I get used to it, the water is warm and comforting. Anyway, wearing clothes in the bathtub isn't half as weird as thinking that in less than an hour — I think, because I don't know how long this actually is going to take — that's not going to matter. Nothing will. I won't be here anymore.

No more pain.

No more feelings.

No more anything.

No more me.

Fill up the glass from the faucet. Open the first bottle. Don't even bother to look at what it is. It doesn't matter anyway. Just pour the pills into my shaking palm, put as many into my mouth as I think I can swallow, and wash them down.

Rinse and repeat.

And repeat.

And repeat.

And repeat.

And keep on repeating.

Turn off the water when I start to feel dizzy.

Because . . . I don't . . . want to . . . drown . . . just want to . . . die . . .

PART THREE

NOW

SYDNEY

MY SISTER has had what her shrink calls "a setback" since
the police told her there is no Christian DeWitt — and she
realized she tried to kill herself over some guy who never
even existed. A "setback" is apparently shrinkspeak for saying that after getting a teensy bit better, she's now as much
of a mess as she was before — maybe an even bigger one.

Mom and Dad were discussing if Lara should go back
into the psych ward, but she was all, "If you even think
about locking me up in that place, I'll try to kill myself
again," so that plan got nixed. She gets to stay home but is
still living under Lara Watch. No closed doors, not even to
shower or pee or sleep. No Internet or phone without parental supervision. No privacy, period.

She told me last night that I'm lucky, because I get to
close the door when I go to the bathroom.

Seriously, Lara?

"*Luck* has nothing to do with it," I said. "Mom and Dad
just know *I'm* not going to do anything in there except the
normal things people do in a bathroom."

She looked like a baby seal who'd just been hit with a
club on a frozen beach in the Arctic Circle — wounded,

blinking big eyes staring at me, asking how I could be so cruel.

So then I felt bad about hurting her, but at the same time I was mad about feeling bad because I didn't think I'd done anything wrong. I was just telling the truth, stating the obvious. Someone has to do that around here, and it's pretty clear that someone isn't going to be either one of my parents.

I'm doing homework on the computer — another thing Lara can be jealous of because I don't have to have Mom looking over my shoulder — when the doorbell rings.

"Can you get that?" Mom says. "I'm in the middle of something."

I don't bother to point out that I am, too. Mom's got cabin fever from being stuck here babysitting Lara all day, and she's worrying about how this is affecting her political career. I know this because her campaign manager was here one day when I came home from school and they were talking about it, and then I heard her stressing about it to Dad. And then I heard him getting all pissed about the fact that she was even thinking about politics when Lara was so sick, and she just got mad back because *he's* not the one who is having to take off from work to keep an eye on a fifteen-year-old 24/7 and . . . well, it went on from there.

It's just easier to get up and do it than argue with Mom when all that's going on.

When I open the door, Mrs. Connors is standing there carrying a foil-covered casserole dish. Since *it* happened, all of our neighbors have been trying to out–Martha Stewart one another. It's like they're all competing to bring us the best casseroles as a way of showing their concern. But there's another reason, too, besides neighborly compassion. It's also because they want the latest dirt so when they bump into people in line at the supermarket they can say: "Well, I was at the Kelley house today, and I heard . . ."

"Hi, honey," Mrs. Connors says, holding out the dish. "I brought you some lasagna so your mom doesn't have to cook. I'm sure she's got enough on her plate with . . . everything that's going on."

"Yeah," I say, taking the dish from her. I remember Mrs. Connors's lasagna. It's not as good as Mom's. But with the mood my mother is in, any edible food is good as far as I'm concerned. "She's pretty stressed out. Thanks."

"How's . . . Lara doing?"

It's like she's afraid to say Lara's name. It's like that with everyone who comes by. I want to scream at them to stop whispering her name; that she *didn't actually die.* She's just super messed up, that's all.

"Okay, I guess."

"But she's not back at school yet?"

Doesn't anyone talk to each other in that house? I mean, Bree must know that Lara hasn't been in school.

"No, not yet."

"She's not feeling up to it?"

What is this, a police interrogation?

"Um, no. Not yet."

"Well, give her our love," Mrs. Connors says, which is kind of weird, given that Lara and Bree aren't really friends anymore. She turns and is halfway down the steps before she calls back over her shoulder, "And give my best to your mom."

"I will," I tell her. "Thanks for the lasagna."

I take the dish into the kitchen, where Mom's reading city council briefing papers and sipping a glass of chardonnay. There's no evidence of any dinner preparation in sight.

"Mrs. Connors brought over a lasagna. Should I heat it up for dinner?"

"Sure, throw it in the oven," Mom says, reaching for the wineglass. "That was nice of Mary Jo."

"She was asking a lot of questions about Lara."

Mom drains half of what's in her wineglass in one gulp. I hope all this stress isn't turning my mother into a wino.

"*Everyone* who brings over food to help me out so I don't have to cook asks a lot of questions about Lara," she says with a sigh. "We're the talk of the neighborhood. I'm sure everyone is dissecting my mothering skills and judging me on where I went wrong."

The phone rings, and as Mom answers I realize how much she just sounded like my sister; Mom, too, is worrying about what everyone thinks about her, stressing out about how they are judging her.

"You're coming by when? Tonight? I don't know if my daughter . . . Oh, okay. I understand."

She hangs up and dials again right away.

"Pete, I need you home. The police are coming. They have a lead and they need to ask us some questions . . . Half an hour. Okay, bye."

Mom downs the rest of the wine and starts clearing her papers off the table. After she has stacked them into a precise, neat pile that she puts into her briefcase, she looks out the sliding back door to the patio, where Lara is curled up on a chair in a Snuggie, reading a book, so she can be constantly observed by Mom like a goldfish in a bowl.

"What kind of lead do they have?" I ask.

"They didn't say. Only that it's something about who might have created the Christian DeWitt profile," Mom says, biting her cuticle. She hasn't had a manicure since The Bathroom Incident and it shows. It was something her campaign manager pointed out, believe it or not. He said it didn't make for good *visuals*, whatever that's supposed to mean. "I better tell Lara. I hope it doesn't set her back even more."

She goes out the sliding door and closes it behind her. Lara stiffens as Mom walks over, clearly miffed that there's an interruption in her rare and precious alone time. Mom starts talking and tries to stroke Lara's hair, but my sister moves her head and Mom's hand falls on the back of the Adirondack chair. It's like watching a bad ABC Family special with the sound on mute, but this is *my* family drama and I can't change the channel or turn off the TV. The only thing I can do is go back and try to finish my homework before the police arrive.

———

Dad and the police arrive at the same time, which means we don't have warning that they've arrived. Just a "Hi, I'm home!" and the next thing I know my father's walking in the room with Officer Timm and some other guy in a jacket.

"Mom, the police are here," I call into the kitchen so she isn't as surprised as I am.

Dad kisses the top of my head and says, "Hi, sweetheart," and then tells the police to follow him into the kitchen. I trail in after them. If they have some kind of lead on who was sick enough to do this to my sister, I want to know about it.

Lara is still out on the patio. She's watching us now: a silent, Snuggie-wrapped observer. Mom opens the door and tells her to come inside. She stands up and shuffles into the house, clutching the Snuggie around her as if she's trekked across the frozen tundra rather than just taken a few steps across our flagstone patio.

Without saying a word and barely acknowledging the policemen, she sinks into a chair and pulls the Snuggie tighter around her. If she could disappear into it like a turtle into a shell, I bet she would.

Jacket Guy, who says his name is Detective Souther, and who apparently has been here once before, asks Lara how she's doing.

She shrugs, avoiding eye contact with him. "Okay."

Mom is standing behind Lara, shaking her head no and mouthing, "Not good."

"The reason we wanted to come by is that we may have a lead on the Christian DeWitt profile," Detective Souther says, tapping his pen against his notebook. He stops suddenly and looks straight at Lara. "Have you had any issues with neighbors?"

"Neighbors?" Mom gasps. "You mean . . . someone we *know* did this?"

"We're trying to narrow down our field of inquiry," the detective says, which doesn't answer her question.

"Have there been any problems with neighbors?" Officer Timm echoes.

"No," Mom says. "In fact, all of our neighbors have been so supportive and kind since this happened. I haven't had to cook dinner once."

"We're going to have to buy a new freezer just to hold all the casseroles," Dad jokes.

I suddenly wonder who decided that casseroles are the currency of support and kindness in a time of crisis? Why didn't they have the good sense to make it cookies instead? I could really go for some chocolate chip ones right now. Or brownies. Really great fudgy brownies.

"What about you, Lara?" Detective Souther asks. "Any issues with kids on the block?"

Lara has been staring out the window, as if she wasn't even paying attention. She still won't give the detective eye contact but looks over his shoulder at the clock on the wall and says no so softly we can barely hear her.

"What about Bree?" I ask.

Lara looks at me as if she's a resistance fighter I've just betrayed to occupying forces. I stare back at her, because seriously, what is the point of pretending anymore?

She looks away first.

"Bree who?" Detective Souther asks.

"Breanna Connors," I say. "She and Lara were best friends until a year or so ago. Our families were friends. And then Lara and Bree fell out, and now nobody is allowed to be friends."

"That's not true, dear," Mom protests. "Mary Jo brought over the lasagna that's in the oven for dinner."

The detective is scribbling as we speak. I imagine his notes. *Neighbor Mary Jo Connors made a lasagna.*

Being a detective must get super, super boring.

"Yeah, but we never hang out with them anymore," I argue. "And we used to all the time when Lara and Bree were friends."

"Even if we've drifted apart from the Connorses, I can't see Bree doing something like this," Dad says. "They're a good family. Sean Connors and I built that tree fort together, the one you can see out back. Lara and Bree practically lived up there when they were younger, didn't you, pumpkin?"

Lara Pumpkin is back in zombie land, tuning the rest of us out.

"But Bree posted that picture of Lara the day she . . . *that day* . . . on Facebook," I argue.

"The one on the stretcher?" the detective asks.

"Yeah, and then people made all these sick comments," I say, glancing at Lara because I'm worried about causing her another "setback" by talking about all of this. But if I don't, how will they figure out who did it?

"It was disgusting," Dad says. "I just don't understand what possesses kids these days. There's no judgment, no thought —"

"Dad," I say, "it's police time, not rant time."

"Sydney, that's enough," Mom snaps.

I shut my mouth and go back to disappearing into the background.

"So you haven't had problems with any other neighbors, at school or out of school?" the detective tries again, determined to get Lara's attention.

"Not that I know of," Lara says, still staring out the window. She laughs, bitterly. "Well, except for all the kids who liked the mean stuff Christian wrote on my wall. I didn't stop to check if any of them were my neighbors before I . . . well, *you know.*"

Detective Souther puts down his pad and pen and says Lara's name gently. She finally looks him in the eye.

"Here's the thing, Lara. Facebook gave us the information that the person who posted as Christian DeWitt did it from an IP address in this neighborhood. We've got the court order for the Internet service provider to tell us more specifically which customer of theirs it was. I was just hoping you might be able to give us a clue to speed things up."

"You're saying one of *our neighbors* did this?" Dad is so upset he springs halfway out of his chair, but Mom pulls him back down to seated and glares at him.

Lara opens her mouth like she's going to say something, and I hold my breath without realizing until she closes it without uttering a word and shakes her head no.

"Are you sure there's nothing you can think of?" Officer Timm asks.

Lara nods, but she's done. She's gone back into zombie mode. I want to slap her. Doesn't she realize that if she talks, it'll help find out who did this faster so we can all get on with our lives? Doesn't she realize that this is messing up *my* life, too?

"Well, thank you for your time," Detective Souther says, and he and Officer Timm get up to leave. "Please call anytime if you think of anything that might help us with our investigation."

"Will you arrest them when you find out who it is?" Mom asks.

"It depends on how much of a case we can build," the detective says.

"But you saw the things this person wrote!" Mom exclaims. "My daughter was tricked into believing that this Christian character cared for her and then he —"

Mom stops as Lara's chair scrapes back loudly and my sister runs out of the room, leaving the Snuggie behind like a shed snake skin. We hear her footsteps running up the stairs and then her door slam. Lara's not supposed to be in her room with the door shut, but she's clearly upset enough that she doesn't care about breaking the rules.

My mother is torn between following Lara and asking the detective more questions. So guess what happens?

"Sydney — go up and see how your sister is doing," Mom orders. "And make sure she keeps her door open."

No *Please*. No *Would you mind, dearest, wonderful,* not screwed-up *daughter?* Just *Do it, Syd.*

I detour to get my schoolbooks from the family room and head upstairs.

Part of me wants to leave Lara alone, to give her some space to cry or punch a hole in the wall or just do whatever she wants to do with the door closed for a few minutes. But I can't, because what if hearing Mom talking about Christian or realizing that whoever did this might be someone we know has made her upset enough to try to hurt herself again?

If she did that, it would be my fault because I didn't go to her.

Because I wanted her to have time to be mad.

Because I was mad myself.

So instead I knock on the door, softly. "Lara? It's Syd. Are you okay?"

She doesn't answer and my heart starts beating an irregular rhythm in my chest. *Not again.*

I try the door handle, praying that she hasn't locked it.

It turns.

Now that I can breathe again, I push the door open.

"Lara?"

She's lying on her bed, clutching her stuffed Hedwig to her chest, staring at the ceiling. She doesn't answer me or even look in my direction as I walk in, put my books on her desk, and sit cross-legged on the end of her bed.

"Mom didn't mean to," I say. "It's just the way she is. If there's a problem, she has to be the one to fix it."

That's when I see the tears rolling silently down Lara's cheeks.

"I'm the one problem she can't fix," she whispers.

I want to say the right thing to her, but I don't know what it is. I'm not a grown-up. I'm not a shrink. I don't know the answers. I've got my own problems, and if I'm going to be totally honest here, my sister is one of them.

"Maybe . . . maybe she can't fix you," I say.

That definitely wasn't the right thing. It just makes Lara's tears flow faster, harder.

"I don't mean that . . . like . . . you're *unfixable*," I try to explain, to undo the damage I've done. "I guess . . . what I'm trying to say . . ." *What am I trying to say? I don't even know . . .* "I think what I'm trying to say is that maybe . . . only *you* can fix you?"

The tears keep coming, and Lara's eyes are still fixed on the ceiling. Am I making things better or worse?

I hear Dad letting the police guys out the front door, and Mom's footsteps coming up the stairs. Great. She's probably going to be mad at me, because I made Lara cry more instead of making her feel better.

"Look, what do I know? I'm just the stupid little sister," I say, shrugging and sliding off the bed.

I pick up my books from the desk and walk to the door just as Mom enters.

"Lara, honey? Are you okay?"

I look back at my sister. She's placed Hedwig over her face, as if to shut out the world — or our mom, I'm not sure which.

But that's not my problem now. It's hers. I've got to finish my homework, if I can even concentrate after all this drama. Honestly, it's amazing I'm getting halfway decent grades considering how crazy life is here.

My bedroom window faces the street, and I press my nose against it and stare out at the neighbors' houses, wondering which window conceals the sicko who did this to my sister.

Is it old Mrs. Gorski or Spencer Helman or Bree Connors or maybe one of the Glovers?

Windows reflect back at me, some light, some dark.

I shiver, pulling my head away from the window and yanking my curtains shut so no one can see in. I always thought we lived in a nice neighborhood with good families. Our neighbors have been rallying around us since Lara tried to kill herself, showing support and bringing us casseroles. But the detective said the person who pretended to be Christian lives right here, among us.

Could it be our neighborhood isn't so nice after all?

BREE

A WEEK after Lara got taken to the hospital in an ambulance, Mom had me delete the Christian DeWitt Facebook account. I wasn't all that sad to say good-bye to him. Flirting with Lara had gotten awkward and old. And seriously — I never really thought she'd do it. Try to kill herself, I mean. Mom also made me delete the picture of Lara on the stretcher from Facebook. She was all about "covering tracks" and "not being so obvious." I was really pissed about that because it's the most likes I've had on any post.

When I complained about deleting the Lara picture, she yelled at me. "*Breanna*, the good Lord gave you brains. Could you use them for a change?"

Her ragging on me for not being the sharpest tool in the Connors shed is nothing new. Mom knows Liam is the smart one. My brother can do no wrong in Mom's eyes. Me, on the other hand — I can do no right.

Seriously, it's not like I was the only one posting stuff about Lara's trip to the ER. Lots of other kids had status updates that night like Did you hear Lara Kelley OD'd? and stuff like that.

At least I didn't make it sound like she *died*.

I've been thinking about what would have happened if Lara had . . . you know. I hadn't really thought she'd go as far as trying to commit suicide. I mean, I knew Lara was super insecure and everything, but *killing* herself? That's so *extreme*. I was really mad at her, but not enough to want her to die. I guess I just wanted her to hurt as much as I did. It didn't seem fair that she was on top of the world all of a sudden. That wasn't the way things were supposed to be with us. I was always the leader of our pack. Even when it came to making the rules for the tree fort, I was the one in charge.

And then she'd laughed at me. I just wanted to restore things back to the way they should be.

I saw Liam go out to the tree fort the other night. When the flickering light came on in the tree fort window, I realized, with relief, that it wasn't a stinky hobo living out there, or some random freak. It was just my stinky, freaky little brother.

He was out there for about an hour. When he finally got back to his room, I went in and asked him why he'd been up there.

"None of your beeswax," he said, like we were still little kids.

"You've been going out there a lot. I've seen the light in the window."

"Maybe I just needed to get away from you," he said.

"Fine. Be a jerk," I said, spinning on my heel to leave his room. But at the doorway I turned back, because I had to know. "Are all our posters still up?"

"You mean the stupid boy bands?" Liam said. "Yeah, they're still there."

For some reason, that made me happy. It's not like I even like those bands anymore — at least not that I'd admit to anyone — but even so, I was glad that they were still smiling down from the wooden walls of the tree fort.

I guess maybe it's because even though I thought everything was so confusing then, I've realized that compared to now, it was way, way simpler.

———

The following evening, the doorbell rings and I answer it to find a uniformed police officer and a guy in a jacket holding up a badge.

Omgomgomgomgomgomgomgomgomgomgomgomg.

"Hi, is your mother home?" Badge Guy asks.

Relief. Maybe he's after Mom for a speeding ticket or something. She has this problem where she thinks she's that race car driver Danica Patrick.

"Yeah. I'll go get her."

I leave them standing on the doorstep and run into the kitchen.

"Mom! There are two cops at the door. They want to talk to you."

My mother drops the paring knife she's holding and puts her hands on the counter, her head bowed and eyes closed. She takes a loud, deep breath and then straightens up and says, "Did they say what it's about?"

"No. They just asked if you were home and said they want to talk to you."

"If they ask you anything about that Christian thing, you say nothing," Mom says. "Do you understand? *Nothing.*"

Wait. Is she telling me to lie to *the police*?

"But, Mom . . ."

"*Nothing.* I want you to keep your mouth shut. For once in your life, Breanna Marie Connors, just *do what I tell you.*"

She goes to the door and I wait in the kitchen, freaking out. Hoping that this is about her, and not me. Or maybe, I think, maybe someone else saw Liam lurking around in the tree fort at night and got scared and reported him. Maybe that's it. I don't know what to do if it's not about those things. I'm supposed to obey my mother, but lying to the police? I've watched enough *Law & Order* reruns to know that's Serious Business.

Mom comes back in the kitchen, grim-faced.

"They want to speak to you, Breanna. In the living room."

This was just supposed to be a prank to teach Lara a lesson. It was never supposed to get this serious. Not hospitals. Not suicide attempts. And *definitely* not *the police*.

Mom makes a zip-it gesture as I walk past her. All my life, I've been brought up to believe the police are the good guys. So if I lie to them, does that make me one of the bad guys?

But on the other hand, I don't want to end up in juvie over a stupid joke. I'm not the kind of girl who goes to juvie. Isn't juvie for really screwed-up bad kids? Definitely not for girls like me.

Badge Guy introduces himself as Detective Souther. Uniform Guy is Officer Timm.

"We're looking into the Lara Kelley incident," the detective says.

"Oh, I know, isn't that terrible?" Mom says. "That poor girl."

It strikes me then what a seriously awesome liar my mother is. I guess maybe that's a quality she needs to be the real estate queen of Lake Hills. "Everything I touch turns to sold."

Maybe that's why she's so disappointed with me. Everything *I* touch seems to turn to dog crap.

"The two of you were close friends at one time," he says to me.

"Yeah," I mumble. "In middle school."

"Speak up, Bree," Mom snaps.

"In middle school," I repeat more loudly. "Not so much now."

"Was there a specific fight, or did you just drift apart?" Officer Timm asks.

"They drifted apart," Mom says. "Poor Lara has always been . . . troubled. It became a little too much for Bree, having to act as therapist as well as friend. She needed to have a life of her own."

"Understandable," Detective Souther says. "How long ago was that, would you say?"

I open my mouth to say a little over a year ago, when we started high school, but Mom is there first.

"They started drifting apart the summer before high school. And of course once Bree got to high school, there were so many new faces, it was only natural she'd want to spread her wings and make other friends."

These guys are going to think I can't speak for myself. Mom couldn't make it more obvious if she tried that she doesn't trust me to say the right thing.

"I have a teenage daughter," Officer Timm says. "These things happen. One minute they're best friends forever, the next week it turns out 'forever' meant until they had a fight."

"We didn't fight," I say. "It wasn't like that. It was more . . . just . . . gradual."

"So has there been any antagonism between you and Lara Kelley at the present time?" Detective Souther asks.

What is this, the PSAT or something? *Antagonism?*

"No, we weren't pissed off at each other, if that's what you mean."

Mom gives me a *look* and I get it. *Cut the attitude, Breanna.*

"Do you know a young man by the name of Christian DeWitt?" the detective asks.

I've never actually been punched in the stomach, but I imagine this is how it feels. Like all the air is suddenly sucked out of your lungs and there's a second of total panic because you can't breathe and you wonder if this is it and you're going to die before you pull yourself together and manage to inhale.

I stand on the edge of the cliff, poised — this is the moment where I either listen to Mom and lie to the police, or I tell the truth.

I only hesitate for a moment before I decide to jump into the chasm. Because despite the fact I'm fifteen years old, and I'm supposed to be learning how to become my own person, when have I not done what my mom tells me?

"No," I say, but I can't help the slight tremor in my voice. "Never heard of him."

"Are you sure?" the detective asks, looking me straight in the eye.

I know if I look away, he'll think I'm lying, so as much as it's wigging me out to maintain eye contact, I do.

"Totally sure," I say.

I am going to burn for eternity for this. But I obeyed my mother, and honoring my mother is one of the Ten Commandments, so does that give me points for something?

Even though it's not that hot in the living room, I feel myself start to sweat in the brief, awkward silence that follows. I surreptitiously rub my hands against the side of my jeans, but don't break eye contact, determined to win the game of blink.

"Well, that's interesting," Officer Timm says. He takes a folded-up piece of paper out of his pocket and opens it up. Then he walks over and holds it out in front of me. "Because you were friends with him on Facebook."

It's a printout of Christian's friend list. And there, among them, with a big red circle around it, is my profile picture.

But I deleted his profile! He's not there anymore. How did they get that? And now what do I do?

I stare up at Officer Timm, tongue-tied with panic.

My mother doesn't miss a beat.

"You know how these kids are," she says, her voice as calm and smooth as a lake on a still summer's day. "They all friend people they don't know. I've warned Bree and Liam about it more times than I can count, but they still do it."

Mom looks at me sternly.

"I'm sure Bree didn't even remember she'd friended him. She has so many friends on that site. I'll have to go through them with her and make sure she cuts back." She smiles at the policemen, shaking her head. "You can't be too careful these days, can you?"

Wow. I take it back when I said Mom was a good liar. She's a FREAKING EPIC LIAR. Like, Super Liar of the Universe.

Just then, her cell phone rings. She looks at the number.

"Excuse me, I have to answer. These clients are about to make an offer on a big property. Let me see if I can call them back."

She answers with her "Everything I touch turns to sold" voice.

"Mary Jo Connors. Yes, hi, Ralph — any chance I can call you back? I'm in the middle of something . . . Oh. I see . . . Okay, hold on a minute."

Mom presses Mute and says, "I have to take this now. I'll be out in the hall. It won't take long."

On her way out, she purses her lips, reminding me to zip it.

And then I'm left there, alone with the two policemen, scared that I'm going to say the wrong thing.

"So here's the thing, Breanna," the detective says. "We're pretty sure the person who created the Christian DeWitt profile lives in this house."

I can't stop the panicked look that crosses my face before I realize what I've done and try to arrange my features into what I hope is an "I have no idea what you're talking about, Detective" expression.

"How?"

"Do you know what an IP address is?" Officer Timm asks.

"It's something to do with the Internet," I say, twisting the silver-and-onyx ring I'm wearing on my right hand. Now that I think about it, Lara gave it to me for my birthday in middle school.

"It's the numerical label assigned to computers on a network," Officer Timm explains.

I stare at him blankly. I have no idea what that means.

Detective Souther must see the look on my face because he says, "We know from an IP search that the person who contacted Lara lives in this neighborhood."

I swallow hard.

"We had to get a warrant to find out from the Internet service provider exactly which house it was," he continues. "And I'm going to make a bet that when we get that information, it's going to show that it's yours. If you tell us it was you, it'll go a lot easier for you than if you deny it and we find out anyway."

I hear Mom's voice in the hallway, talking to her client about their bid. She tells them they should go in slightly under asking, but not so far that they'll think it's insulting.

I don't know what to do. Mom wants me to lie. But it feels wrong to lie to the police. And what's the point of lying if they're going to find out it was me anyway?

My head is throbbing, and I feel sick to my stomach.

"Just because it was someone in this neighborhood, doesn't mean it was me," I say, picking at a cuticle on my thumb.

"You posted a picture of Lara being taken out of the house on a stretcher on your Facebook profile," Officer Timm says. "Why would you do that to someone who was your friend?"

He sounds just like Liam, but he's not my younger brother, someone I can ignore. He's a policeman, wearing a uniform, with a gun in his holster and handcuffs attached to his belt. This is real life. This is serious business. I never thought about any of this when I posted that picture.

I never thought, period.

And now I'm terrified.

"How do you k-know that? I d-deleted that picture!" I stammer.

"Ever hear of something called a screenshot?" Detective Souther says with no small amount of snark. "Lara's father took a whole bunch of them the night Lara tried to kill herself. He wasn't a happy man when he saw what people were doing to his daughter. Can't say I blame him."

"I . . . don't know why I did it . . . ," I say. "I thought it would . . . you know, get a lot of likes."

I see the looks on their faces. They hate me. They think I'm a really awful person.

Officer Timm mutters something under his breath, shaking his head.

"You might as well tell us, Breanna," the detective says. "We know it was you."

Mom! Get off the phone and get back in here! What should I do? THEY ALREADY KNOW!

But my mother is still out in the hallway, arguing with her clients over a five-thousand-dollar increment in their bid. Doesn't she realize my whole life is at stake here? For once, I'd just like to feel more important to my mother than the next deal.

"It will go much better for you if you're honest with us, Breanna," Detective Souther says. "No matter what anyone might have told you."

I feel tears well up, even though I'm trying to will them back because I know they'll make me look guilty.

"If you tell us the truth, we can work with you," the detective continues.

He's the good guy. The police are the good guys. I'm not a bad guy. I'm a good person. If I keep lying to him, I'll be the bad guy. It's better if I tell the truth.

My face feels like it's five-hundred-degrees hot. The first tear boils over and trickles down my cheek.

Mom's commiserating with her clients about how long it's taking the city council to *not* pass the tax incentives. At least she doesn't mention Mrs. Kelley by name.

"You can be honest with us, Breanna," Officer Timm says, and he doesn't sound like he hates me now. He sounds nicer, more friendly, like he's trying to help me do the right thing. "It's okay."

More tears fall, and I taste salt on the corner of my mouth. I wipe the tear away with the back of my hand, and despite Mom telling me to zip it, to tell them *nothing, nada, zilch*, I say quietly, "It was me."

And even though I'm scared about the trouble I know I'm going to get into, about the punishment I know I'm going to face, it feels better than continuing to lie when they already know the truth.

"Did your mother know about this?" Detective Souther asks.

It's one thing to admit to them that it was me. I can't tell them that Mom did it, too. But to cover for her means lying. I stare down at my hands and say nothing.

Hang up, Mom. Hang up and come back. I need you more than your clients do right now.

I glance toward the door. My mother is still on the phone. She's telling the clients if they're really worried about the five grand, to split the difference but go up to $2,575, because that sounds better to the seller. "It's all mind games," she says.

"Breanna? Did your mom know about the fake profile?" the detective repeats.

I look back at the policemen and decide that if she's leaving me here by myself, I get to make my own decisions. And I decide to keep on telling the truth.

"Yes. She did," I say in a low voice so Mom doesn't hear.

"You're doing the right thing by telling us the truth," Detective Souther reassures me.

"My mom's going to be really mad at me," I say quietly, wiping away tears with my sleeve as I throw another nervous glance toward the door.

"Just how involved was your mother?" Officer Timm asks.

Come on, move over. I want to be Christian for a while . . . Oh, come on, Bree. It's just a little fun.

"I . . . she . . ."

I feel like I'm going to throw up. Mom's in the hallway talking about how if only they had those tax breaks.

That's when I crack.

"She p-pretended to be Christian a few times," I admit. "So did Marci. My friend . . . Marci Liptak."

It looks like this was something they *didn't* know, because they look at each other, and Officer Timm, who doesn't have as good of a poker face as the detective, seems shocked and even . . . angry.

"What made you do it?" Detective Souther asks.

"Do what?" Mom says sharply, walking into the room. "Made her do what?"

"Breanna told us the truth, Mrs. Connors. That she created the Christian DeWitt profile, and that both you and she — and another teenager named Marci Liptak — engaged Lara Kelley in conversation as DeWitt."

My mother turns to me, her face already flushing red with fury.

"Can't I trust you to do *anything* right, Breanna?" Mom says in a voice as cold as her anger is hot, completely unmoved by my tears.

I'm used to disappointing my mother. It feels like I've done it all my life. And I realize in that moment that maybe I am as stupid as she always tells me. Because deep down, I'd had this small shred of hope, some sick deluded fantasy, that she'd say I did the right thing by telling the truth.

LIAM

I'M IN my bedroom doing my homework with the headphones on when I get a text from Spencer.

> Dude, why's there a cop car outside your
> house? Saw it when I was walking the dog.

Wait, what? I text back.

I take off my headphones and look out the bedroom window. Sure enough, there's a Lake Hills police car parked on the street in front of our house.

> IDK. Gonna go check it out.

As I get to the bottom of the stairs, I hear Mom say, "Can't I trust you to do *anything* right, Breanna?"

When Mom yells, you know she's mad, but when she speaks in that cold, quiet voice, you know she's *really* mad. Like "stay out of her way if you know what's good for you" mad.

And then I hear Bree sobbing, so I detour to the kitchen. As much as I want to know what this is all about, going into the living room doesn't seem like a smart move right about now.

Instead, I call Dad.

"Where are you?" I ask him. "Are you on the way home?"

"Uh-huh. I'll be there in a few minutes. Do we need milk?"

"No," I say. "The police are here talking to Mom and Bree."

"*WHAT?*" Dad exclaims. "What about?"

"I don't know," I tell him.

He curses. "I'll be there as soon as I can."

"Hurry," I urge him before hanging up.

My phone buzzes. Another text from Spencer.

So? What's going on?

I ignore it, waiting for Dad to get home. And then I hear Bree come out of the living room bawling, and her footsteps as she runs up the stairs to her room.

Figuring it's the quickest way to find out what's going on, I head back upstairs and knock on her door.

"Go away!" she cries.

But I don't. I slip into her room, closing the door behind me.

She's curled up on her bed, with her knees up to her chest, clutching Bertie, her worn, old teddy bear.

"I t-told you to g-go away," she hiccups between sobs.

My sister and I aren't super close like some siblings, but it's clear something pretty bad has just gone down.

"What happened?" I ask. "Why are the police here?"

My questions just make her start crying harder again. I don't know what to do. Bree's totally freaking out about whatever happened in the living room, and I have no idea what it is.

I sit down on the bed and squeeze her ankle.

"It'll be okay," I say, even though I have no idea if that's true. It's just what people always say when someone is freaking out to make them stop.

"No it w-won't," she says. "N-nothing is g-going to be o-okay."

"What's this all about?"

"M-Mom's right. I *am* s-stupid. B-But I had to t-tell them the t-truth."

"The truth about what?"

"About L-Lara."

Lara? What could the police have to do with Bree and Lara? I mean, they were friends and they aren't now, but that's not a crime. That's just girls, from what I can tell.

And then I remember the night Lara was taken away in the ambulance . . .

"Is this about that picture you posted? The one the night Lara tried to kill herself?"

Bree uncovers her face and gives me a look like *I'm* the stupid one. She swallows, like she's trying to get a grip, and says, "No, Liam. It's not about that. The reason the police are here . . . the reason why everything isn't going to be okay is because . . . I'm the reason that Lara tried to kill herself."

I stare at her, trying to understand what she means. How can my sister be the reason Lara tried to kill herself?

"What are you talking about? She did that because she was upset about that jerk Christian guy."

"*I'm* 'that jerk Christian guy.' He never existed. He was fake, right from the beginning."

The horror of what Bree's just said crawls over me like I've just stepped onto a nest of fire ants. I stand up and back away from her bed, my breath catching in my chest.

"You mean . . . that awful guy . . . who wrote all that stuff about Lara . . . was *you*?"

My sister nods slowly, staring back at me with eyes red from weeping, her face stained with tears.

"What is *wrong* with you?" I ask just above a whisper. "Why would you *do* that?"

Bree doesn't answer. She just puts her head down and starts crying again.

I realize that I've grown up with Bree and I have no idea who she really is. Because the sister I thought I had wouldn't do something that sick to anyone, especially someone who used to be her best friend.

I leave Bree to her crying and head for my room. And then I'm hit with a wave of nausea that sends me toward the bathroom instead. Because I've just imagined Sydney's reaction when she hears about what my sister did.

LARA

I'M BOTH excited and nervous about Luis and Julisa visiting today. Ashley and a few girls from cheerleading came by last week to drop off fashion magazines and flowers, but I was taking a nap, and to be honest I was glad Mom let me sleep, because I wasn't ready to see them yet. But Julisa and Luis are different. I know them better.

Even so, it's hard. Julisa bursts into tears when she sees me and hugs me so tight I think my ribs will break.

"Don't you dare scare me like that again," she says, her tears dampening my shoulder.

"I won't," I tell her, hoping that I mean it.

Luis stands behind her, uncharacteristically awkward, clutching a bunch of bright yellow tulips. He smiles tentatively as I look at him over Julisa's shoulder.

"Hey, Lara," he says.

Julisa releases me from the bear hug, and he hands me the tulips. "You have no idea how happy I am to see you right now," Luis says.

"Thanks. Tulips are my favorite," I tell him.

"I know," he says, looking down at the carpet.

"*How* do you know?" Julisa asks the question I am wondering.

Luis looks straight into my eyes. "You told us last spring. When we went to the concert in the park."

I can't believe he remembered. A group of us went to a free concert in the park downtown last spring. It was a beautiful sunny Sunday, and they'd set up a stage under a tent. The daffodils and tulips were out, and the leaves were back on the trees and everything seemed hopeful again — especially for me, because I'd made new friends after Bree dumped me.

That he cared enough to remember something so small about me makes me cry.

"What's the matter?" he asks, worried, as tears stream down my cheeks. "I'm sorry — I thought they would make you happy."

"Th-they d-do," I sniff. "I j-just c-can't believe you r-remembered."

Luis looks totally confused. "I will never, ever understand girls," he says with a sigh.

Julisa puts her arm around me. "*Tontito*, all you need to understand is that Lara likes the flowers, okay?"

"But if she likes them, why is she crying?" Luis asks, running his hand through his thick, dark hair.

The poor guy is so bewildered I can't help giggling, despite my tears. I'd probably be confused, if I were him.

"It's complicated," I say, glancing at Julisa, who starts laughing, too.

Luis finally throws up his hands, says something in Spanish I don't understand, and joins in the laughter.

I realize how happy I am to see them. And that it's the first time I've really laughed like that since . . . since that awful night.

———

Later that night, I'm in bed trying to think of a third thing for my Gratitude List when the phone rings. I'd already written the first two:

1. *Luis remembered I like tulips and brought me some.*

2. *Mom was so busy with work that she didn't bother me for an entire hour and a half. I got to be alone, even if she could watch me out of the kitchen window.*

I'd gone outside to read — luckily the visual problems I had after the overdose turned out to be temporary — but instead I ended up just listening to the leaves rustling, as the breeze blew them from the branches to meet their fallen comrades below, and to the geese honking as they flew south from Canada in a perfect V. I also listened to the thoughts in my head, the whats and the whys and the hows and the whos, and even though they made me sad and mad, at least I could just sit there with them and have them go through my head without anyone trying to "process" them. They were just there.

But I'm stuck on the third thing. My life is very limited at the moment. I go from home to Linda's office and back home again. I'm not allowed on the Internet, except to do the schoolwork my teachers send home, and when I do that, Mom is in the same room and constantly looking over my shoulder to make sure I'm not on Facebook or chatting with anyone. What she doesn't understand is that now that I know that Christian wasn't real, I'm afraid to start all that up again. Because what if I make the same mistake again?

I miss my cell phone more than Facebook or Instagram or anything else. My parents haven't even let me have that back yet, because I might go online with it, so I can't even text my friends. I said they could turn the data off, but they said there's always Wi-Fi and, besides, I have to "earn the privilege."

I'm a lab specimen under constant observation. It's as irritating for Mom as it is for me. She's really resentful about how time keeping an eye on me is taking away from her work and the campaign. She's trying to be a good mom so she doesn't come straight out and say it, but it comes out in lots of little ways.

Sometimes, she takes me for a walk around the neighborhood to "get some fresh air," but really so I get some exercise. I've already done enough damage to her campaign by being mentally unstable. I can't compound it by getting fat again.

I wonder if Mom will ever stop thinking of me as her "problem child."

I wonder if I'll ever stop being one.

When I hear the phone ring so late, I'm afraid that someone is in the hospital. Or worse, has died. That's what those calls usually mean. Late-night calls are never about good news.

My stomach clenches. Is it Grandpa, who has angina, or Nana, whose cancer has been in remission? *Please don't let Nana's cancer have come back. There's enough bad stuff going on right now. Pleasepleasepleaseplease!*

Dad's angry shout of "WHAT?" so loud that I hear Syd stir in her sleep next door tells me the call isn't about death or illness. It's something else. For once I'm glad about my "open door" restriction, because I can hear what's going on.

Finally!

3.   *Open Door Policy helps me eavesdrop better.*

"WHERE DID YOU HEAR THIS?" Dad yells.

I hear Mom telling him to stop shouting, because he'll "wake the girls."

Um . . . a little late for that, Mom.

Syd stands in my doorway, bleary-eyed and bed-headed.

"What's Dad shouting about?"

"Haven't a clue," I tell her.

She comes in and collapses in a huddle on the end of my bed, her head resting on my stuffed Hedwig.

"What kind of sick —"

"What is it, Pete?" Mom interrupts him. "Who's on the phone?"

"A reporter from the *Lake Hills Independent*," Dad tells her, then recommences his rant.

"PETE! Tell them no comment and hang up, now!" Mom hisses at Dad.

"No comment! Good-bye."

Syd and I look at each other as we hear the phone slam back in the cradle.

"I'm going over there right now and I'm going to rip them to pieces with my bare hands!"

I've heard my father angry before, but I've never, ever heard him like this.

"Who's he going to rip to pieces?" Syd asks. "What's he so mad about?"

"I don't know," I say. "But he's really starting to freak me out."

"Me too," Syd says, cuddling Hedwig.

I slide my toes under her for warmth, and she doesn't protest. She encircles my ankle with the hand that's not holding my stuffed owl.

Mom is telling Dad to calm down, that he can't take things into his own hands.

Dad comes stomping down the hallway, with Mom on his heels.

"Pete, you have to let the police deal with this," she pleads. "It won't do anyone any good if you go vigilante."

That's when I know that this is about me.

Pulling my feet from under Syd, I jump up from the bed, and run out into the hall.

"What happened? What was that phone call about?"

Mom's hand flies to her mouth. She looks paralyzed with fear.

Dad turns to me. He's in his tartan pj bottoms and a faded Chicago Bulls T-shirt and slippers. Is he planning on going out of the house to exact retribution on someone like that? *Tell me you're not planning on leaving the house like that, please, Dad?*

"You want to know what that phone call was about? It was a reporter from the *Independent*. She wanted to know my reaction to the news that it was our neighbors and former friends who'd set up that fake account."

Neighbors and former friends?

No . . . It can't be. He can't mean . . . No way. Bree would never do that to me. Not Bree. Never. *Christian* couldn't be *Bree* . . . He *flirted* with me.

I feel sick.

"*Wait* . . . you mean . . ."

It's too hard to process, much less *say* the words I'm thinking.

"Yes," Dad snaps. "I mean the Connorses. Your best friend, Bree, and her mother, Mary Jo. *That's* who you've been talking to all this time."

Christian . . . who used the L *word . . .*

Then told me the world would be a better place without me in it . . . was really . . . *Bree*.

My best friend, Bree.

My *former* best friend, Bree.

And her *MOM*.

Did they sit there laughing at me while they did it? Was messing with my head all some big joke to them?

I almost *killed myself* because of Bree and Mary Jo Connors.

How . . . can . . . this . . . be . . . real?

The dizziness comes over me so suddenly I have to put my hand on the wall to stay upright.

"I'm going over there right now," Dad says.

"You can't, Pete. It's eleven-thirty at night," Mom tells him, gripping his arm. "You'll wake up the entire neighborhood."

"You think I care?" Dad shouts, pulling his arm free of her grasp. "What kind of neighborhood is this when you can't even trust the people you thought were friends? Huh, Kathy? Answer that for me."

He turns on his heel and stomps down the stairs. A few seconds later we hear the front door slam so hard, the framed school pictures of Syd and me lining the wall of the stairway rattle against the wall.

Mom heads toward her bedroom. "I better go out there before he gets himself arrested," she says in a voice clipped with anger.

Why does it seem like she's angrier with Dad than with the Connorses?

She comes out, tying the knot on her bathrobe, her bare feet stuck hastily into a pair of pink running shoes.

"I'll be back," she says, her face grim, as she marches down the steps to save Dad from himself.

"Are you okay?"

Syd puts her hand on my shoulder, tentatively, like she's afraid I'm going to shake it off. But I don't. I'm grateful for it.

I shake my head no, not trusting myself to speak.

"I bet . . ." Syd puts her arms around me cautiously, like I'm an unexploded hand grenade that could go off any minute, and gives me a gentle but awkward hug.

Syd's afraid I'm going to lose it again.

"I'm doing better than Dad," I say, patting her back.

"No kidding," Syd says, pulling away from me. "He's scary."

And that's when we hear the commotion in the street. Shouts and screaming.

Syd and I look at each other and run down the stairs, through the door, and out into the street, neither of us caring that we're in our pj's and barefoot. The grass is cold and damp beneath my feet, and it sends a chill up my body, but not nearly as much as the scene in front of the Connors house. Dad is trying to get to Mrs. Connors like he wants to strangle her, and Mom and Mr. Nunn from next door are holding him back. Mr. Connors is standing between Dad and his wife, his fists clenched, ready to deck Dad if he gets any closer. Liam stands behind his mother, watching wide-eyed.

Mom is screaming at Dad to calm down and go home. Mr. Connors is telling him he's crazy. Mrs. Connors shouts that she's calling the police. Syd clutches my arm, and I hug her back for comfort and warmth.

And then I see Bree, watching the scene from their living room window. She has her cell phone in her hand, and she's probably recording this whole thing to put on Facebook. Putting my family's worst moments on Facebook seems to give her pleasure for some screwed-up reason. Why else would she have posted that picture of me on the stretcher?

Up and down the street, people are turning on their outside lights and coming out to check out the source of the noise, to see what the heck is going on.

More shouting.

"Hey, do you mind putting a sock in it? You just woke up my kids!" That's Mr. Campbell from three doors down.

Mom grabs Dad's collar so she can pull his head toward her. "Pete, you're making a scene. We have to leave. *NOW.*"

People are holding up cell phones. This whole surreal scene is being captured for posterity or YouTube, whichever comes first.

And as none of us Kelleys are ever allowed to forget, Mom is running for reelection.

Syd starts crying. "Dad, come inside," she wails.

I'm hugging her, not sure if I'm giving or seeking comfort. Despite all the tears I've shed since the night I took those pills, tonight my eyes are dry. Other than the cold grass under my bare feet and the wind that occasionally blows my hair across my face, I hardly even feel. Because this . . . this *scene* I'm a part of now . . . it's not real. It can't be. It's too *surreal*. It's a movie that I'm watching, that's about my life, with familiar characters acting in unfamiliar ways.

And then we hear the sirens approaching. That's when Mom loses it, too.

"Pete, get in the house," she screams. "You're making things worse."

"Listen to Kathy, Pete," Mr. Connors snarls. "Get off my property. Go home and leave my wife alone!"

When the police car pulls to a stop in front of the Connors house, the red and blue lights create a strobe effect, flashing off the houses, the gawking and videoing neighbors, my parents and Mr. and Mrs. Connors.

A police officer gets out and walks over to where my parents and the Connorses are standing. Mrs. Connors is still holding the cordless phone she used to call 911, brandishing it like a weapon in my father's direction.

Dad, who has been like an attacking Rottweiler held back by Mom and Mr. Nunn, droops visibly when he sees the blue uniform. Mom and Mr. Nunn drop their hold on him, and he glances over at Mom, who doesn't meet his gaze. She is marble — cold, hard, impassive, but I know underneath she is calculating the damage to our family image and her campaign and figuring out how to repair them both.

Can something like this even be repaired?

Mom catches sight of Syd and me shivering together on our front lawn and gestures for us to go inside. Syd wipes her tears away with the sleeve of her pajama top.

It's like being at a sleepover when everyone else wants to watch a horror movie. I've seen enough that I don't really want to watch any more, but I still want to know how it ends. But Mom gestures again, this time mouthing, "Go inside *now*," and knowing the kind of mood she's going to be in after this, it's better to just go with it.

"Come on, Syd. We have to go in."

"But what about Dad?"

"Mom says."

We head back to the house. My sister casts a look back at my parents, and when I look back, too, I notice that Liam's gaze is focused on us, not at what is going on with our parents and the police.

"My feet are freezing," Syd complains when we get inside.

"Do you want me to make you some hot chocolate?"

She gives me a strange look. Under the kitchen lights, I can see the dried tear tracks that stain her cheeks, still tinged pink from the chill outside.

"What?" I ask.

Syd opens her mouth like she's going to say something, but closes it and looks down at her bare feet, which have bits of grass still stuck to them. "Nothing," she mumbles. "Hot chocolate would be nice."

I know she was going to say something else, but I don't have the energy for twenty questions. Whatever's on her mind, Syd's gonna have to just spit it out.

I've just finished pouring the boiling water into the mugs when the front door opens and slams shut.

"How *could* you, Pete?" Mom shouts. "Do you realize you've probably single-handedly sunk my reelection campaign?"

"I'm sorry . . ."

"A citation for disorderly conduct? What kind of example —"

"Seriously, Kathy? That . . . *woman* almost killed our daughter and you're worried about the election and setting examples?"

My former best friend and her mother punked me and I tried to kill myself over a guy who didn't even exist, my dad's been cited for disorderly conduct by the police — I'm sure the video of him losing it on our neighbor's lawn in his pajamas is all over YouTube as we speak — and my mother's reelection campaign is probably over as of tonight.

Everything is a complete disaster, and it's all because of me.

Syd grabs my wrist as soon as I put down her mug of hot chocolate.

"Don't."

The fierce urgency in her voice shocks me. "Don't what?"

"Don't do that thing you do. Don't go all zombie on me right now."

Her eyes burn into me, trying to force me out of the numbness I'm trying so desperately to retreat into.

"You always do that. You always disappear when things get hard," she says. "I'm sick of it. It's not fair."

I think, *I'm not disappearing. I'm trying to save myself.*

I say, "I'm right here, Syd."

Syd rolls her eyes and blows a raspberry of disgust through her lips. "Sure, Lara. Okay, Lara. Whatever you say."

She slides out of her chair, taking the mug of hot chocolate with her, and storms out of the kitchen, while I listen to our parents fighting and try my best to slip back into the comforting void, alone.

BREE

I THOUGHT when Mr. Kelley went crazy on our lawn in his pajamas and got cited by the police for disorderly conduct, it would take some of the heat off Mom and me.

Well, that's just another example of how stupid I am.

What actually happened was that it brought *more* attention to us. There's a huge front-page spread in the *Lake Hills Independent* under the headline "Mother-Daughter Bullying Team."

Mom and me a team? That's got to be the biggest joke ever. The truth is, she's the crazy coach and I'm the player who always gets yelled at for no reason.

There were reports on the local news stations with the same "Bullying Team" tagline. Not that the Kelleys got off easy, either, which didn't make me feel any better. There was video footage of Mr. Kelley ranting on our front lawn in his pj's. When Mom watched the news yesterday morning during breakfast, she laughed at that.

"There goes Kathy Kelley's political career," she cackled.

"Zip it, Mary Jo," Dad said. "That's enough."

Dad's been pretty quiet since the front lawn ruckus, but it's not his normal, laid-back quiet. It's a brooding, tense silence as he goes around the house with a furrowed brow, and without his usual good humor.

I don't pay much attention to politics, but I think Lara's mom has been a good councilwoman. She always seems to be talking about making sure the schools have enough money, which sounds important to me. I can't understand why Mom is so happy about her career going down the toilet, especially since she worked on Mrs. Kelley's campaign when she first ran for office.

It can't be all because of that stupid tax abatement thing that Mom's always complaining about, can it? I suddenly wonder if that's the reason Mom worked on the campaign. I always thought it was because she and Mrs. Kelley were friends.

Just before dinner, the doorbell rings. Mom tells me to get it. When I open the door, a well-groomed lady is standing there holding a microphone. Behind her is a cameraman, pointing the lens of his camera over her shoulder in my direction. One of those trucks with a satellite dish is parked at the curb outside our house.

"Are you Breanna Connors?" she asks.

"Yeah. Wait, are you filming this?" I ask, wondering if I should be talking to her at all, or if I should just shut the door in her face.

She ignores my question.

"Is your mother home?"

"She's making dinner," I say, trying to avoid looking at the cameraman, but then wonder, if they *are* filming, if that would just make me look sketchy.

"Well, can you get her?"

Fine, snippy Reporter Lady. Be that way.

"Moooom!" I shout without moving from the doorway. "There's a TV reporter here to see you."

"You were Lara Kelley's best friend. Why would you do this to someone you allegedly cared about?"

She sticks her big black microphone right next to my mouth, staring at me accusingly, and I freeze, panic stricken. I don't want a microphone in my face. I don't want to be there at all. I want to be in my room, with the curtains closed, hiding under the covers, shutting the rest of the world out.

"I . . . didn't . . . mean . . . to."

"You didn't mean to create a fake profile to trick her?"

"No. I just . . . I didn't . . ."

"What's going on here?" Mom says. "I didn't give my consent for you to interview my daughter. She's a minor."

They need Mom's permission to interview me? Normally that would make me mad because I'm old enough to make my own decisions, but at this moment I just feel relieved.

"I apologize," says the reporter, but she doesn't look or sound the teensiest bit sorry. "Do we have your permission to interview your daughter, Mrs. Connors?"

I hold my breath, hoping Mom won't agree.

"No," she says, and I exhale my relief. "Get lost."

Mom turns to me. "Go finish your homework."

I'd already finished it, but I use the excuse to escape into the family room.

Still, I notice that I don't hear the front door slam shut for another five minutes.

———

"Don't answer it," Mom says when the phone rings during dinner. "It's probably another one of those nosy reporters."

We all sit listening to the answering machine. Sure enough, it's a reporter from CNN. Practically as soon as he hangs up, the phone rings again. This time it's a woman, who says she works for Nancy Grace on Fox.

"For crying out loud, Mary Jo," Dad says, getting up and turning both the answering machine volume and the phone ringer to silent. "This is giving me indigestion."

"What do you expect *me* to do about it?" Mom asks.

Dad opens his mouth to retort, but the doorbell rings again.

Liam jumps up to get it.

"Ignore it," Dad says.

"But, Dad, what if it's —"

"I said, *ignore it!*" Dad shouts.

Liam sits back down, muttering, "Fine," but then the doorbell rings another time.

I exchange a glance with Liam. How are we supposed to eat dinner if the doorbell keeps ringing and Dad won't let anyone answer it? Between the phone, the doorbell, and the obvious tension between my parents, I've pretty much lost my appetite anyway.

Then I see movement in the corner of my eye. It looks like there is something — or someone — outside the kitchen window.

I scream.

"What on earth?" Mom exclaims.

"There's someone outside! I saw them!" I shout.

"That does it," Dad says. He runs out to the garage and comes back a few minutes later with Liam's baseball bat. Striding over to the back door, he flings it open, turns on the outside light, and starts shouting at the camera crew to get off his property right now or he will call the police.

"And if I see you step foot on my property again, I'll do more than make a phone call," he says, waving the baseball bat around menacingly.

He looks and sounds crazy, not like my normal, level-headed teddy bear of a dad.

After he slams the kitchen door shut and locks it, he closes the blinds in the kitchen.

"Go shut the curtains in the front of the house," he orders. "Keep the lights off while you do it."

I creep into the living room, feeling like I'm in some action movie and our house is surrounded by bad guys. There is a little bit of light from the street, but in the shadows I scrape my ankle against the corner of an end table, deep enough to draw blood.

When I get to the window, I peer out before pulling the curtain cord.

What I see turns my stomach. It is unreal. It is the kind of thing that happens to other people, not people like us.

There is a cluster of TV trucks lining the street between our house and the Kelleys'. Reporters and camera people and guys with lights, blocking the sidewalk and our driveways. Some of our neighbors across the street are on their front porches, watching the commotion.

I yank the cord, shutting them all out, and stumble my way through the darkness back to the light of the hallway.

"Did you see what's out front?" Liam asks as he emerges from the dining room.

I nod slowly, waiting for him to say something about how it's all my fault, but he doesn't. He's pale under his freckles. He looks as scared as I feel.

"The neighbors are going to love us," Dad mutters as he sits back down at the kitchen table. "And I'm not talking about the Kelleys."

"You're always so worried about what everyone is going to think, Sean," Mom says.

Dad glares at her.

"Maybe if you and Bree had worried about that a little *more*, we wouldn't be in this mess," he snaps.

I stare down at my plate, feeling like the worst daughter in the world. It's one thing disappointing Mom. I'm used to doing that. But Dad . . .

Suddenly, my parents' cell phones start buzzing.

"They must have decided to try our work numbers," Mom says.

"Great," Dad says sarcastically. "This is going to do *wonders* for business. People are already making comments when they come into the store to buy parts."

"Don't start, Sean," Mom warns him.

"What do you mean 'Don't start,' Mary Jo? I didn't start this. I didn't even *know* about this until the police showed up," Dad says, his voice rising with the anger he's obviously been keeping under all that quiet. "*Bree* started this. And when you discovered what she was doing, instead of giving her consequences, you didn't just *encourage her*, you *took part in it yourself.*"

"Oh, so it's all my fault, is it?" Mom shouts at him. "Is that what you're saying?"

"What I'm saying is, that because the two of you didn't think, the legal consequences are just the beginning. I'm worried about the business. You know how long and hard I've worked to build Connors Plumbing Supplies into what it is, and I don't want to see it go down the tubes because of pure stupidity. And how do you expect to pay the bills if the business falls apart?"

My stupidity.

I stare down at my plate, fighting tears as Mom argues back.

"Your business! What about *my* business? You're not the only one paying bills around here, Sean."

Dad slams his fist on the table so hard the plates jump. My father has never, ever done anything violent like that before, and it even shocks Mom into silence. It freaks me out so much my hands are trembling. Liam looks from my father to my mother, wide-eyed, as if he doesn't know who they are anymore.

"Let's just eat," Dad says, his voice gruff but quieter now.

We eat the rest of dinner in uncomfortable silence, broken only by the sounds of the outside world trying desperately to get in.

———

Liam and I are doing the dishes after dinner while Mom and Dad watch the news in the living room. My brother is still giving me the silent treatment, like he's been doing ever since the cops came, only speaking to me when absolutely necessary.

All of a sudden we hear Dad exclaim a slew of curse words, and Mom shout, "Turn it up!"

Liam and I exchange a brief "What was that?" glance, then race into the living room to see what's going on.

Their eyes are glued to the TV. To the evening news. The *national* news. The news that they show on TVs all across the United States of America.

The box in the upper left-hand corner of the screen next to the newscaster's head has a picture of Mom — the one that's on all those awful bus shelter ads around town that make Liam and me cringe every time we see them — and underneath it, in big horror-movie-style letters, the caption "Monster Mom."

"I'm going to sue the pants off them," Mom fumes. "They can't slander me like that."

I listen close to hear what they'll say about me. If Mom is a monster, and I'm her daughter, what does that make me? *Monster Spawn?*

There's a shot of the outside of our house and of the high school. It's hard to hear everything the newscaster is saying over Mom's ranting and Dad telling her to calm down. Something, something, "cyberbullying tag team shocked the community." Then there's Mr. Kelley in his pj's again, the same footage from the local news, something about "outraged father" blah blah blah "cited for disorderly conduct."

When the news announcer moves on to the next story, Dad picks up the remote and turns off the TV.

"Hand me the phone, Sean," Mom says. "I need to call a lawyer. They can't do this to me. It's libel. They're going to ruin my business."

Only Liam is brave — or stupid — enough to point out the obvious.

"It's not libel if you actually *did* it, Mom."

I hold my breath, waiting for the explosion in 3 . . . 2 . . . 1 . . .

"What, now my own kid is turning on me? Get out of here!" Mom shouts.

Dad gives us a look that says we'd be better off upstairs. So we go.

"Thanks a lot, Bree," Liam says. "School's going to suck even more now."

"It's not like *you* did anything."

"Duh! I *know that!*" he says. "That's what sucks. I did nothing, but I'm still lumped with *you* and *Monster Mom.*"

He stalks the rest of the way up the stairs and slams his bedroom door. Normally, my parents would have yelled about that, but Mom's too busy threatening to sue the TV, and Dad's too busy trying to calm her down.

Thanks a lot, bro. Way to make me feel like a total leper. I know Liam is mad at me. I know he thinks what I did was wrong. But it's hard enough knowing that the rest of the world is going to think I'm a monster without my own brother hating me.

Getting to sleep is almost impossible. I toss and turn, worrying about what is going to happen, how people are going to react.

When I finally get to sleep, my dreams are filled with nightmares of me being chased by enormous black microphones, all asking, "Why, Bree? Why would you do this?"

———

The TV trucks are still there the next morning.

I beg Mom to drive me to school so I don't have to walk through them to take the bus.

"I can't. I've got a showing," she snaps. "At least *this* one hasn't canceled."

"People are canceling showings because of . . ." I trail off, not wanting to actually call her the name I'm sure she's being called behind all the doors in our neighborhood. Behind doors all across America.

"Because people don't want Monster Mom as their broker."

"I'll take you," Dad offers. "How about you, champ? Do you want a ride?"

"Nah . . . I'll take the bus," Liam says.

"Are you sure?" Dad says. "You don't want to have to walk through that mob outside."

"I'm sure. I'm going to leave early and cut through the Nunns' backyard. I'll get on the bus at the next stop down."

I know why he's doing it. He'd rather be anywhere that I'm not, because he wants to avoid being known as Monster Bro.

"How're you holding up, Breenut?" Dad asks me when we're alone in the car. "This is all pretty insane, huh?"

"Yeah," I mumble, looking out the window.

"I had a bunch of really nasty voice mails on my cell when I woke up this morning," Dad says. "There are some sick people in this world."

"The news made it sound like Mom's the one who's sick. And me." I look at him and ask the question that's been haunting me all night. "Am I, Dad?"

My father doesn't respond right away, and I turn to look at him, wondering if he thinks I'm some kind of sicko, too. He's biting the side of his lip, the way he always does when he's gearing up to tell Mom something he's afraid might set her off.

"I wouldn't say you're sick, Breenut. You're a teenager who made some . . ." He pauses, searching for the right words. "Very *foolish decisions.*"

He means *bad* decisions. Because he thinks I'm bad.

Dad's the one person in my family who even slightly understands me, and even *he* thinks I'm a screwup.

"As a result, we've decided to take away your computer privileges. From now on, if you need the computer to do your homework, you'll have to wait till I get home from work to supervise."

"But, Dad —"

"There's no negotiating on this, Bree."

I want to ask him what Mom's punishment is going to be, but I know that'll just make him angrier. Still, the unfairness of it means I have to fight the lump welling in my throat to get out the next question.

"What do you think's going to happen?"

Dad glances away from the road to look at me for a second.

"I wish I knew, honey. We're in uncharted territory here."

I wanted him to reassure me, to say everything is going to be okay, even if he had to lie. But Dad's never been a fibbing kind of parent. Like when Grandma died, he didn't say she "went to heaven" or was "with God now" or any of the stuff people normally say to kids so they can avoid saying the *D* word. He just cuddled Liam and me on either side of him and told us that she died. Flat out. She died, but she loved us and it was okay to feel sad because we were going to miss her. That he was feeling sad because he missed her, but we should also remember all the fun things about her, because that's what she'd want us to do.

And then he told us all these funny stories about things Grandma did when he was a kid, which got Liam and me remembering stuff, too. I still cried later that night when I went to bed, but that was okay, too. Dad held me, my tears soaking into his shirt, and his eyes were wet, too.

"The one thing I do know is that things are going to get worse before they get better," Dad continues. "With all this press coverage . . . the voice mails . . . emails . . . just since the news last night I've had over a thousand emails through my website. None of them . . . pleasant."

"Daddy, I don't want to go to school. I don't feel well."

"Here's the thing, honey: You made a big mistake. You did something that was pretty stupid and very wrong. And now there are consequences." He looks at me with such sadness and disappointment in his eyes that it's much worse than if he were shouting. "I wish you'd taken a little time to stop and think about the consequences before you did what you did, but you didn't."

He sighs. "And neither did your mother, unfortunately." He reaches over and pats my leg. "Be strong, Breenut. You'll get through this." He pauses. "We all will. Somehow."

It's like he's trying to convince himself, as well as me, which tells me how totally screwed I am just as we pull into the school parking lot. My stomach turns over and I'm afraid the Cheerios I had for breakfast are about to come up in a totally uncheery way.

"Please . . . can't I just come to work with you? I can help in the stockroom or something."

Dad pulls up next to the curb and puts the car in park. "Honey, no problem, big or small, gets solved by running away from it. When you make mistakes, the only way to face them is head-on."

He reaches over, pulls my head toward him, and kisses the top of my hair, despite my reluctance. "Hang in there. See you later, alligator."

I get out and slam the car door. I have this half-regurgitated-Cheerio feeling that meeting mistakes head-on is how people end up with brain damage.

Marci and Jenny are sitting in the usual place on the wall. Marci's mouth is moving as she watches Josie Stern walk by, and I bet you anything she's making fun of her purple hair. If I were standing there, I wouldn't tell her to stop, even though I think it suits Josie. It's just easier to agree — to disagree would risk Marci turning her sharp tongue on me, which I'm afraid she's going to do anyway now that I'm the Monster Spawn of Monster Mom. Does Marci know that I told the police about her? Does she realize I gave them her name because I was scared? If she's mad at me, I don't blame her. It's becoming more and more obvious that I'm a horrible friend to everyone.

I think about going around the long way and sneaking in

the gym entrance to avoid finding out. But then Jenny turns and sees me. She waves, so I'm trapped. I walk over, slowly, waiting and dreading.

"It's Bree Connors, our local celebrity!" Marci says really loudly so everyone standing nearby can hear. "Hey, bestie! Can I have your autograph?"

I swallow the Cheerios back into my stomach with relief. I guess the police haven't spoken to her yet. And I should have figured that Marci would think being the bestie of a nationwide TV story was a better gig than ragging on me. She puts her arm around me.

"How are you doing, Bree?" she asks. "Are you, like, *totally freaking*?"

"It's not a whole lot of fun at the moment," I admit.

"Can you believe that video of Lara's dad losing it on your front lawn in his pj's?" Marci says. "I was *dying*!"

"It was pretty surreal," I say. "Especially when the cops showed up."

"Maybe that's where Lara gets it from," Marci says. "Being crazy, I mean."

Jenny's just been standing there, not laughing, not saying anything. But then, unexpectedly, she speaks up.

"I don't blame him," she says. "I'd go crazy, too, if you and your mom did what you did to my kid. If I had a kid, that is."

"Who are you, getting so judgmental all of a sudden?" Marci asks.

Jenny ignores her and instead looks straight at me. "I'm sorry, Bree, but what you did was terrible. Lara almost *died*. Doesn't that bother you?"

Jenny's always been so quiet and mild, more of a follower than a leader. But now her blue eyes flash with an angry, indignant fire, and it's directed straight at me.

"Of . . . course . . . it bothers me. I . . . never expected her . . . to, like . . . try to *kill herself*."

"What *did* you expect, exactly?"

"Jeez, Jenny, lighten up!" Marci says. "It was a joke, okay? It's not Bree's fault Lara is a psycho who couldn't take it."

Jenny stares at Marci, as if she's seeing her, really seeing her, for the first time. Then she turns on her heel and stomps away into the building.

"Wow, what got into her?" Marci says. "It must be that time of the month or something."

I don't respond, because deep down I'm pretty sure Jenny is the one who's right about me, and I wish I had the courage to say so.

———

When I see Jenny coming toward me in the hallway after second period, I'm about to turn the other way and escape to the bathroom to avoid her, but she calls my name.

"Bree . . . have you heard your outgoing voice mail message?" she asks.

There's a strange look on her face that makes me get that unCheerio feeling again. "Um . . . no. Why would I? I don't call my own cell," I say.

Jenny takes out her phone. "I called you to apologize about this morning. I wanted to leave a message instead of texting because . . . well . . . I know things must be rough for you with everything that's going on, and well . . . I was kind of harsh," she says. "I'm sorry."

Hearing her say that brings a lump to my throat.

"You were honest," I tell her. "But . . . thanks. I didn't get your message yet. I leave my phone off in class."

"Then I think you better hear this," she says.

She dials my cell number and hands me her phone, her face creased with concern. Instead of my usual "Hi, it's Bree, you know what to do, so do it after the beep," my out-going message says something else. Something that makes my blood run cold.

It says, "I'm Breanna Connors, the sociopath who almost killed my best friend. Leave me a death threat," in a voice that isn't mine.

My hands are trembling as I hand the phone back to Jenny. I dig my own cell out of my bag and turn it on. There are seventy voice mails. I push Play and put it on speaker so Jenny can hear. "I'm coming for you, sicko. I know where you live" is the first one. I go to push the button to delete it, wanting it off my phone, out of my life, out of existence, but Jenny pushes my finger away.

"No, Bree! You have to keep it for the police!"

I know she's right, but I don't want to carry my phone around with that on it. It's so scary. What if it's true? What if someone's really out there, waiting and watching, wanting to hurt me for what I did to Lara?

By the third message, I'm crying. By the fifth one, I'm completely hysterical.

"Don't listen to any more of them, Bree," Jenny says, gently wrestling the phone out of my grasp. "Let's go to the principal."

She puts her arm around me and helps me walk down to the office. My legs are shaking so bad I can hardly walk, and it's hard to see through my tears, but Jenny's arm is solid and strong, and she keeps repeating that the adults will know what to do, that they'll call the police and everything is going to be okay and no one is going to hurt me and that I shouldn't worry about what those crazy messages say and I'll be safe and so will my family.

I don't believe for a second that everything is going to be okay, but I need to hear her say the words. I don't believe her, because if they can find out my cell number and figure out how to change my outgoing message to tell people to leave me death threats, how can I ever be really safe again?

SYDNEY

I WANTED Mom to drive me to school today, but of course she had to stay with Lara, who didn't sleep well last night because of the press attention, and Mom doesn't want Dad to drive me like he did yesterday because he almost punched out a photographer who tried to take a picture of us. He has to keep away from the press in case he does something stupid and messes up her campaign even more.

So I have to fight my way through the savage media hordes all by myself. They stick these big black microphones in my face and ask me questions about Lara and Bree. I push their mics away, saying, "Leave me alone, you're going to make me miss the bus!"

But they keep surrounding me like a pack of rabid dogs, until Mrs. Gorski comes out of her house with a broom and yells at them.

"Leave the poor child alone!" she shouts, waving her broomstick at them like some crazy old witch. She's wearing a flowered nylon housecoat and a pair of purple Crocs, which look ginormous at the end of her thin chicken legs. But Mrs. G. has never looked better to me, even in her Barney Crocs with her white hair sticking up in all directions.

She marches to the bus stop by my side, wielding the broom like a weapon, ready to use it on anyone with a camera or a mic who dares comes too close.

"Thanks, Mrs. G.," I say.

My words come out damp and wobbly. Having this tiny old lady with her flyaway hair and her housecoat ready to fight for me, armed with only a household cleaning tool and her personality makes me feel more like the real Sydney and less like the beef jerky one.

The other kids at the bus stop give me a strange look when I get there, but I don't know if it's because of the news or because of Mrs. G. marching beside me with her broom and her purple Crocs.

Liam isn't here. I don't know if he was here yesterday. I didn't see him in school. Maybe *his* parents are willing to drive him.

Mrs. G. keeps up a steady stream of conversation, telling me about how her daughter who lives in Cleveland is coming to visit with her one-year-old grandson this weekend and how she can't wait to see him and she wishes they lived closer. Even though I'm only half listening, I'm grateful because it means I don't have to answer any questions or wonder what the other kids are thinking. In fact I'm so grateful that when the bus pulls up, I hug her before I get on.

"Hang in there, *bubbeleh*," Mrs. G. says, embracing me with her bony arms. "All this *mishegas* will be over soon, and they'll move on to the next thing. You'll be okay. Trust me."

I don't have a clue what *bubbeleh* or *mishegas* mean, but I want like anything to believe her when she says that I'll be okay.

———

Two stops past our normal one, Liam gets on the bus, and it suddenly goes quiet. Then kids move to the aisle so that even though there's an empty space next to them, he can't sit down.

He quickly covers the flash of hurt on his face with a mask of indifference. But I know. I can tell by the way his skin flushes under his freckles. I can tell by the way his jaw is set. I've known Liam Connors long enough to tell.

Even though I've got every reason to be mad at the Connorses, more reason than any of the other kids on this bus to hate Liam, I don't. He can't help being Bree's brother any more than I can help being Lara's sister. We're both stuck in this sucky situation by accident of birth. In that brief instant before the mask came up, he looked as tired, angry, and miserable as I feel. So I slide over to the window and gesture to the seat next to me.

I hear muttering. "What the?" . . . "Why would she *do* that?" . . . "Isn't that *Lara Kelley's sister*?" but I try to tune it out. They don't know our history. They don't know what it's like to be me — or to be Liam.

Liam looks surprised, but he plops down next to me in the seat.

"Thanks," he mumbles, giving me a quick, grateful glance, but then he keeps his eyes trained on the backpack resting on his knees as if he's afraid to let the mask slip.

"How's it going?" I ask, and then curse myself for asking because it's a seriously stupid question.

"Oh, everything's just *swell*," he says, dripping sarcasm. "Someone posted our phone number online at two o'clock in the morning, and it started ringing off the hook with people leaving obscene messages and death threats for Mom and Bree. Dad finally ripped all the plugs out of the wall."

As mad as I am at Bree and Mrs. Connors, as much as I want them punished for what they did to Lara, death threats are pretty extreme. Especially when Liam didn't do anything wrong.

"That's horrible," I say. "Are you . . . you know . . . scared?"

Liam shrugs. "I don't know. The policeman who came by at four this morning said the obvious thing to do is change our phone number and just be vigilant. They'll investigate to see if any of them are really credible, but even if they can arrest someone, they can't protect us twenty-four seven."

He gives me a sideways look and, despite everything, manages a weak smile. "You're not planning on bumping me off, are you, Syd?"

That he can still joke with me, while crazy people are threatening to kill his mom and his sister, tugs at my heart. He's my friend, no matter what's happening in the world around us. I have to keep reminding myself of that.

"Not this week," I say. "But I'll have to check my assas-sination schedule for next week."

And then I get a real Liam smile, one that goes all the way to his eyes. "I'll watch my back, then."

I don't want to take away his smile, but I have to ask. "How's Bree doing?"

The light disappears immediately, and he starts picking at a loose thread on his backpack strap. "She's a disaster. Especially after what happened with her cell yesterday."

"What's that?"

"Someone hacked it and changed her outgoing message, asking people to leave her death threats, then posted the number online. When she turned it on after second period, there were already seventy messages. She got totally hysteri-cal and Dad had to go to school and pick her up." He pulls hard at the loose thread and rips it. "They were *seriously* nasty — at least the few I was allowed to listen to."

I can't help myself. "Worse than the stuff that people wrote on Lara's Facebook wall?"

Liam stiffens. "At least people weren't threatening to *kill* her."

I know he's her brother, but it's like he's forgotten that Bree's the one who started it all. If it weren't for her, none of us would be living through this nightmare. Dad wouldn't have a citation for disorderly conduct, Mom's reelection campaign wouldn't be on the rocks, Lara would be cheering at football games and getting on with her life instead of being such a mess, and I'd have had the chance to audition for the eighth-grade musical and maybe have gotten a lead instead of just being on crew and once again being reduced to playing a bit part in my sister's drama.

If his life sucks right now, well, so does mine. And so does Lara's. And Mom's. And Dad's.

"Maybe not, but people — no, not people, *Bree* — basically told Lara *to kill herself*," I tell him. My voice cracks, as I try to hold back angry tears. "And she tried to do it."

Liam stares at me, his green eyes dark and wounded. What does he expect? That I should feel sorry for Bree?

I feel bad for *him*, because he's caught up in this just the way I am, but Bree's different. She brought this on herself the moment she created that fake profile and started messing with my sister's head.

"She's *my sister*, Syd."

I look away from him, out the window, the scenery blurred as the first tear trails down my cheek. "Well, Lara is *mine*."

We don't speak to each other the rest of the way to school.

———

Maddie and Cara are talking about *Beauty and the Beast* at lunch, because that's mostly what they talk about these days. Cara ended up getting the part of Belle. I'm really happy for her, but whenever they talk about the musical — I can't help feeling left out, even though I'm doing crew. It's just not the same.

I also can't help wondering what would have happened if Lara hadn't tried to kill herself. If I hadn't been stuck at the hospital. If I'd been able to go to auditions instead of being caught up in Lara's drama.

Maybe it could have been me. It's not like I'm mad at Cara — if anyone other than me had to get the lead, I'm glad it was her.

But the thing is . . . I wanted the role sooooo badly. Even if I didn't get the part, at least I wanted the opportunity to try out. All that practicing for weeks leading up to auditions. And because of Lara — no, because of *Bree* — I didn't even get that chance.

It makes me mad at Bree all over again. And at Liam. Is he crazy? How can he expect me to feel sorry for Bree? I mean, it's not like I *want* people to make death threats. That's going totally overboard. But she deserves something bad to happen to her because of what she did. She shouldn't just get to keep on going on with her life like nothing ever happened. Because we don't have that option. Not Lara. Not me. Not anyone in my family. Especially now.

"*Ohmigosh*, did you see the latest about Bree and her mom on the news?" Maddie says between bites of carrot.

Jeez, Maddie, didn't anyone ever teach you not to talk with your mouth full?

"You mean *Monster Mom*?" Cara giggles. "Wouldn't that be a great new reality series?"

"Yeah, sure," I say. "If it weren't *actually my life* at the moment."

The smiles fade from my friends' faces.

"I'm *sooooo* sorry, Syd — I . . . just spaced," Cara says. "I'm not used to stuff on the news having anything to do with people I actually know. You know . . . *real people*."

"Trust me, this is all *too* real. For my family *and* the Connorses," I say.

They both gape at me.

"Wait — are you sticking up for Breanna Connors after what she did to Lara?" Maddie asks. "Because that's messed up."

"Totally messed up," Cara agrees.

I don't know what I'm doing. I've been confused every minute of every single day since we found Lara unconscious in the bathroom. I alternate between being confused and mad. Mad at everyone and everything. Mad about why everything in our family always revolves around Lara. Confused about why life is so freaking unfair all the time. Wondering why people have to be jerks instead of being nice to one another.

"No . . . I'm not sticking up for her . . . exactly. It's just . . . I don't know."

How do I explain that as much as I hate Bree and Mrs. Connors for what they did, the person who probably understands what I'm going through the most is Liam? Or at least *was* Liam. They wouldn't understand. I don't think anyone would. It's hard enough to accept it myself right now.

"Never mind. I've got to go. I'll see you later." I get up and clear my stuff.

"I'm sorry if I upset you, Syd," Cara says. "Really, I am."

"It's okay," I tell her. "Things are just . . . you know."

"Yeah, I know," she says.

But the thing is, Cara doesn't know. Neither does Maddie. Neither of them have the faintest idea what it's like. How can they?

The only person who really understands is the brother of the one who started all this. And now that I'm mad at him, I feel absolutely and totally alone.

It's not till I reach the nearest bathroom that the realization hits me: I'm turning into my sister, Lara — a walking, talking buzzkill.

———

I'm working on my homework later that afternoon when I get a text from Liam.

Need to talk. Can u meet me in the tree fort?

My thumbs hesitate over my phone. Part of me is still mad at him and wants to stay that way, because it's easier than trying to figure out the mess of feelings I have for him if I'm not. Also, if there are any press people lurking around, and they catch a picture of us together . . . I can't even think about that.

But the other part of me, the one that feels so incredibly alone in this insanity — that part wins out.

K. Be there in 5.

I finish the problem I was working on, then go brush my hair and put on lip gloss, even though it's only Liam and I'm just meeting him in the tree fort. *So why am I bothering?*

Slipping out the back door, I check for camera people, but they seem to be congregated around the front of the house. Still, I keep to the back of the yard and detour around the rusting swing set that none of us use anymore, just in case.

Liam's already there when I climb up into the tree fort. It's dusk and there's no electricity up here, so he's lit a few candles. In their flickering glow, I can see the fort is noticeably cleaner and less cobwebby than the last time I was there.

"It looks cleaner up here."

"Yeah," he says. "You should see me with a feather duster. The spiders were quaking in their webs."

"Well, it's a lot nicer being up here without getting them in my hair, that's for sure."

And then we just look at each other in an awkward silence.

I break eye contact first, unsure of what to make of what I see there.

"Syd . . . I feel bad about this morning. You know . . . on the bus?"

I meet his gaze again. His green eyes glow, reflecting candlelight and what I think is . . . what I hope is . . . honesty.

I nod, afraid to say anything. And then he reaches over and takes my hand, warming my cold fingers.

"I totally get it that this is all Bree's fault. And my mom's. I really do. I know that because of what they did, Lara almost . . ." He swallows, and I'm temporarily distracted by his Adam's apple, so it's not till I look back to his eyes that I realize how upset he is about this. "Almost *died*, and I get how sick that is."

Then he kind of tugs my hand, pulling me toward him, and we are in an awkward hug. I'm suddenly aware of how close his lips are to mine, and I wonder if Liam wants to kiss me. Because I want to kiss him. And then he's leaning in, a brush of lips, soft and warm on mine, with the candle in between us, like a warning that I might get burned.

I pull away and bite my lip. I wanted that kiss, but this is all just so messed up. My first kiss ever — and it's with Liam Connors, whose sister almost caused my sister to die.

"I know how hard things must be for you, Syd. I just . . . I just wanted you to understand that things are pretty messed up at our house, too."

"I know," I say. "And I know it's not your fault." I sigh. "Are you still getting the death threat calls?"

"We haven't plugged the phones back in yet," Liam says. "We're not going to until we've changed the phone number to an unlisted one. But in the meantime, someone hacked Dad's business website and redirected it to a porn site."

"Eww — that's disgusting."

"It's more than disgusting. It's shut down his online business until he can get someone to fix it," Liam says. "Not to mention how it's hurting the reputation of his store. He says this could end up ruining everything he's worked for his entire life — because Mom and Bree were idiots."

What does he want from me? Sympathy? Comfort? Understanding?

"Bet that went down well with Mary Jo," I say.

Liam laughs bitterly. "Oh yeah. I'm surprised you couldn't hear the shouting from your house." He moves the index finger of his free hand back and forth through the tip of the candle flame.

"Stop!" I exclaim. "Doesn't that hurt?"

"This?" he asks, doing it again, grinning. "No. Try it."

I shake my head. I already feel like it's dangerous enough being up here with him. Kissing him, even. I don't need to make it even more real by sticking my finger through a flame.

"I spent a lot of time doing this up here last night when Mom and Dad were fighting, and the phones kept ringing off the hook, and Bree was crying," Liam says, running his finger through the flame again. He looks back to me from the flame. "We have to change all our phone numbers. They haven't hacked my cell yet, but the police said they could sooner or later, so Dad's canceling everything tomorrow."

"That sucks," I tell him. It does suck for him about the phone, because it's a pain to have to change numbers, and I feel bad for Mr. Connors, because it wasn't like he was pretending to be Christian DeWitt, either. But . . . I slide my fingers out from Liam's, unsure of how he'll react to what I'm about to say. "The thing is, Liam, it's no picnic at our house, either. Lara's a mess, and we have to tiptoe around her in case she relapses. My dad . . . Well, his being on the news going psycho on your lawn in his pj's — that was fun."

Liam laughs until he realizes that I wasn't trying to be funny, and his smile fades.

"And then there's Mom, who's desperately trying to figure out how to salvage her election campaign because having an Emotionally Damaged Daughter and a Psycho Husband ruins her Perfect Wife and Mother cred, don't you think?"

"Do you . . . think she'll withdraw?"

I laugh. "Kathy Kelley? *Withdraw?* As if! My mom doesn't withdraw. She just figures out a new angle."

Liam smiles. "I thought I was the World's Most Cynical Teen, but apparently not. It's you, Syd."

I wonder if he'll kiss me again.

"Do you ever wish you could change your name or be adopted by another family?" I ask. "A *normal* family? Like one that isn't in the newspapers or on the national news or doesn't have to pretend to be perfect because they're running for public office?"

"Or isn't doing screwed-up things like setting up fake Facebook profiles and almost causing their former best friend to kill herself?"

"Yeah, that kind of family," I agree. "One that does normal stuff together like have barbecues and build tree forts. Like our families used to do before everything got screwed up."

"Do you think life can ever get back to normal after this?" Liam asks. "Or will I always be Son of Monster Mom?"

"And will I always be the sister of the girl who tried to kill herself over the fake Facebook guy?" I say. "With all these news stories being online, we can't even go off to college and escape this now. It's going to follow us wherever we go."

"I'm not going to let Bree's stupidity ruin the rest of my life," Liam says. "I'm going to do something so amazing that people will remember me for being me, not because I'm her brother." Then he laughs ruefully. "The problem is, I haven't figured out what that amazing thing is yet."

Liam's so brave and determined that I don't doubt for a second that he'll do it.

"You will," I tell him, taking his hand. "I know you will."

He smiles at me and shifts over so he's sitting next to me. Then he puts his arm around my shoulder, and I snuggle next to him, resting my head on his shoulder. We sit looking at the flickering candle flame, just being there in our little tree house of sanity.

LARA

I **HATE** the Gratitude List. I hate Linda's office. I hate Linda.

Days like today I wish the pills had worked so I wouldn't be stuck sitting here in this stupid office, talking about the stupid Gratitude List with my stupid therapist.

"I'm sure the last few days haven't been easy for you, with this being all over the news," Linda says. "How are you feeling?"

If I were feeling good, would I be forced to come here to see you, Shrink Lady?

"Okay, I guess."

I don't want to talk to her today. I don't want to be in her faux homey room with all the well-worn toys that are supposed to fool messed-up kids into thinking that they're not being therapized.

But therapists don't get paid big bucks to give up easily.

"How have things been at home?"

"What, since Dad got cited for disturbing the peace in his pajamas and they had video footage of him on the news? Oh, Mom's *thrilled* about that," I tell her, trying not to sound too bitterly sarcastic because that just convinces her that I'm still messed up and I need even more time in therapy. "It's done *wonders* for her election campaign."

"So your parents are fighting?"

I should have kept my mouth shut. Every time I open my mouth I inadvertently give her more clues about "what is wrong with Lara."

"Parents fight. There's nothing abnormal about that."

She stops writing on her notepad. It worries me when she scribbles notes about the stuff that comes out of my mouth. I'm always wondering what it was I said that was so padworthy.

"Have they been fighting more than they normally do?"

"I guess," I admit. "Just another thing that's my fault."

"What makes you say that?"

"Because all the stuff they fight about . . . none of it would have happened if I hadn't been stupid enough to talk to Christian. You know . . . if I wasn't idiot enough to believe that someone that hot could like someone like me."

The therapist is scribbling again.

"Lara, can you tell me . . . what did Christian give you?" Linda asks.

What part of he didn't even exist *doesn't she understand?*

"He didn't *give* me anything," I say. "*He* was Bree and her mom doing this for whatever messed-up reason they had for doing it. Giving me presents definitely wasn't one of them."

Linda takes a deep breath and leans back in her chair. I get the feeling that today, at least, I'm annoying her as much as she annoys me. *Yay! We're even!*

"I'm not talking about *presents*, Lara. I'm asking you to think about what you got from those chats emotionally," she says. "It must have been something, or you wouldn't have kept chatting with him over a period of weeks." She leans forward again, and the tight grip of her fingers around the pen betrays her frustration with me. "So you must have gotten something from your interactions — even if he did turn out to be a fictional friend."

"We talked about stuff," I say.

"Like what?" she asks. "What kind of 'stuff'?"

"I don't know. School. Our families . . . Although I guess he . . . I mean Bree, was lying about his, like everything else, because the people he was describing weren't the Connorses."

"What was it about Christian that made you feel so attached to him?"

It's too humiliating to admit, even to just her and these four walls, that I couldn't believe such a hot guy was interested in me. That was just what made me do something I knew I wasn't supposed to do — friending someone I didn't know in real life in the first place. But his looks weren't what made me feel close to him.

"It was how he listened to me," I tell her. "He made me feel . . ."

I miss him.

Without warning, the realization hits me. It's like a piece of me cracks, and then I'm sobbing. Deep, shuddering sobs that rack my body so hard it hurts my chest. She's taken her shrinky flashlight and pointed it into the dark corners of my mind, shining a light on the last thing in the world I wanted to think or talk about. By making me even consider for a moment how much I miss Christian, she's opened the floodgates on all the pain I've been trying with every ounce of my being not to feel.

And I hate her even more for doing it.

She gets up from her chair and hands me the box of tissues, even though they're on the table right next to me. I take one, and then another and then another. Are there enough tissues in that box, in the entire universe, to soak up all the pain I have inside?

Linda is back in her chair, with pen and notepad good to go, waiting for my sobs to slow to sniffles. When I've blown my nose into the eleventh tissue, she says, "That brought up some strong emotions. What are you feeling right now?"

I use tissue number twelve to wipe the mascara from under my eyes, which I'm sure are raccoon-like from all the tears. It also gives me a reason to delay answering the question I've grown to hate in all its variations — *What are you feeling? How are you feeling? Are you feeling okay?*

"I feel s-sad," I sniff.

"Why?"

I should have known she wouldn't let it go at that.

"Because . . ."

I hesitate. How do I admit I miss a person who never really existed? That's going to make me sound even crazier than everyone already thinks I am.

"You probably won't understand."

"Try me," she says.

It's hard to know who I can trust anymore. I'm afraid to trust anyone. But I figure she's bound by doctor-patient confidentiality and the truth is, there's no one else I can really talk to about Christian.

"I know this is going to sound crazy, because he wasn't even a real person, but . . . I miss Christian. I miss him a lot."

I swallow, willing myself not to start crying again. "And when I feel that . . . when I'm alone in my bedroom crying because I miss him and I feel so lonely, I know I'm the stupidest girl who ever existed," I tell her. "Because he was Bree. Or her mom. And none of the nice things they made him say were even true."

"Feelings just are, Lara," she says. "It doesn't do you any good to judge yourself for having them."

"But how can you miss a fake person?" I argue.

"It's not the person you miss," she says. "It's what he gave you emotionally."

I start ripping the tissue into little pieces in my lap as I consider what she's said.

"What do you miss the most about your chats? How did chatting with him make you feel?"

And then I can't stop the tears again, as I'm once again hit with the emptiness and the loss.

"He . . . made . . . me . . . feel . . . special," I sob. "Like . . . I was actually . . . worth something."

She lets me cry without probing further, and I'm grateful

for that. I'm grateful that I'm allowed to experience these feelings without her making me analyze them anymore. Because right now I'm exhausted just from having them.

"Lara," she says, and her voice is softer and gentler than it has ever been before. "You *are* worth something. Maybe we need to work on you owning that before you get into more relationships."

I shake my head. "How do I own something I can't see?"

"That's what we're going to work on," she says. "Helping you to see your strengths."

I think it's a useless exercise because I don't have any strengths, but she sounds so confident about the possibility of it happening that I feel a tiny whiff of hope, as faint as the breeze from a butterfly wing.

Even that is a step up from the utter despair I've felt ever since Christian told me the world would be better off without me in it. Is this progress?

———

Mom is on her cell in the waiting room when I get out. We walk out of the office, and when I push the elevator button she shakes her head and points to the stairs, gesturing to the phone.

"It's *Nightline*," she mouths.

Oh no. Not more TV.

I try to tune out as we walk down the three flights of stairs, but it's hard to avoid the sound of Mom's overloud cell-phone voice in the echoey stairwell.

"Yes, it really is sick, and as a parent, one of the most frustrating things is that there's no adequate legal remedy available," Mom says. "That's why I'm planning to work with existing antibullying organizations to lobby for Lara Laws, trying to persuade states to add specific cyberbullying language to their existing bullying statutes."

I stop so abruptly Mom almost trips over me on the stairs. "What are you talking about, 'Lara Laws'?" I hiss.

She mutes her phone. "Wait till I'm done," she says. "I'll explain everything."

I don't want to wait. It's my name she's tossing around here. I don't want my name on a law. I want it all to go away so I can try to forget it ever happened.

"But, Mom —"

She waves her hand at me to be quiet, and I turn and stomp down the rest of the stairs as noisily as I can, making sure to slam the door at the bottom.

The brisk autumn air outside the building does nothing to cool my anger. Neither does the length of time I have to wait by the car as Mom stands in the lobby finishing her phone call. By the time she comes out to the car, I'm fuming.

Mom acts like nothing happened.

I get in the car and slam my door. "So are you going to tell me what these Lara Laws are about, or am I supposed to find out by watching *Nightline*?"

Mom starts the car and backs out of the space like I haven't even spoken. It strikes me that maybe there's a good reason I feel like I don't matter. *Note to Linda . . .*

"Earth to Mother? Why are you using my name without my permission? I have a right to know what this is all about."

"I'll tell you what this is all about," Mom says, her voice calm and even. "It's about helping you and other kids like you. It's about making sure that if any adult is as sick as Mary Jo Connors, there are legal ramifications to make sure she ends up behind bars."

Mom says this is about me, but it isn't. It's about her. If it were about me, she would have told me sooner. I would have been a part of it. Instead I'm just the convenient excuse for her next political project.

"Call it something else," I say. "I don't want it named after me."

The only sign Mom gives that I've pissed her off is how tightly her hands clench the steering wheel.

"What else would we call it?" she asks.

"How about the Psycho Parents Law?" I suggest.

My mother is not amused.

"I'm doing everything I know how to help you, Lara. It would be nice to have a little appreciation once in a while," Mom snaps.

"If this is really about helping me, how come you didn't ask my opinion first?" I say. "Why didn't you even tell me about it?"

Mom doesn't respond right away. Her eyes remain on the road ahead; her lips are tightly compressed. In my imagination, I can hear the cogs of her brain working, coming up with the way to frame this that she thinks will play best to the angry-teen-daughter constituent.

"Lara, honey, you've been in a fragile state since your . . . hospitalization. We've been trying to protect you. The last thing Daddy or I want to do is cause you more anxiety when you're in such a delicate state of mind."

"Really, Mom? You thought that using my name for some new law you want to get passed without asking me about it was going to *help* my *delicate state of mind*?"

"Of course I was going to talk to you about it, Lara," Mom says.

"Yeah — *after* you talked to freaking *Nightline* and the rest of the country."

Mom doesn't say anything for a moment. When she does speak, her voice cracks like she is on the verge of tears.

"I'm doing the best I can here, Lara. You're my daughter. These people hurt you, so badly that you tried to kill yourself, and the police and the prosecutor are telling us that their hands are tied because of the existing laws. I can't just sit here and do nothing. And I had to consider your mental health."

"I might be depressed and confused, Mom, but I'm not a baby," I tell her. "I don't want you to use my name. I'm never going to be able to put this behind me if you're going on nationwide TV talking about Lara Laws, am I?"

"Making sure this doesn't happen to other people can help you put it behind you, Lara," Mom says, and now I see a tear rolling down her cheek. But somehow knowing that she's hurting, too, and it's my stupidity that made it happen doesn't make me any less angry. Only more.

"No, Mom. It'll help *you* put it behind *you*. Not *me*. *You.* Stop pretending this Lara Laws thing has anything to do with me."

We ride home the rest of the way in silence, the distance between us much wider than the front seats of a car.

———

I need to escape from Mom when I get home, so I take my book and my Snuggie and go out to the patio, even though it's cold. I'd rather freeze in solitude than be warm in the house with her. It works for a little while, but then I'm distracted by voices. I look up and see my sister climbing down the ladder from the old tree fort. But she wasn't up there alone — because following her down the wooden rungs is *Liam Connors.*

Isn't there a single person in this world I can trust anymore?

He touches her cheek tenderly before they part, and Syd smiles up at him, her face glowing and happy.

It makes me want to throw up.

I grab my Snuggie and book and run up to my room. Why should I care about the stupid rules when everyone else in the world is breaking them? I close the door and throw myself onto the bed, crying into my pillow so no one will hear.

Betrayal is only part of the sadness. The worst part — and it's painful to admit this, even to myself — is that I'm jealous. I'm jealous that she has what I *thought* I had with

Christian. A relationship with a boy who cares about her. For real, not pretend.

I'm crying into my pillow because it'll never happen to me now because of Liam's sister and his mom — and because I was stupid enough to think that it could happen to me in the first place.

———

I wait till we're all sitting together at the dinner table before I casually mention that Syd was hanging out in the tree fort with Liam earlier.

Dad chokes on his casserole. His face turns reddish purple, and I have to thump him between the shoulder blades to dislodge the food.

"What the heck are you thinking, Sydney?" he explodes when he's finally able to get air back in his lungs. "What possessed you to talk to the Connors boy after what they did to Lara?"

"*Liam* didn't do anything," Syd protests. "He's just caught up in this mess because of his crazy family. Just like me."

My parents glance at me to see how I'm taking that, because obviously, *I* have to be the crazy family she's referring to, right? It couldn't possibly have *anything* to do with *them*.

"Sydney . . . ," Dad says in a warning tone, but Syd's on a roll.

"Why *shouldn't* I see him? He's my *friend*. Where's the rule that says *we* have to stop being friends just because of Lara and Bree?"

"It's not that," Mom explains in her diplomatic politician voice. "But . . . surely you can see it's awkward . . . *under the circumstances.*"

"Yeah, *circumstances* that neither Liam or I had anything to do with," Syd says. "And just like always, we're supposed to go along with the program, just because you guys say so!" She slams her knife and fork down on the table. "Well, *FORGET THAT!*" she shouts, pushing her chair back and standing up. "Just because you're all screwed up, why should Liam and I suffer?"

She storms out of the room, crashes up the stairs, and slams her door so hard it rattles the light fixture.

"Pete, you have to talk to her," Mom says. "She can't keep associating with Liam. Not now. Can you imagine what would happen if the press got wind of it?"

I remember the look on Syd's face when I saw her and Liam together earlier.

My sister and Liam are friends, but they're more than that. And even though I'm jealous, even though what she has highlights everything that I lost when Christian turned on me and I found out he wasn't real, I don't want that taken from her.

"No," I say suddenly. "Syd's right."

My parents stare at me. You'd think I'd suddenly grown a third head. Maybe I have, and this time I finally got one with a working brain.

This whole thing has been so messed up for everyone — for me, for Mom, for Dad, for Syd. Maybe until now, until I admitted to missing Christian today, I've been so wrapped up in my own misery, how much I am hurting, that it was the only thing I could see. Christian may have been fake, but one thing he said about me was true: I'm not a good friend.

Thinking back, I can start to see what he meant. I don't want to, but it's there. Especially with Bree. And it hits me that maybe she tried to tell me, but I just wouldn't listen. Like, there was this one night when we were in eighth grade, I got back from a really bad day at the therapist, and I was complaining to Bree about how I hated school, my parents, and basically my entire life. She didn't say anything while I cried about my awful day and even more awful life.

When I finally stopped, she said, "It sucks that you're going through all this, Lara, but did you ever think of asking me how *my* day went?"

At the time, I just got mad. I thought she didn't care about me, that she just didn't understand how bad things were. I was so upset I hung up on her. But now I realize that Bree had a point, the same one that Syd made at dinner. I've been wrapped up in my own pain for so long, I haven't paid much attention to anyone else's. Even the people who care about me the most . . . or those who used to.

But I can start to change that tonight, right here, right now, by standing up for my sister. Maybe that can be my way of starting to move forward, the way trying to make a new law is for Mom.

"It's not Liam's fault," I say. "He's a victim, too. Like me. Like Syd. You can't blame him for what Bree did. Or what his mom did."

Mom and Dad exchange a glance. Apparently it means that Dad should do the talking.

"We know that, honey," Dad says. "But it's a complex situation."

"What's so complex about Liam and Syd wanting to stay friends? They really *like* each other."

Mom looks at me sharply. "You mean 'like' as in . . . a *crush*?" she asks.

"Maybe. Or maybe just friends. I don't know."

Mom shakes her head, rubbing her temple. "This is all I need. The visuals of my daughter dating the son of the woman who cyberbullied you while I'm calling for legislation to make it a criminal offense . . ."

And that's when I can't take it for another minute longer.

"Visuals? Do you even hear yourself, Mom? We're your *daughters*, not props for your political photo ops!"

"That's not what I meant, I —"

But I don't stay around to hear her explanation of what she meant. I'm already halfway up the stairs. I'm going to talk to Sydney, to apologize for ratting her out and to see if I can make it up to her, somehow.

Even if I can't make up for the past, I can try to do better in the future.

SYDNEY

I'VE GOT my headphones on, and I'm blasting music that matches the beat of all the angry words in my head. Now I know why people punch walls and things. Not that I'd do that, because I can imagine how much it would hurt, plus my parents would freak if I damaged the wall — or my hand. But I've got so much mad I'm not sure the four walls of my room can contain it, and maybe punching a hole in the wall would let it out.

Or maybe I could climb to the top of a really tall mountain and just scream and scream until I lost my voice. The problem is, despite its name, Lake Hills is pretty flat. It should be called Lake Hillslope. Or Lake Mounds. *Hills* is really stretching it.

Whatever you call this place, my life in it is unfair, and I'm so sick of it. And just when I had something good happen in all the awfulness, guess who ruined it, as usual? Lara, of course. Because that's what she does. I'm starting to wonder if her goal in life is to ruin mine.

The music's turned up so loud, I don't hear her come in, so when she touches me to get my attention, I shout in surprise.

"Jeez, Lara, did you ever hear of knocking?" I say, pulling the headphones out and pausing the music.

"I did knock. But you didn't hear me." Lara gestures to the headphones.

She has a point.

"What do you want?" I ask, unwilling to concede anything because I'm so mad at her.

"I just . . . Can I sit down?" she asks.

"I guess," I agree, reluctantly sliding over, but only a little so she has to perch on a little corner at the end of the bed.

"Syd . . . I just . . . I want to say I'm sorry. Really sorry. For . . . everything."

I'm not sure I can believe what I'm hearing. My older sister is *apologizing to me*?

"Uh . . . what do you mean?"

She looks at me, confused. "Um . . . what I said. That I'm sorry."

What is she sorry for? For ratting me out to Mom and Dad? For trying to kill herself? For making me miss auditions for *Beauty and the Beast*? For the fact that everything ends up being about her in this house?

"Wait . . . did Mom tell you to do this?"

"What?" Lara seems genuinely surprised I asked. "Why would you even think that?" she asks, her cheeks flushing.

I shrug. "Maybe because the only times you've ever apologized to me in my life are when Mom's made you?"

Lara flinches, and her eyes glaze with tears.

I wonder if she's going to turn and run, or do that thing she does where she disappears into Lara Land.

But she doesn't. She lifts her chin and says, "Well, she didn't make me *this* time. I decided to do it myself. I *wanted* to do it."

And then she takes my reluctant hand and squeezes, hard, until I look her in the eye. When I do, she repeats, "I'm sorry, Syd. For everything. I mean it. I know things have been hard for you because of me. I'm sorry."

Who are you and what have you done with Lara?

"I hope someday I can make it up to you," Lara says.

A tear traces its way down her cheek.

And I feel like she just punched a hole in the wall for me, but with her words instead of her fist, because the anger inside me begins to escape.

I say, "Thanks," and I sit up and hug her.

My sister has said "I'm sorry" to me so many times, but this time is the one that matters most. This time, she means it.

LIAM

SYD CALLS and tells me to take Dad's offer of a ride rather than fighting the press, even if it means being in the car with Bree. She says it will be less awkward than facing the looks we'll get if we sit together on the bus again.

"Oh. Okay. Sure," I say, but I'm gutted because I think that she's already having second thoughts about kissing me. I've been replaying that kiss over and over and imagining more, but maybe she's been thinking it was all one big mistake, never to be repeated, ever.

But then . . . "I got into a major fight with my parents at dinner," she continues.

"What about?"

"You," she says. "Lara saw us. And she snitched."

"Uh-oh," I say.

"'Uh-oh' is right," she says. "My parents were all, *What possessed you to hang out with him, Syd? It's awkward under the circumstances, Syd,* and I was like, *Yeah, circumstances that have nothing to do with either of us.*"

I smile, happy that she stood up to her parents for me. "Wow. Thanks."

"And you know what's the craziest thing of all?" she

says. "After ratting me to Mom and Dad, guess who then stuck up for us and said they should back off?"

"*Lara? No way.*"

"Way! I couldn't believe it, either," Syd tells me. "And what's even more amazing is the talk we had afterward. She came up to my room and said she was sorry for everything I've had to go through because of her."

I try to imagine *my* sister saying something like that. Epic fail.

"*Seriously?*"

"I know, right? At first I was like, *Who are you and what have you done with Lara?*"

I laugh.

"But then, once I realized she really meant it, that maybe all this therapy stuff she's been doing has actually made a difference, we talked. I mean *really* talked. It was pretty cool."

I wonder what it would take for Bree to apologize to me. To any of us. Most of all, to Lara and the Kelleys. I wonder if I'll ever understand what made my sister do the things she did.

———

We drop Bree off at the high school first the next morning.

"Keep your chin up, Breenut," Dad says. "Don't forget — go to the principal's office and call me or Mom if you have a problem."

Bree still doesn't have a new cell. After what happened with her voice mail, she doesn't seem in a hurry to get one, which is crazy because Bree's life used to revolve around that phone.

Bree gets out of the car slowly, like she's half-asleep still.

"Hey, Bree, could you hurry up? I have to get to school, too, you know," I remind her.

Dad gives me a hush-up look in the rearview mirror.

"Bye," Bree says, shutting the car door and shuffling off, shoulders hunched and head down.

"Can you try to show a little compassion for your sister, Liam?" Dad asks.

"What, like she showed for Lara?"

Dad's lips set into a thin, grim line in the rearview mirror. "Bree did wrong. Very wrong. I'm not denying that," Dad says. "And she deserves some consequences. But hacking her cell phone? Death threats? She's fifteen years old, Liam, and she's your sister. Can't you cut her some slack?"

I'm so mad at Bree, it's hard to let go of it, even though I hear what Dad's saying. But I mumble, "I guess," and figure I'll try.

———

That's until I hit the bathroom in between second and third period. I'm at the urinal taking care of business when four kids from the football team walk in, and Shane Perry says, "Yo, it's Bullying Bree's brother!"

Just my luck to be standing there, pants unzipped, mid-stream when four guys trap me in the bathroom.

Hurry up and finish, I tell my bladder, because all I want to do is zip up and get out of there. But it keeps on coming.

Meanwhile, they walk up behind me.

Steve Malloy says, "My sister's a cheerleader at the high school. She said your sister pretended to be a guy and made Lara Kelley try to kill herself."

He shoves me, and pee goes up the wall.

"Who does that?" Steve asks.

Not me. And could you at least let me put my junk away before you beat me up?

I finally finish and start trying to put myself back in my pants, but Todd Adams punches my arm really hard.

"Yeah," he says as emphasis. "Who does that?"

"It wasn't me," I say. "It was Bree."

Whose fault it is I'm getting beat up right now.

"And your mom," Joe Anderson says. "Your mom is seriously cray-cray."

I manage to get put away and zipped, just before Anderson and Malloy pin me against the wall.

Now I'm freaking out. I'm about to get seriously messed up. And there's no way I can win four against one.

"That girl almost died," Adams says, pulling my hair as he gets up into my face. "Doesn't that make you feel bad, Connors?"

Spittle gets on my face as he says the *s* in *Connors.* I want to throw up.

"Of course it makes me feel bad," I say, trying not to gag from the spittle.

"Not bad enough," Shane Perry says. And he punches me in the stomach, hard, just as the bell rings for next period.

Anderson and Malloy let go of my arms and split with the rest of them, and I sink to the floor, clutching my stomach and trying to breathe.

All I can think of while I'm lying there is how much I hate my sister, because it's all her fault that this happened.

BREE

WHEN I finally get to sleep, if I can sleep without dreaming, I'm able to escape for a while from the mess I've made of my life. Not just my life. My whole family's life.

When the alarm goes off to wake me for school, I turn it off, fighting off tears, because I don't know if I can face another day.

I wonder if this is how Lara felt.

Swinging my legs over the side of the bed, I try to summon up the energy to get moving. Get up and get dressed. Brush my hair. Put on makeup. Try to look my best on the outside, even though I feel awful on the inside. Go downstairs. Eat food that tastes like nothing, even though I'm not hungry, just so Dad doesn't give me a hard time because I haven't eaten.

"Come on, let's go," Dad says, picking up his car keys and his briefcase.

"I might take the bus today," Liam mumbles, staring down into his cornflakes.

"Go with your father, Liam," Mom orders. "There's still some press outside."

"I don't care," Liam says, looking up and staring Mom

down defiantly. "I don't want to go with them. I'll take the bus."

"Bree, go wait in the car," Dad tells me.

"Liam just wants to take the bus so he doesn't have to be with me, right, Liam?" I say.

"It doesn't matter why," Mom says grimly. "He's not taking the bus, and that's final."

Liam picks up his backpack and storms out to the garage to wait in the car, slamming the door behind him.

"Your brother got roughed up in the bathroom at school yesterday," Dad says. His knuckles are white around the handle of his coffee cup. "Four guys against one."

"Because of . . ."

"Yes, Breanna — because of the situation that you and your mother created for this family. Because the two of you didn't think about how the repercussions of *your* actions would affect *all* of us."

"Don't start with that again —"

"Quiet, Mary Jo."

My father doesn't shout, but I almost wish he did, because his cold, precise anger is worse than my mother's loud fire. I slump down in my seat.

"I'm sorry, Dad."

"I know you're sorry, Bree. But this is too big and it's gone way too far for 'I'm sorry' to fix."

Dad tells me this like it's something I don't already know.

But I do. When I begged him to stay home from school, he told me that actions have consequences and I have to learn to live with them. He doesn't have to worry. I'm being taught a lesson again every single day.

———

Marci and Jenny aren't waiting for me out front like they usually do, so I have to walk into school alone. There's a bunch of football players and cheerleaders sitting on the wall by the front door.

Don't let Ashley Trapasso be one of them.

I walk past, hoping they don't notice me, but they do.

"It's Bullying Bree," Ashley calls out. "Who are you and Monster Mom planning to pick on next, Bree?"

Don't look. Just keep walking.

"They better not pick on anyone." It's Tomas Garcia, the quarterback of the football team. "Otherwise we're going to come over and pick on them."

Other voices saying, "Yeah," "Too right," and calling me and Mom curse words.

Don't look. Just keep on walking.

Sticksandstoneswillbreakmybonesbutnameswillnever hurtme.

Why do they even teach us that stupid rhyme? It's such a lie. Names *do* hurt.

I'm shaking by the time I get to my locker.

No one says, *Hi, Bree.*

No one says, *What's up, Bree?*

No one asks, *Are you okay?*

It's like I've become the Invisible Girl — unless people want to say something bad.

I see Marci down the hallway and wave, but she turns away like she hasn't seen me. Or maybe she has and she's pretending she didn't. Maybe the police finally went to her house and she's mad at me for telling. The thought of Marci finding out makes me want to hurl.

I start to wonder if I am invisible. But as I walk to my first class and hear the names people call me, I'm reminded that people can see me all too well.

That's when I start to wish I really were invisible.

———

At lunch, I see Marci and Jenny sitting at a table with Diane Taylor and Liza Sanchez. I go over to sit with them, but when I get to the table, Marci looks at me and says, "Sorry, Bree, there's no room."

She moves her chair to the side as if to emphasize the point.

"It's okay, I can move over if you find a chair," Jenny says.

Marci gives her a dirty look. But the look she gives me is even worse. That's when I know without a doubt that the police went to her house. I realize this is the end. Marci's decided the perks of being friends with the celebrity bully have lost their luster, and she'll never forgive me for betraying her. She's better off hating me like everyone else.

Even though she did it, too.

At least Marci didn't make a scene. I just don't think I can handle another person pointing out how awful I am. I turn away, trying not to cry in front of everyone in the middle of the cafeteria because that would be fatal. I walk with my lunch tray straight to the cafeteria door.

"You can't leave with that," says Mr. D'Anastasio, the teacher on lunch duty.

So I throw my lunch in the garbage, tray and all, and walk out of the cafeteria, ignoring Mr. D'Anastasio's angry shout. Fighting the tears that threaten to cloud my vision, I head straight for the main office to call Mom to take me home.

Dad thinks I should have consequences. Well, I've got them. I hope he's happy.

———

When Mom talks to the principal about what's going on, he says there's a zero-tolerance policy on bullying but then shrugs.

"Look, I understand your concerns, Mrs. Connors, and obviously this isn't kind behavior, but it's not bullying as defined under the law . . . and *under the circumstances* I can't say this is entirely unexpected."

"So what you're saying is my daughter brought this on herself, is that what I'm hearing?" Mom says, her voice shaking with anger.

"No, Mrs. Connors, I'm just saying that given your

daughter's actions toward Lara Kelley, I'm not surprised that there is backlash from other students," the principal says. "It doesn't make it right, but that's the way it is."

"Well, if that's your attitude, you better get my daughter transferred to another school, pronto, or you're going to have a lawsuit on your hands," Mom says. "Come on, Bree. I'm getting you out of this place."

For the first time in my life, I'm glad that my mother is a Great White Shark Mom, because maybe it means I won't have to come back to this school.

———

School isn't the only problem. The death threats have kept on coming, even though we disconnected the landline and got an unlisted number. After Mom tells Dad about what happened at school, Dad makes Liam and me delete all our social media accounts — Facebook, Twitter, Instagram, Tumblr, you name it. It upset me a little, but I could understand why Dad was making me do it, and to be honest, I hadn't been checking them much because I was afraid to see what people were writing. Liam, on the other hand . . . I've never seen him so mad.

"WHAT DID I DO?" he shouts. "*Nothing*. That's what!"

The nasty look he gives me is worse than the kids at school. Because he's my brother, part of my family. He's supposed to love me. That's what families do.

"This is all your fault, Bree. I hate you!"

I guess "supposed to" doesn't matter when our family is falling to pieces, and I'm the one to blame for pushing us all off the cliff.

"Liam, we're dealing with more than enough haters outside of these walls," Dad says, his voice quiet but firm. "We don't need them on the inside."

"Too bad you didn't tell *her* that," Liam spits out, gesturing to me angrily with his thumb. "Or *Mom*. Before they started hating on Lara. Before they made her try to *kill herself*."

I wrap my arms around my waist, as if they can offer a shield from his angry words. But nothing does. My brother's disgust with me is like nuclear radiation; it seeps through all my feeble defenses.

"People make mistakes," Dad says, sighing heavily. "You can't hate your sister forever because she made one bad decision."

"Try me," Liam argues, his eyes cold and narrowed. "Not all mistakes end up with death threats and people leaving dog crap in our mailbox."

"Okay, so I made the Biggest Mistake in the History of the Universe," I say, feeling like I'm going to cry for the zillionth time since I heard those messages on my cell phone. "I'm *sorry*, all right?"

"*Are* you, Bree? *Really?*" Liam asks. "You didn't seem that sorry when Lara tried to kill herself. It's like you're just sorry 'cause you got caught."

Maybe it's because he hurt me so badly when he said that. Maybe it's because he fired an arrow, and it hit a bull's-eye in a truly dark place. Maybe it's because, deep down, I know in some small way he's right. Maybe it's because it hurts so much that my brother seems to hate me, and that just makes me want to hurt him back.

"Well, what are *you* doing hanging around with Sydney Kelley?" I ask. "I saw you two coming down from the tree fort together last night. How sick is that when Mom had to call the cops on her dad, and her parents want to put Mom and me in jail?"

I know this came as a total shock to Dad based on his expression as he turns to my brother and asks, "Is this true, Liam? Have you been hanging out with Sydney? Do you realize how inappropriate that is?"

If I thought Liam was mad before, that was just the warm-up. Dad's question is the spark that ignites the serious fireworks.

"*I'm* the one making things inappropriate? Because I'm hanging out with Sydney?" he shouts at Dad, and it's gross because he's literally spitting with rage. "I didn't ask to be part of this freak show. But I had no choice. I am stuck smack in the middle of it."

"It's not easy for anyone right now —" Dad says, but Liam's not in the mood for excuses.

"You know what they call me at school? *Son of Monster Mom. Bullying Bree's Brother.* I hate every . . . single . . . minute. If I had enough money . . ."

He gives a bitter laugh, which ends up sounding like a sob. "Forget that — if I had the *courage*, I'd run away and change my name so no one would know I was related to you."

He says the last part looking straight at me, with such disgust and loathing that I can't believe he's the little brother I've grown up with and lived with my whole life.

I can't face him anymore. I can't face the world anymore. It's bad enough that everyone at school hates me. It's bad enough that all these people who don't even know me hate me.

I run to my room and throw myself on the bed, crying, wondering if this is all I can look forward to in the future — if I'll always be hated because I'm Bullying Bree, the Monster Spawn of Monster Mom, pariah of Lake Hills.

"Didn't you ever stop, for just one minute, to think about the consequences of what you were doing?" Dad had asked me last night when he came to kiss me good night and found me crying.

"I d-don't k-know," I sniffed.

"It's a simple yes or no question, Breanna," he said, smoothing the hair back from my hot, damp cheek.

What Dad doesn't get is that nothing is "simple" anymore. Especially not that.

"Did you ask Mom that?" I asked him. "Because she did it, too."

I've been thinking about that a lot.

What would have happened if Mom had acted differently when she caught me pretending to be Christian?

What if she had punished me instead of joining in?

What if she hadn't just grounded me, but she'd called Mrs. Kelley and told her what was going on and made sure they broke things to Lara gently because of her history?

Would Lara have tried to kill herself?

Would we be getting death threats?

Would Liam hate me?

Would I hate myself?

But here's the question I ask myself most of all, especially at night when I stare up at the ceiling, trying to get to sleep: Should I have been the one to take all those pills instead of Lara?

SYDNEY

MOM WON reelection to the city council by a "comfortable margin" despite Dad's televised pajama rant. Her opponent tried to bring up her parenting skills in a debate and was booed down by the audience. Over a celebratory dinner at home tonight, Mom says that even if he hadn't been, she'd been prepared. After discussing it with her campaign manager, she'd decided that the best way to deal with the issue was to face it head-on so she could "frame" it to her advantage. Lara and I secretly roll our eyes at each other.

After dinner, I follow Lara to her room and ask her how she feels about being an "issue" to be "framed."

To my amazement, she actually puts her hands around her face like she's making a picture frame and *laughs*.

"It's just never-ending fun and giggles," she says in a comically bright voice.

But then she puts her hands down and shrugs, the smile fading from her eyes. "Whatever . . . it's Mom. She deals with life her way. I have to learn how to deal with it in mine."

"But . . . what if her way makes your way . . . I mean, what if she makes you crazy?"

"I have to try to talk to her about it. Like I'm doing about this Lara Laws thing. I get that passing a law is her way of trying to help. But we're trying to get her to understand that naming it after me is going to stop me from moving on."

"Who's 'we'?" I ask.

"Linda," Lara says. "She's not as bad as I thought she was in the beginning. She says I can go back to school soon."

"Wow. That'll make Mom happy," I say. Mom has made no secret of how difficult it was making it for her to campaign when she had to babysit Lara all day. She'd started dragging Lara around with her when she went door-to-door. "But what about you?"

"I don't know," Lara replies. "Part of me is relieved I won't be stuck at home with Mom watching my every move anymore."

"At least you can pee and shower with the door closed now," I remind her. She'd been allowed that privilege back the previous week.

"Oh yeah! And I won't miss having to go door-to-door canvassing with Mom," Lara says. "Although, I have to admit, it made me see a different side of her."

"What do you mean?" I ask.

"I guess to me it always seemed like this political stuff was all about her, because of the way it affects *our* lives," Lara says.

"What, like having to pretend we're the Perfect Family of Perfect Town all the time?" I say with a heavy dose of snark.

"Yeah, that," Lara says. "But when I was campaigning with her, I heard people thanking her for the things she'd done to help them and their families. I realized she really *does* want to try to make people's lives better. I mean, it doesn't make it any less annoying about the Perfect Family stuff, but at least I started to see something good that comes from all her politicking instead of hating every single thing about it."

"Or maybe you're just starting to understand where all Mom's crazy stuff comes from," I say.

Lara laughs for a second time. Which makes me think she's finding herself again, gradually, but a stronger, better version. I've missed that Lara.

"Definitely," she says. "But maybe understanding where the crazy comes from makes it a little easier to deal with."

I pick up Hedwig and make her pretend fly around my knees. "So are you scared? About going back to school?"

"Of course I am," Lara says, looking at me like I'm an idiot. "I'm terrified. Scared to face the stares and the whispers. You know, *That's the girl who tried to kill herself over some guy who turned out to be her next-door neighbor pretending.* Wouldn't you be?"

"Totally. But at least you won't have to face Bree now that she's transferred."

"I know. That's a big relief. It would be even harder to go to school if she were still there." Lara wraps her arms around her knees. "It's going to be hard enough facing everyone else."

"Do you wish you could go to a different school, instead of going back to Lake Hills High?"

"We talked about that," Lara says. "But even though there are bad things about going back to Lake Hills — like dealing with the people who I thought were friends and weren't — at least I'll still be with the people who really *are* friends, rather than starting over totally."

She sighs. "Do you want to know the worst part of going back to Lake Hills?"

"What?" I ask.

"Dad," she says, grimacing.

"Don't tell me he's still on you about The Spreadsheet."

"He's totally insane!" Lara exclaims. "*You need to know who these jerks are so you can be wary of them when you go back to school.*"

Lara's imitation of Dad makes me giggle, but her expression sobers me up quickly.

"I take it you still don't want to look at it," I say, remembering the scene that night in the hospital when Dad tried to force her to do it.

Lara shakes her head no. "It's too painful. I remember a few names of people who liked Christian's post from that night before I took the pills, but believe me, it's not because I want to."

I don't want to disagree with her now that we're finally getting along and she seems to be doing so much better. But I kind of agree with Dad on the list thing.

"But if you don't . . . like, if you just try to forget it all, then how will you know who to trust?" I ask her. "I mean, if they were that mean to you once, what's to stop them from doing it again?"

"I know, I know," Lara says, dropping her head to her knees. "I've heard it all a million times from Dad. *Forewarned is forearmed, Lara. You need to know to protect yourself.*"

She raises her head and looks me in the eye. "Syd — the names I *do* remember . . . they might not have been my best friends, but they were people who I thought at least *liked* me. Why would they do something like that? *Why?*"

I don't have an answer for Lara then. None of us do. And that's what's so hard for everyone — especially my sister.

——

Liam and I keep meeting up in the tree fort, despite the objections of our parents.

"It makes me feel like we're Romeo and Juliet," I tell Liam as we snuggle together in the candlelight.

"That's cool — as long as I don't end up poisoned and you don't stab yourself," Liam says with a wry smile.

"Okay, like Romeo and Juliet but with a happy ending," I say.

"That would be a story with a different title, I think," Liam says.

"Liam and Sydney, then."

"I hope that one has a happy ending." Liam sighs.

"Is everything okay?" I ask him. "I mean, I know everything isn't okay, but . . . you seem upset."

He runs the hand that isn't around my shoulder through his hair. "I'm just sick of taking crap for what Bree did. How much more of this do I have to put up with?"

I don't have any more answers for him than I do for Lara.

"Haven't a clue." I sigh.

"I wish I had a Time-Turner or a TARDIS so I could go back in time and tell Bree to think it through before she made that stupid profile," Liam says. "Dad says I have to find a way to forgive her, but I'm still way too mad."

"I'll bet," I say. I can't find it in my heart to forgive Bree yet, either. I mean, I feel bad about the death threats and stuff, but I'm glad she had to change schools. Glad for Lara's sake and, if I have to admit it, glad that she has to suffer in some way because of what she did.

"Mom's business has crashed to a grinding halt," Liam says. "So much for being the real estate queen of Lake Hills. No one wants to list property with Monster Mom. Dad's business is suffering, too. And it's not like he had anything to do with it."

No wonder Liam has a hard time forgiving his sister.

"I keep wondering if it makes me a bad person," Liam says. "Dad says she's my sister, and family is so important, and we have to support each other, especially because she's getting so much grief from the outside."

I feel all his muscles tense with anger.

"But so am I," he says. "And it's not like *I* did anything wrong. And that's not all. We have to cut to basic cable because we can't afford the movie channels anymore, and Dad's talking about all these other 'sacrifices' we have to make. All because of Bree."

As bad as things have been for our family, at least we're slowly starting to heal. Lara's back at school and Mom got reelected. And maybe I didn't get to audition for the fall musical, but I'm going to be first in line to audition for the spring talent showcase.

"You're not a bad person, Liam. I'd be mad, too."

I kiss his cheek. It's soft and chilly from the autumn cold. "It'll get better eventually," I tell him. "Remember when the press people were here? At least they're gone."

They were camped outside our houses for almost a week until some politician sent an "inappropriate" photo of himself to a woman who wasn't his wife, knocking "Monster Mom" and "Mother-Daughter Bullying Team" off the front page.

"I hope you're right," he says. "And I just hope *eventually* comes soon."

BREE

THE KITCHEN timer goes off, and I step into the shower to rinse my hair, turning the water as hot as I can stand it. I watch the water swirl into the drain, dark and muddy, as it washes the excess color from my hair. When the water finally runs clear, I comb through the conditioner and wait for two minutes like it said on the instructions, wondering as I wait how I am going to look, what my parents are going to say, whether this is going to make a difference.

After I blow-dry and look in the mirror, I look like me, but different. My hair is inky black, not light brown like Mom's or chestnut like Dad's and Liam's. My skin looks pale in comparison: white and almost translucent under the mirror lights. I like it. It feels more like the me I am now instead of the Bree I'm trying to escape.

If I can ever escape her. That's the million-dollar question. Transferring schools only helped a little because everyone at my new school knows what happened. When you've been a national news story, it's hard to get a fresh start short of getting into the Witness Protection Program and getting a whole new identity. Important crime witnesses qualify for that, but high school cyberbullies don't.

So every day I face the whispers, the looks, the cold shoulders when I try to make new friends.

The only light on my horizon is dance team, which makes me feel a part of something. My teammates still don't invite me to sleepovers or to go shopping with them at the mall, or anything out of school — real friend stuff. But at least they say hi to me in the hall and let me sit with them at lunch, and when we won a competition I was part of the group hug just like everyone else. At least they don't shun me. It's a start.

When I transferred to the new school, Mom tried to get me to try out for cheerleading.

"No. I'm done with cheerleading," I said. "I'm trying out for dance team. I already talked to the coach and she said she'd let me, even though it's midyear."

"What do you mean you're *done* with cheerleading?" Mom said. "You love cheerleading!"

"No, Mom. I don't. *You* love cheerleading," I said. "I am sick to death of cheerleading. I'm glad I didn't make the team at Lake Hills. And I'm not going to try out at West Lake."

My mom opened her mouth to say something, but Dad put his hand on her arm to stop her.

"Mary Jo, it's okay. Maybe exploring a new activity is just what Bree needs right now," he said.

Mom closed her mouth and ate the rest of her dinner in stony silence, while Dad tried to keep up the conversation to lighten the atmosphere.

The weirdest thing about that whole night was Liam. He'd been speaking to me only when necessary, barely making eye contact, like he couldn't stand to look at me because he hated me so much.

But that night at the dinner table, after I said I wasn't going to do cheerleading anymore, he actually looked me in the eye and grinned. I smiled back, but I don't know why he did it. It's not like it lasted — he's still really angry with me most of the time. But it was something.

Since then, we've sat watching TV — basic cable because we had to cut all the movie channels — and have laughed like we did before at stupid stuff, until he remembers he's mad at me again.

Everyone is in the kitchen when I go downstairs — Dad's reading the Sunday paper, Mom is looking at the help-wanted section, and Liam's eating a bowl of cereal. I slip in quietly and go to get a bowl for my cereal, waiting for someone to notice.

"Morning, hon," Dad says, but he barely glances up, so he doesn't. Liam doesn't pay any attention to me, as usual.

But of course my mom notices.

"Breanna Marie Connors, what on earth have you done to yourself?" she shrieks.

Knowing that my mother hates my hair just makes me love it all the more.

Liam stares at me, a mouthful of unchewed cereal in his mouth.

"Well, that's a very . . . different look, Bree," Dad says, lowering the paper to the table. "What brought this on?"

I can't tell from his measured tone if he's mad at me or not.

"And how could you do this without asking us?" Mom adds. There's no doubt from her voice that *she* is.

"It's *my* hair, so it's my decision," I say.

"However, you are fifteen years old and we're still your parents," Dad reminds me.

I guess he *is* mad. I don't care.

"I needed a change," I tell them. "I want to be someone different. Someone besides Bullying Bree."

"Yeah, like dyeing your *hair* is going to change things," Liam says. "Right."

Thanks for nothing, Liam.

I raise my chin defiantly. "It's something. It makes me feel more like myself when I look in the mirror."

"You look like a drug addict," Mom says. "It washes you out completely."

"Wow. Thanks, Mom," I tell her, swallowing the lump her words bring up in my throat. "I can always count on you to build up my self-confidence."

"Would you feel better if I lied to you?" Mom asks. "Okay, fine. You look like Miss America. There, happy?"

"No, but —"

"It's not a parent's job to sugarcoat things, Bree," Mom says. "It's our job to tell you how the real world works."

"By making me feel like I'm never good enough?" I

throw back at her. "Because if that's the case, you're the best mom ever."

"Okay, that's enough, Bree. Upstairs," Dad orders me.

"But I haven't even had breakfast!"

"Now!" he demands.

I hate my family. I hate my life. I hate everything and everyone.

Making as much noise as I can stomping up the stairs, I head up to my room and slam the door hard enough that one of the ornaments on my desk falls over. Luckily, it doesn't break. I've messed up enough things in my life as it is.

I fling myself on the bed, clenching my fists so tight that my fingernails dig into my palms. I want to explode, but I'm too numb, like my detonator's gone missing. Only those half-moons in my palms remind me I can feel, that my pain is real.

There's a knock on the door. It opens before I decide whether to say "go away" or "come in."

It's my dad. It was only a courtesy knock, telling me sure, it's my room, but I'm only fifteen years old and he's still the parent, so he's coming in no matter what I say.

I sit up and curl into a ball, holding my knees, as he walks over and sits on the bed next to me. He's carrying a bowl of cornflakes, which he hands to me.

"Thought you might be hungry," he says.

Shrugging, I take it from him. I've kind of lost my appetite, but I take a bite or two to make him happy, then put the bowl on my nightstand.

Dad's regarding me sadly.

"Things are really tough for you," he says.

"You think?"

"Believe it or not, honey, we're on your side. We want to help you. I could do with less attitude."

"Mom wants to *help me* by telling me I look like a drug addict?"

Dad takes my hand, which is still clenched into a fist, and holds it between his two hands. They are large and warm and comforting, despite everything.

"Breenut, when you created that fake profile, you acted before you thought," Dad says. He hesitates. "And sometimes . . . sometimes Mom speaks before she thinks."

The relief of Dad admitting that Mom was wrong to say that makes me unclench my fists. He strokes my hand, turning it over. First he sees the deep marks in my palm where I'd dug my nails into the skin. Then he sees the other marks. The ones I made last night when I dragged a sharp pair of scissors across the skin on my forearm.

"Honey, what did you do?" he asks, sucking air through his teeth as he touches the marks gently with his finger.

"Nothing," I say, turning my face away. I can't meet his gaze.

"This isn't *nothing*, Breenut."

When I don't respond, he says, "Look at me, Bree."

I turn my face toward him and see concern.

"What's going on, Bree? The hair . . . hurting yourself like this . . ."

"I don't know."

He shakes his head. "You must *know*," he says. He sounds . . . angry. "People don't just do things like this out of the blue without knowing why."

"I already *told* you about the hair. You just don't *listen*."

There's something inside me that's so big it scares me. But no one sees it. No one hears it. I don't have the words for it. All I know is this:

"I just . . . I need what hurts to show on the outside as much as I feel it on the inside."

I look away, because I don't expect Dad to understand. I've given up on being understood. I blew that right when I pretended to be Christian. One stupid mistake and I've messed up my entire life, forever.

"Bree," he says, and his voice sounds strange. Strangled.

I turn to him and there are tears rolling down his cheeks. The only time I've ever seen my father cry before is when Grandma died. He holds open his arms and something breaks open in my chest. Suddenly, the numbness is gone and in the comforting warmth of my father's hug I sob — great, messy, painful sobs so big they feel like they're going to break my ribs.

Dad strokes my hair as I cry and tells me it's okay, that he's going to arrange for us all to go to a family therapist, that he thinks we need outside help to get through this, that it's more than we can handle by ourselves.

"I know some people say asking for help is a sign of weakness, but I don't hold with that," Dad says. "The smartest, strongest thing a person can do is to know when to get help."

"But d-doesn't that make me c-crazy, just like L-Lara?" I sniff.

"Haven't you learned not to call her crazy?" Dad says.

"Mom always does."

"Well, that's another thing we need to change around here," Dad says. "Calling people names."

I pull away and ask him the question that plagues me every moment of every day.

"Did I mess up my life forever? I mean . . . will people ever forget about this?"

Dad's the one who is most likely to tell me the truth.

His hesitation in answering tells me the most.

"Things will get better. I can't tell you how, or when. It might take a very long time. But we'll get through this."

He doesn't know. None of us do. The future, once so full of possibility, is now a dark and scary place. But hopefully, like Dad says, maybe with help we can get through it, however long it takes.

EPILOGUE

TWELVE MONTHS LATER

LARA

TO SAY life is back to normal would be a lie. It's probably more accurate to say we're living the "new normal."

Mom is still trying to get Lara Laws passed in the state legislature and is using the notoriety of our case to lobby for similar laws across the country. She and Dad are still furious that Mrs. Connors and Bree weren't prosecuted for what they did, and they want to make sure there's a law in place to protect people. But after we talked about it in family therapy, she agreed to change the name to BIC Laws — against "Bullying in Cyberspace." Doing that allows her to heal in her way and me to heal in mine.

Healing for me is still a work in progress. Before I went back to school, Dad kept nagging me to look at the list of people who'd liked Christian's mean post on my wall or had made awful comments. I didn't want to, any more than I had in the hospital. In the end, I compromised by taking the list to therapy and looking at it there — away from the house, away from my parents, in a place where I could just feel whatever I needed to feel about it.

What did I feel when I finally let myself look at the names on that piece of paper?

Betrayal. Anger. Disgust.

But that was a positive sign, according to Linda. Because I was starting to feel angry, instead of sad. Because I was getting mad at the people who were behaving badly toward me, instead of directing the feelings toward myself and feeling sad and suicidal. Because gradually, I was learning not to let those people have control over me anymore.

When I finally did go back to school, I was glad I knew those names. Some of the same kids who'd liked the picture of me on the stretcher, who'd written things like "Corpse Girl" and "Is Lardosaurus dead?" came up to me and acted so genuinely friendly and concerned that if I hadn't seen Dad's list I would have believed they really cared. Just like the same trusting idiot I was before this all happened. Like I was with Christian.

People can be so two-faced.

Or maybe there's another explanation. Maybe they really *do* feel bad about what happened. That's something Linda brought up when we talked about it. Maybe, after I ended up in the hospital, they thought about what they'd done. Maybe they hadn't realized that the words they'd typed so casually caused me so much real pain.

The problem is, I can't read their minds, and that's what scares me the most — that I don't know how I'm supposed to trust anyone ever again. Linda keeps reminding me that it's a process. Ugh, the dreaded *P* word again. I keep asking her why someone can't just give me a pill to cure this — I'd even take an operation. Why does everything have to be a long, drawn-out "process"? People always say, "It gets bet-ter." What I want to know is *when?*

And then the person who bullied me got bullied, too. You'd think I'd be happy about the poetic justice of that, but the weird thing is, I wasn't. I mean, sure I was mad at Bree. I still am. But knowing that people were being so cruel to her didn't make me feel any happier. As strange as it seems, it only made me feel worse.

It was as if the whole thing took on a life of its own that had nothing to do with me anymore. People who wanted "vengeance" on my behalf were as mean to her as she was to me. Did it make it better, any less cruel because they didn't know her, because they hadn't been her best friend once upon a time?

Maybe. Maybe not. Either way, everyone ended up hurt. She hurt me and they hurt her. Liam got hurt. Syd got hurt. Our parents were hurt. Did any of it help in the end, other than all of us hurting?

Even though I'm relieved that I don't have to see Bree every day, I still see her going to and from her house once in a while — it's hard to completely avoid someone when you live right next door. I have frequent, imaginary conversa-tions with her in my head. They're always short conversations. I ask her, *Why? What did I do to make you hate me so much? Why did you do it?*

The conversations are short because she never answers. Because even when I try to imagine reasons why she would hate me enough to trick me with Christian, to write the things she did, I come up blank. Even a year later, after all this therapy, I still can't figure it out.

That, more than anything, is what still makes me crazy and prevents me from moving on.

"Come on, Lara," Dad shouts. "We've got to leave if we're going to get to the game on time."

It's the big Lake Hills versus West Lake football game today.

Liam and Syd are both freshmen at Lake Hills now, although Liam told us the Connorses might have to sell their house and move to a smaller one because Mr. Connors's plumbing supply business still hasn't picked up from the hit it took after the bad publicity. Mrs. Connors's real estate business is dead. She's working at Walmart for minimum wage. They're struggling to afford the mortgage.

I take a last look in the mirror, adjust my purple-and-gold hair ribbons, and head downstairs. Syd and Dad are already in the car.

"Hurry up!" Mom says, handing me my pom-poms.

We pull out of the driveway and just as we pass the Connors house we see their car starting to back out of theirs.

"Is Bree going to the game?" Mom asks.

"Yeah," Syd says. "She's on the dance team. They're performing at halftime with the West Lake band."

My mom glances back at me, her forehead furrowed with the "worried about Lara but don't want to say anything to upset her" look.

"Mom, we live next door to each other. I already see her once in a while without totally losing it, so I think I can handle her dancing on the football field without having a relapse," I say.

Syd gives me an encouraging grin.

"I wasn't thinking you were going to have a relapse, Lara, honey," Mom says. "You've made such good progress. I just . . . don't want you to be *upset*."

I try to imagine how I'll feel if Bree and I actually come face-to-face — like if we bump into each other randomly in the crowd. Will I ask her why, or just act like nothing ever happened because what's the point? Will I say hello or walk straight by her like we never met?

Until it happens, I'm not sure how I'll react. Maybe today's the day I'll find out. Or maybe not.

When we get to school, my parents and Syd go to sit in the stands, and I head down to the sidelines to meet the rest of the squad. We start doing crowd warm-ups, even though the stands are still half-empty and not everyone on the team is here yet. It gets people psyched up, and moving keeps us warm.

Mom and Dad are sitting together, but Syd's not with them. She's sitting in a different section a few rows down with Liam. They seem relaxed together, and happy. Even if their relationship doesn't last, at least something kind of good has come out of this whole mess. For that, I am grateful.

But as much as I try to be happy for them, it only reminds

me of my loneliness. I've been too afraid to get involved with anyone since Christian, too scared to trust people, even the ones I can see right in front of me.

Knowing that Liam's here, I can't help turning around and glancing at the opposite sidelines to see if the West Lake dance team is there. They are, and they're wearing black-and-silver track suits. But I can't pick her out.

Maybe she didn't come. Maybe she couldn't face being back here.

I could understand that. People might have moved on, but they haven't forgotten.

Luis and Julisa wave to me from the stands. They've been so supportive of me. I couldn't ask for better friends.

"See you at halftime, after the show!" Julisa shouts.

I give her a thumbs-up and wave my pom-poms in their direction.

Luis smiles and shouts, "Cheer hard!" Ever since he remembered about the tulips, I've started noticing little things about him. Like what a great smile he has, and how even though he and Julisa might bicker about little things, he always sticks up for her.

When the game starts, I don't know if it's because I think Bree might be there, but I cheer even louder, kick even higher, and smile even bigger than I normally do. I want to show everyone that Lara Kelley is doing just fine. Lara Kelley didn't let this destroy her — even though she almost did at first.

We're up 14–7 at halftime, when the West Lake band, their cheerleaders, and the dance team take the field. I search for Bree, and I think maybe I spot her. I have to admit, their routine is pretty good.

Then it's our turn and, for the first time in a while, I'm really nervous to perform. It's the halftime show. All eyes on us. And I don't want to mess up any tumbles or do the slightest thing wrong, because Bree might take it as a sign that she damaged me in some way. That somehow she won. But then, as I think that, I see myself sitting in Linda's office. Hear her telling me that's an unproductive thought that I need to learn how to toss.

So I pretend it's a piece of paper and mentally throw it in a pretend garbage can as the band starts up. Taking a deep breath, I just let my muscle memory take over and do what we've been practicing over and over.

It's all good.

Luis and Julisa meet me on the sidelines when we come off the field.

"You hungry?" Luis asks. "I'll buy you a wrap."

"Sure," I say.

"What about me?" Julisa complains. "Are you buying *me* a wrap?"

He looks at her like she's crazy. "You're my *sister*," he says. "Buy your own wrap!"

"Oh, come on," I tell him. "Be a good twin and get one for Julisa, too!"

"I get suckered into everything," he says, sighing before heading off for the food cart.

"I have to run to the bathroom," I tell Julisa. "I'll meet you back here."

"Meet me at the food cart," she says. "I'll go keep Luis company in line, since he's treating."

As usual, there's a line for the girls' room. I'm standing behind a group of girls in black-and-silver tracksuits. I wonder if they know Bree.

"How does it feel being back at your old school?" one of them asks the black-haired girl standing with her back to me.

"Weird," she says. "*Really* weird."

My heart starts thumping in my chest, and my palms are damp. It's Bree.

"I never thought I'd come back here, ever," she continues. "Not after . . . what happened."

I stand there, frozen.

And then Christine, one of the other cheerleaders, comes out of the bathroom, and says, "Hey, Lara," and Bree turns around, looking at me, wide-eyed.

Her face looks thinner and paler against the stark black of her hair.

I feel a flood of nerves explode within me, and I have the urge to bolt. Instead, I quietly say, "Hi, Bree."

"Lara," she says. "Hi . . . I was wondering if I'd . . . see you here."

"Yeah . . . me too," I say. "You —"

Hurt me so much . . . Made me try to kill myself over a guy who didn't even exist . . . Made me afraid to trust anyone including myself . . .

"— look different with dark hair."

"I did it a while back," she says, fidgeting a little. "Mom hates it."

The girls she's with are watching and listening. They know what happened, and they've figured out that I'm Lara Kelley.

The girl who fell for Bree's trick. The girl who tried to kill herself.

I am that girl, but I'm not just her anymore. I've been working really hard to become more. I straighten my shoulders.

"I liked the routine you guys did," I say, even though what I really want to say is *Why, Bree? Why did you do it?*

"Thanks," Bree says. "We've been practicing that one for a while."

She glances at the line ahead, as if desperate for it to be her turn so she can avoid talking to me anymore. "How are things here?" she asks. "With you?"

I had to work so hard every day to get to where I am now . . . I hate you for what you did to me . . . Why did you do it, Bree? WHY?!!!

"Great!" I say, smiling brightly. "Cheerleading's great. Homecoming's coming up soon. It's all good."

I feel like I've turned into my mother. *Everything is perfect with us Kelleys!*

"Oh . . . I'm glad to hear that," Bree says. We're almost at the front of the line, and a stall opens up. "Is it okay if I go first?" she asks her friends. "I'm really desperate."

They tell her to go ahead.

"Bye, Lara!" she says, before escaping into the bathroom stall.

Her teammates look at me curiously, like they're not sure what to make of me. They seem surprised that there wasn't more of a scene.

What they don't realize is that when I get into the bathroom stall, my legs are shaking. I have to take several deep breaths to try to calm myself down before I emerge to go meet my friends at the food cart.

Julisa's in line as I come out of the bathroom. At least it's shorter now.

"I couldn't wait. I left Luis waiting for you by the food cart," she says. "Don't let him eat my wrap!"

"I won't," I say.

The minute I see Luis, he asks, "What's the matter?"

"How can you tell?" I ask.

"Because you're even paler than usual, *gringa*."

Even though I'm freaked out, he gets a giggle out of me.

"I just ran into Bree."

"Is it the first time since . . ."

"Yeah. It was . . . weird."

"Are you okay?"

Am I? I've been imagining that meeting for so long, now that it has taken place it's almost anticlimactic. And I still don't know why Bree did what she did. Maybe I never will. Maybe I just have to learn to move on, regardless.

"Yes," I tell him, summoning up a smile. "You know, I think I am."

He hands me my wrap and shifts from one foot to the other.

"So, before my sister gets back, I wanted to ask you . . . Do you want to go to the homecoming dance?"

He takes me totally by surprise.

"With you?"

"No, with Iron Man," he quips, smiling, his warm eyes lighting up. "Yes, with me!"

I don't know if it's because I just saw Bree, or if it's just because I'm a coward.

"I'm sorry . . . I can't. I've got to get back."

And I turn and run back to the sidelines.

I immediately regret it.

———

Syd says I should have said yes and just gone. She says it's like trying to get back on a bicycle to ride after falling off. But if you fall off a bike and you break your arm, the doctor can tell you how long it's going to take to heal. So many weeks wearing a cast, so many weeks of physical therapy, and, boom, you're good to go.

But when someone lies to you and makes you afraid to trust, it's different. No one can tell you how long it'll take for that damage to heal. You can't just take a pill or wear a cast or do so many reps of weights in physical therapy. I'm still seeing my therapist, and although I'm better than I was, I know there's still a long way to go.

Syd and Liam are in the living room watching a movie, a bowl of popcorn balanced between them. He has his arm around her, and when she feeds him a piece, he kisses the tips of her fingers as she places the kernel to his lips.

When they laugh about something — and I don't know if it's because I'm sick of feeling like the third wheel or because I'm ready to feel happy for me, and I realize to do that I need to take a ride on the bicycle — I make a decision. When I get to my room, I text Luis and ask him if he's found a date for the homecoming dance yet and say if not, I've changed my mind and I'd love to go with him. I apologize for being a coward yesterday.

It's okay, he texts back. And I do have a date. Her name is Lara Kelley. :)

Last year at this time, I was obsessing about going to a dance with an imaginary boy. Now I'm going to a different dance with a real one, one who I know, who knows me, and who I think I'm beginning to trust.

Sometimes I feel like I'm never going to get over this, but maybe I am making progress after all. Maybe this really *is* a "process" and healing doesn't come all at once — maybe it just creeps up on you a little bit at a time until one day you finally realize you're feeling better than you thought.

My memory box sits on the shelf above my desk. I haven't really been able to look at it since last year. It's just sat there. I take it down and remove the printout of the chat conversation where Christian DeWitt, the guy who never really existed, said *Love you*, which he never did. I rip the paper into tiny fragments and throw them in the garbage.

It's time to make some new memories. Real ones, this time.

Today I'm grateful that the pills didn't work. I'm grateful that every day I'm feeling a little bit stronger. I'm so very grateful that I get the chance to try again.

AUTHOR'S NOTE

I WAS inspired to write *Backlash* after reading news stories about several cyberbullying incidents and the online vigilantism that occurred in the name of making the bullies "pay." As bullying continues to play out more often in a virtual world, it is important to understand the hurt these actions can cause, and the real-life consequences they can have. It's my hope that this book will help start thoughtful conversations around how we can rethink attitudes and combat bullying in our schools, our homes, and our communities.

For more information and resources about bullying and cyberbullying, visit: www.backlash-book.com.

ACKNOWLEDGMENTS

A NOVEL has many parents. Although my name is on the front, taking all the credit, so many others deserve kudos for helping this book become infinitely better than it started out.

My amazing editor, Jody Corbett, kept asking all the right questions, while keeping me endlessly entertained through our margin-note conversations. To the wonderful team at Scholastic — production editors Elizabeth Starr Baer and Stephanie Engel, copy editor Rachael Hicks, designer Sharismar Rodriguez, publicist Saraciea Fennell, and, of course, David Levithan, Tracy van Straaten, and Lizette Serrano — thank you!

Jennifer Laughran is an agent extraordinaire. She tends to her clients with love, humor, and cute dog pictures.

I owe Steve Fondiller big-time for his brilliant advice on revising chapter one. Diana Klemin, Bill Buschel, Susan Warner, Gay Morris, Tom Mellana, Len Vlahos, Alexandra

Stevens, and Karen Ball were early readers, and I can't thank them enough for their helpful feedback.

One of the things I love most about being a writer is being granted the opportunity to ask interesting people questions about their work for research. Sincere thanks to Greenwich police chief Jim Heavey; Sergeant Mark Zuccerella, leader of the Greenwich Police Department's Special Victims Section; Paul Falavolito, chief at White Oak Emergency Medical Services; and David H. Delman, MD, of DHD Medical PC for their generosity and patience. Any mistakes about procedures are all mine.

Adam Bernard allowed me to turn him into an Abercrombie model (not that he doesn't look like one already), Luis Cotto volunteered to be a character in my novel (I hope you like yourself), and Nikki Mutch and Gabe Rosenberg shared my "If dog looks could kill" photo on Facebook so I could then delete it and see if it still existed on their walls. (It didn't.) Being willing to do strange things for your author friends is a sign of true friendship.

I would not be the woman I am today without the love and support of my incredible, warm, and funny family. As Grandma Dorothy used to say, "We come from good stock." You know, kind of like prize heifers. I love you all.

Josh and Amie, being your mom is the best story ever, and I can't wait to see what the next chapter brings.

Hank, thank you for keeping me sane on those "one more wafer-thin mint" days. Okay, stop laughing. I meant sane-*ish*. I love you, and I'm grateful every day we are together.

ABOUT THE AUTHOR

SARAH DARER LITTMAN is the critically acclaimed author of *Want to Go Private?*; *Life, After*; *Purge*; and *Confessions of a Closet Catholic*, winner of the Sydney Taylor Book Award. When she's not writing novels, Sarah is an award-winning columnist for the online site CT News Junkie. She teaches creative writing as an adjunct professor in the MFA program at Western Connecticut State University and with Writopia Lab. Sarah lives in Connecticut with her family. You can visit her online at www.sarahdarerlittman.com.